THE BLOOD WE SHED

THE BLOOD WE SHED
By William Christie

ibooks

new york
www.ibooks.net

DISTRIBUTED BY SIMON & SCHUSTER, INC.

DEDICATION

For everyone who ever wore the Eagle, Globe, and Anchor

William Christie can be contacted at christieauthor@yahoo.com

William Christie is the author of:

The Warriors of God
Mercy Mission

Author's Note

This is a work of fiction, which means I made it all up. The Marine Corps Base at Camp Lejeune, North Carolina, of course, does actually exist. But other than that, any resemblances to actual persons, places, or events is coincidental and unintentional. There is a slight chance that any part of this story which seems too strange to be believed could be based on fact.

ACKNOWLEDGEMENTS

I'd like to acknowledge all the Marines who helped me in so many ways, but since I'd like to see them get promoted again I can't. They, of all people, know the reasons why.

A man is lucky in this life if he has one friend he would die for, and who would die for him. I am a lucky, lucky man, because I found my blood brothers and sisters when the story began, and I still have them now. The Bull and Joan. Jad and Peg. The Zooman. Rick and Melissa. Erich and Vicki. Nelson and Donna. Mark. Dan, wherever he may be. Ske´, for being the kind of character who simply has to go into a book, and Guia, for putting up with him.

Jim and Beth King, as always, for everything. Anne and Howard King, always my second set of parents.

Those who tolerantly listened to more Marine Corps stories than anyone should ever have to, and for other things besides: Jason and Valerie; Philip and Sally and Lee and Kimberly and Neil and Will; the triumvirate of Hope, Anne, and Jackie (not forgetting Hobe).

My dear friend Mary Gilbert, who read the manuscript at a very early and uncertain stage and always has something valuable to say.

My equally dear friends and neighbors John and Shirley Berdie, for whom every new book is a reason to party.

My family, fanatic supporters one and all.

Finally, but most important, my agent, Richard Curtis of Richard Curtis Associates. One of the good guys. And the Zen Master who aimed me toward the final shape of this book. Thanks for everything, Richard.

THE BLOOD WE SHED

"Every man thinks meanly of himself for not having been a soldier, or not having been at sea."

Samuel Johnson, 10 April 1778
Boswell, *Life of Johnson*

CHAPTER ONE

Y ou need to understand two things. First, people get killed every day in the U.S. military. Only the real spectaculars make the news. My own service, the Marine Corps, likes to say that there are no accidents, only screw-ups.

Second, no one likes officers. Sometimes I don't and I am one. But on a blistering July day at Camp Lejeune, North Carolina, humid the way only swampy and sandy coastal low country can be, you'd be surprised how many people would rather crap out in the shade rather than practice shooting their way into a building—even if what they learn is going to save their lives later. That's why there are infantry platoon commanders, to make Marines do what they ought to, not what they want to. And that's why no one likes the bastards.

Echo Company was shooting live ammunition on the MAC ranges. The military worships at the altar of acronyms; they may even sacrifice virgins to them. MAC stands for MOUT Assault Course. And MOUT stands for Military Operations on Urban Terrain. In layman's terms, city fighting.

My platoon, 2nd platoon, was on station 6, the grenade house, waiting for 1st platoon to finish up. I'm Second Lieutenant Michael Galway. Everyone asks about the county in Ireland, but the name couldn't be more common.

The grenade house was set up as a single floor of a building, with entrances, hallways, and rooms. The walls were made from old auto tires stacked vertically, the open center filled with packed sand. The interlocking rubber and sand cylinders kept the bullets and grenade fragmentation from bounding back at you.

Metal silhouette targets were scattered throughout. A squad entered, engaged targets, and moved down the hallway.

You didn't want to just charge into a room filled with enemy soldiers all waiting behind cover and aiming at the doorway. So after the door was breached, one Marine, covered by the rest, tossed in a grenade. As soon as it blew, breaking the concentration of anyone inside, the next two went through the doorway left and right, putting their backs to the near wall. Aiming first at each corner and sweeping toward the center, they shot everyone in the room. The 3rd and 4th members of the fire team covered both ends of the hallway and stood by to reinforce if the room was too big for first two to handle.

This delicate drill had to be done quickly and precisely. There was no room for error with the muzzles of loaded weapons dancing all over the place, nor was it advisable to fumble around with live grenades.

Which was why I took one look at my Marines crapped out under the trees and said to the squad leaders, "I know you're going to start practicing your clearing drills right now."

There was the usual chorus of bitching as the Marines groaned to their feet. The lieutenant was being a dick again. I really didn't enjoy being a dick, but I'd found that it worked a lot better than appealing to the virtue of the average American teenager.

Second Lieutenant Jack O'Brien, the 1st platoon commander, was spending the week at embarkation school to learn how to load ships. So First Lieutenant Bob Gudtfreund, the company executive officer or XO, was the range safety officer for 1st platoon, along with Staff Sergeant Meadows, the platoon sergeant.

I could hear the characteristic wh-whap of grenades going off inside the house, followed by the crackling of rifle fire. I think that stuttered sound was caused by the detonator going off a fraction of a second before blowing the main charge. What struck you when you heard a real versus a movie grenade was how incredibly loud they were. No orange flame — that was for the movies. With close to half a pound of Composition B explosive they were loud even when muffled by rubber and sand. We thought it was motivating, which I guess was why people thought we were crazy.

While the firing was going on inside the house, Staff Sergeant Meadows was debriefing another squad just outside.

I turned my attention back to my drilling squads. WH-WHAP!! The unmuffled roar and blast of hot air struck me like a thunderclap. I whipped my head back to see a blooming cloud of black smoke outside the grenade house. I tried to move in that direction and my legs froze. They wouldn't budge; it was as if my central nervous system had more sense than I did. It couldn't have been more than a second, but it felt like I'd been paralyzed for an hour before I got control of my legs and ran toward the smoke.

The cloud of sand dust and acrid high explosives slowly drifted away to reveal a squad of Marines littered all over the ground.

The first Marine I reached was lying face down, the bottom of his helmet resting on the back of his flak jacket. I grabbed his wrist to feel for a pulse. But how the hell do you feel someone's pulse when your own heart is pounding itself out of your chest and reverberating all the way down into your hand? I rolled him over carefully but the helmet stayed where it was. I almost leaped back. Practically everything from the top of the flak jacket collar to the bottom rim of the helmet was gone, blown away.

I scrambled over to the next one. Sergeant Palermo, one of the squad leaders. He was rolling back and forth, both hands clasping a gaping wound in his thigh just above the knee. Bright red arterial blood jetted through his fingers. I couldn't get to the pressure point on his groin, his equipment was in the way. So I jumped on top of him and kneeled on the side of his thigh above the wound, putting all my weight on it. The blood stopped pumping out each time his heart beat.

In first aid training the victim is always stoically awaiting treatment, but it was like being on top of a bucking horse. Sergeant Palermo was yelling and swearing, and it was all I could do to stay on. "Hold still!" I shouted. I needed a tourniquet, and if I moved he was going to be pumping blood again. I yanked the sling off an M-16 lying on the ground and had to dig in the dirt under his thigh to get it around and above the wound near the groin. The knot was the easy part. Then I stuck Palermo's bayonet in the knot and twirled to twist the sling tight. I tied the bayonet to his leg with one end of the sling.

I ripped a battle dressing out of my first aid pouch, even though we're always drilled to use the wounded man's, not our own. I packed the pad into the wound, then put another on top of it and tied the whole thing on tight with the dangling gauze tails. Finally I looked back up at Sergeant Palermo's face, and thought he was dead. I felt an irrational spasm of anger. Textbook first aid, and the son of a bitch dies on me. No, he was still breathing. He'd just passed out.

More help had arrived and I could pull back and evaluate the scene. The usual turpentine sap scent of the Lejeune pine forest had been replaced by the raw odor of spilled bowel, and blood that smelled like the taste of a copper penny in your mouth.

Doc Bob, the platoon medical corpsman, and a bunch of the Marines were working on the casualties. The Doc was placing dressings on an open abdominal cavity. Someone behind me was puking. I didn't need to see that.

But I did notice the rest of the platoon packed around us in one tight knot, with nothing to do but watch and close to freaking because of it.

I realized I had to do my job, which wasn't first aid. I stood up and took a couple of deep breaths to steady myself. Mood was contagious. If I was calm then it wasn't as bad as they thought. "All right, listen up," I said. I pointed out four Marines, "Go check the grenade house for more casualties." I ticked off two more, "Put all the packs in a pile with the ammo, and guard it." And to the rest, "Spread out, secure the area, and keep everyone away from here."

And in that beautiful Marine way they instantly shook themselves together and dashed off to execute their orders. It was as if I was on autopilot and watching the stream of commands flowing from someone else's mouth. All training.

My acting platoon sergeant, Sergeant Harlin, was just standing there. "Sergeant Harlin!" I barked. "Get me a list of names and numbers from the I.D. tags of the casualties."

Lance Corporal Vincent was right behind me with the platoon backpack radio, his mouth hanging open and wearing an expression of pure horror such as I'd never seen on another face before. The radio was set to the base range control frequency. I wiped my bloody hands on my trousers and grabbed the handset from Vincent. "Blackburn, this is MAC station 6, over."

Blackburn was the callsign of the range control duty officer. His voice crackled over the net. "MAC-6, this is Blackburn, over."

"Blackburn, we have just had a grenade accident. We have emergency casualties, and require medevac by air if possible."

"MAC-6, wait out." He put all the ranges on base in check-fire to keep them off the radio net. And I guess was checking to see if there were any helicopters in the air.

The noise was so bad I had to step back in order to hear the radio. The wounded weren't yelling. They weren't screaming. It was a highpitched animal shrieking. I'd never heard anything like that before; it was the kind of sound that wakes you from a nightmare.

Second Lieutenant Frank Milburn, the 3rd platoon commander, had run over from the Dodge City range with Doc Stone, his corpsman. Thankfully he hadn't brought anyone else, it was enough of a zoo.

The corpsmen only had one bag of intravenous solution each, carried in case of heat casualties. And no pain killers other than aspirin. Battalion surgeons never issued morphine syrettes, because a corpsman losing narcotics was the same career-ender as a Marine losing a rifle. And why would you ever need it? Peacetime mentality.

Lance Corporal Nolan ran up to me, "No casualties in the grenade house, sir.

"Okay," I said. "Stay there and secure the area."

Blackburn came back up. "MAC-6, Blackburn, over."

"Go Blackburn."

"MAC-6, you have one CH-46 inbound, callsign Griffin 1-2. Say the number of casualties and type of injuries, over?"

"Blackburn, seven emergency and two routine. All grenade fragmentation, over." A dead man was a routine medevac. There was no rush over the dead.

"MAC-6, do you have a zone and means of marking, over?"

"Roger, Blackburn, he can put down right on the range. I will control and mark with smoke, over." The red smoke grenade was hooked onto the radio backpack, part of the range safety officer's required equipment.

I plucked it off the webbing and handed it to Vincent

"We've got a helo coming in!" I shouted to the Marines. "Put 'em on ponchos and be ready to move."

The helicopter broke into the net; I could hear the rotors behind the pilot's voice. "Mac-6, this is Griffin 1-2, over."

"Griffin, MAC-6, over."

"MAC-6, can you give me a zone brief, over?"

I gave him the standard landing zone brief, by the numbers: location, size, marking, obstacles, and wind.

Then I saw him. "Griffin, I'm at your 2 o'clock."

"Roger, pop smoke."

I motioned to Vincent. He pulled the pin and hurled the grenade out in front of us. "Smoke out."

"MAC-6, I have your red smoke."

Frank Milburn ran out to guide him in with hand and arm signals. The helicopter settled down right in front of him, the rotors blowing up a blizzard of sand.

The jostling of the wounded Marines being picked up off the ground and carried aboard set of a fresh wave of shrieking that nearly drowned out the sound of the helicopter. Doc Bob and Doc Stone rode along with them. The bird lifted off.

When Griffin 1-2 checked off the net, Blackburn came back up and told me to get on the range telephone and give him names, social security numbers, and blood types of the casualties. I realized they wouldn't want that information going out over a radio net in the clear.

When I returned from the phone Milburn was huddled with Corporal Anderson of 1st platoon. "You need to hear this," Milburn said to me.

Corporal Anderson was a tough little redhead with the face and voice of a 1930's movie gangster. It made seeing him on the verge of tears all the worse. "I told him not to do it, sir! I told him not to!"

"Who?" I demanded.

"The XO, sir."

It was only then I noticed Gudtfreund sitting on the ground, his head in his hands.

Milburn and I walked up to him. I said, "Bob, what happened?"

Gudtfreund just shook his head.

Milburn put a hand on his shoulder. "Bob, what happened?"

But Gudtfreund wouldn't say anything, or take his head out of his hands to look at us.

Milburn gave me a look that said it was useless.

Then, with no warning of his arrival, our company commander, Captain Mark Dudley, was in my face. "What happened?" he shouted, spittle flying. Milburn was right there but it was all directed at me. "What the fuck happened?"

"First platoon had a grenade go off outside the house, sir," I said. "I don't know how it happened. We have two dead and seven wounded."

His tone shifted from belligerent to bewildered. "Two dead?" As if begging me to correct myself.

"Yes, sir. All casualties were medevaced by helicopter. They should be at the Naval Hospital now. Corporal Anderson and his squad were in the house when it happened. They're waiting out in back."

That brought the volume back up. "Were you the range safety officer?" he demanded. I was not the Captain's favorite.

"No, sir," I replied. "The XO was."

Without another word to me, Captain Dudley ran over to Gudtfreund. When he got the same response that we did, he jerked the XO to his feet and dragged him out of earshot.

I realized I was so dry I could barely peel my tongue off the roof of my mouth. I chugged an entire 1-quart canteen.

It was my first chance to really stop and think about what had happened. There were no television displays of grief. Not by me; not by anyone. Plenty of strong emotions, though. Sadness made even deeper by the knowledge that it had obviously happened due to someone's mistake. Relief, too. That it hadn't been my mistake, and that I'd done my job right and gotten through it. Though I think I might have puked my guts out if I hadn't been so preoccupied. That had to be the secret of leadership in war—being too busy to lose it. There was more than a little exultation, too. I was still high from the adrenaline.

And a secret part of me would always be humiliated about not being able to get my legs moving right after the explosion. That I didn't have any control over it really scared me. Would it happen again, but worse?

Like a silent movie, Milburn and I both watched Captain Dudley gesturing wildly at Gudtfreund, whose arms were spread wide in supplication.

"Dudley knows he's fucked," Milburn said. Training accidents, especially fatal ones, were career-enders for commanding officers.

We were on the range for hours more. The Provost Marshal took control of the scene and all the ammo. Gudtfreund and Corporal Anderson's squad were all whisked away for formal interviews.

Captain Dudley marched the company back to barracks. His career was over and, ironically, mine was saved. The story probably isn't what you'd expect.

CHAPTER TWO

Everyone else had the weekend off. I was back on base at 0800 on Saturday morning for duty as the battalion Officer of the Day. For the next 24 hours I was the Colonel's personal representative. The duty was manned seven days a week, but weekdays the OD was posted in the morning by the battalion XO and then went about his normal routine, only taking over after everyone left for the day. On the weekends it went from 0800 to 0800, which was why it was usually reserved for the most junior lieutenants.

I had a small office in the headquarters building with a desk, a phone, a locker, and a metal bunk bed rack to sleep in. I also had a green clothbound logbook to record everything that happened during my tour. Along with a vinyl binder hopefully full of the answers to any questions I might have. Not to mention an M9 Beretta 9mm automatic pistol and a ring of keys to every lock in the battalion area. The key ring was a great metaphor for the Marine way of doing things. It was attached to a shaft of wood the size of my forearm. That wood had probably gotten bigger every time some poor OD mislaid the keys.

The job wasn't as dramatic as the pistol made it out to be. Answer the phone and deal with any problems. Fill out the papers if a Marine had to go on emergency leave. Tour the area. Make sure the food in the regimental chow hall was up to snuff. The Marines restricted to the area as a result of company punishment had to come by on a schedule and sign in to prove they were still there.

It was boring, really boring. My staff duty was Staff Sergeant Lornell, the S-2 (Intelligence) chief. Old for a staff sergeant—promotions came slow in some occupational specialties. In the Corps a Staff NCO who was burned out and had lost his motivation was called "tired." Staff Sergeant Lornell might have been tired, but he could still talk the bark off a tree. After a while it felt like being married. Making a tour was an excuse to get out of the house.

The troops lived in three-story motel style brick barracks arrayed behind the headquarters. Three-man rooms with their own bath, each one facing out onto an open air roofed walkway on each floor. Every company had a duty NCO in an office inside the barracks. And an enlisted firewatch patrolling the walkways and perimeter of the building.

An OD didn't have to exercise a lot of judgment, because the typical battalion commander prohibited just about everything. That way no matter what happened he could tell the commanding general he had a standing order against it. So far all I'd had to do was tell a couple of Marines to turn their stereos down.

At 0200 in the morning I was asleep in the lower rack of the bunk bed in the office. Privilege of rank, but it also meant I had to roll out and answer the phone.

I picked it up and gave the required greeting: "Officer of the Day, Lieutenant Galway speaking, may I help you sir?"

An excited voice blurted out, "Sir, this is the Fox Company duty. We've got a Marine threatening to kill his roommates with a knife."

"Where's he now?" I said, grabbing for my blouse.

"Still in his room, sir."

"I'll be right there," I said, fumbling for my cammies. I told Staff Sergeant Lornell what was going on while I pulled on my boots and pistol belt.

"I'll call the MP's," he said.

"You know the building number for Fox Company's barracks?" Right then I couldn't have remembered it for a million dollars.

"I've got it," he said. "Be careful, sir."

I went out the door at a dead run. It wasn't hard to find the right room. The duty, the firewatch, and two Marines in their skivvies were standing out in front of it. It was a steaming summer night, but they were both shivering

Incoherent screaming inside. Someone was literally bouncing off the walls. "Is he in there alone?" I asked.

"Yes, sir," said the duty NCO.

Unfastening the holster flap and keeping my right hand free to draw my pistol, I opened the door a crack and took a peek. The Marine was now on one of the racks, totally naked, still screaming, and slashing at his abdomen with a knife. I saw blood. Great, just great.

I quietly shut the door and considered my options. In the movie the OD would swagger into the room and disarm the nut case with a fancy Kung Fu move. But there could be only two actual outcomes. Either I'd get stabbed or he'd get shot.

I didn't think Lieutenant Colonel Sweatman, our battalion commander, would have too much heartburn over me getting stabbed. But I knew he'd be royally pissed if I shot a Marine, no matter the circumstances.

So I reasoned in a very cold-bloodedly practical Marine way that even if the wacko managed to disembowel himself, it would take him at least 15 minutes to die. And the MP's would show up before then.

But he threw a monkey wrench into my plans by deciding that he wanted out of his room.

I couldn't lock him in from the outside. All I could do was grab the doorknob with both hands and brace one foot against the brick wall. He was yanking away with all his might from the inside and I was holding firm on the other.

By now we'd attracted a crowd of rubberneckers. If he got out with that knife I'd have to shoot him.

But the MP's finally showed up, three of them. I described the situation while holding onto the doorknob for dear life. In other circumstances it would have been comical.

On a silent count of three I let go of the knob. The door flew open, and the sudden lack of resistance sent the Marine flying back into the room. The MP's piled in with me right behind them.

They blinded him with a flashlight beam for the crucial second it took to pin the knife arm with a baton and knock the blade loose. The Marine went crazy, and the sweat and blood on naked skin made him as slippery as a greased pig.

All four of us were on him. Every time we got a grip on an arm we'd lose it. The MP's were cracking him with their batons in between using them to try and pin him down; I was wrapped around his legs so he couldn't get up, and at the same time doing my best to twist his feet off his ankles. And for all the effect it was having we might as well have been giving him a massage. We damn near died of exhaustion in the eternity it took to get the cuffs on him. Even then he was so wild I had to scrounge a web belt to tie his ankles together.

The next time I see a video of four cops whaling the piss out of some suspect, I'll feel sorry for the cops.

Even after all that, we had to physically sit on him to keep him from thrashing around. The slashes on his chest and stomach were superficial but they bled like hell. He kept screaming a bunch of gibberish, mostly along the lines of Satan making him do it. I was about to go looking for a sock to stuff in his mouth when the ambulance arrived.

They had to strap him onto a cervical backboard before they could get some pressure bandages on him. Since he had no cervical injuries they didn't bother to strap his head down. And pretty soon all you could hear was the clomping sound of him banging his head against the wooden backboard.

"Next time I won't fail!" he yelled as they put him on the gurney.

"Next time do it when I'm not on duty," I muttered as they rolled him by me.

After a well-deserved breather, we all had to sit down and put the whole thing together.

The Marine in question was Private Dove, a peaceful name in ironic contrast with a non-peaceful nature. He'd been reduced to his current rank after a string of offenses. He was also in alcohol rehab. In the Marine Corps an alcoholic either accepted treatment or got discharged. The treatment was the same as in the civilian world, no whips or dungeons involved. Except the alcoholic was required to take Antabuse. Antabuse was a drug that made you sick as a dog when you ingested even the slightest amount of alcohol.

During the day a Marine reported to sickbay where he took the pill under observation. After hours the OD did the job. Just tons of fun. You had to watch him swallow it and then confirm by checking inside his mouth with a flashlight.

But Private Dove hadn't shown up to get his medication from me, and I'd logged him in accordingly. He'd actually gone out drinking. And by that time he didn't have enough Antabuse in his system to make him sick, or he didn't care. Whether the Antabuse made him psychotic or whether he was psychotic to begin with would be answered above my pay grade.

From the way the media loves reporting, "Former Marine shoots...," or "Ex-Marine attacks...," you'd think that Boot Camp turned young men into psychotic killers. Take my word for it, it doesn't. But if you happened to be a psycho before you joined up, it doesn't make you normal. I don't have any statistics, but my guess is that psychotics are far more likely to join the Marine Corps than the Peace Corps.

Dove's two long-suffering roommates were awakened from their slumber to find him standing naked atop one of their racks, brandishing the knife and announcing, "I'm going to kill you."

They'd immediately and sensibly un-assed the room and notified the duty NCO, setting the chain of events in motion.

"JESUS FUCKING CHRIST!!" Staff Sergeant Lornell exclaimed when I came trudging back to the office covered with blood.

I told him the story before throwing my cammies into a garbage bag and taking a shower. It paid to keep a couple of spare uniforms in your locker.

Then I called the Naval hospital and asked them to give Dove an HIV test. It was negative. Marines had to have one every year anyway.

I'd written term papers shorter than my logbook entry. The entries for a typical tour ran two pages. Basically along the lines of: *1500 hours, OD toured the area, all secure. 1800 hours, OD to chow hall, chow was sufficient in quality and quantity.*

But recording this particular incident took me ten pages. It all had to be perfect, since the log was a legal document that would be figuring prominently in Dove's impending adventures with the Uniform Code of Military Justice.

Major Thom, the battalion XO, had given me an excruciatingly detailed duty brief on Friday, keeping me at parade rest in front of his desk the whole time. He'd finished up by saying, "Galway, when you're on duty you represent the command. Don't fuck the command. Because if you fuck the command, you fuck *me*. And if you fuck *me*, I'll fuck you 'til you're pregnant."

It was just like Officer Candidate School, where the sheer theatrical quality of the ranting and raving always tickled my funny bone. But the consequences of even cracking a grin were terrible. So I faithfully followed Major Thom's orders to call him at home if anything out of the ordinary happened. After all, it was only 0500 on Sunday morning.

At first he was pissed that I'd called him, then halfway through the story he blurted out, "What?" I kept going; he listened quietly then asked where Dove was. I told him, there was a moment of silence, then he said, "All right," and hung up, leaving me no idea where I stood with him.

By the time everything quieted down it was too late, or rather too early, for me to get any sleep.

I had to ask the Staff Sergeant: "Does this kind of shit happen very often?"

He had a good laugh over that. "Sir, I've been in seventeen years and nothing like this *ever* happened to me before. You really got your cherry busted tonight."

Great, I thought. What was my *second* duty going to be like?

CHAPTER THREE

S unday morning was a couple of loads of laundry and a much-needed nap, unfortunately interrupted by a phone summons from Jack O'Brien that put me on the road.

A Marine Corps infantry battalion is a very insular little world. Lieutenants worked together, and lieutenants socialized together.

We usually met at O'Brien's quarters on base. Company grade housing was streets of absolutely identical small homes. They were painted different colors, though. As you went up in rank and accumulated more children and possessions the houses got bigger, though still identical.

I lugged a load of beer and ice from my pickup truck. No gun rack, if that's what you were thinking, but all my worldly goods did fit inside it. Since married second lieutenants with children could afford less than single corporals, everyone always brought something to a get-together. The bachelors usually contributed the alcohol.

At O'Brien's front door I was met by the two dachshunds. One was really smart, and the other…well, she had a great personality. One was being protective and barking at me, and the other was wagging her tail happily to let me know she'd lead me to the valuables if I scratched behind her ears.

I dumped my load in the plastic trashcan and gave Jack O'Brien's wife Lynn a big hug. Their 1½-year-old daughter Bonnie was clinging tightly to her mother's leg in the presence of so many strangers.

When I rubbed her head she smiled shyly and looked up at me with heartbreakingly big eyes. Then I gave hugs to Mary Federico and Tracy Nichols, and they gave me a massive tray of marinated chicken to lug out to the back yard.

The men were gathered around the fire for the burning of the meat. O'Brien in front of the grill with his apron on, and the rest of the hunting party arrayed about him in a semicircle. Jack was big but not tall. A powerlifter, built like a refrigerator. And while I resemble a Spanish seaman shipwrecked from the Armada, he was what the world thinks an Irishman ought to look like.

Frank Milburn might have stepped off a recruiting poster. His body was shaped like a perfect V from the broad shoulders to the narrow waist. Even his face was the All-American quarterback type the Corps favored for the recruiting ads. Of course I was jealous.

Jim Nichols was about the same height as O'Brien but not as burly. The kind of guy who, immediately after you'd met, found a way to let you know that he'd been first in his class in The Basic Officer Course, always called The Basic School. And of course everyone found a way to break his balls about it. Nichols would start talking about being a corporal in Desert Storm, and Milburn would always say, "Jim, a supply clerk with the Air Wing wasn't in Desert Storm. You were in Saudi Arabia." Nichols was prior-enlisted, what the Corps calls a Mustang. He was now an infantryman, everyone suspected, because the Commandant of the Marine Corps was always an infantryman.

Jim's wife Tracy had just had a baby, the third of three girls. The gossip was that this would continue until she had a boy. O'Brien liked to say that Jimmy needed to get his X and Y sperm formed up into a column of twos.

Those were the Echo Company lieutenants who'd made it through the grenade accident. O'Brien had 1st platoon, I had 2nd, Milburn 3rd, and Nichols weapons platoon.

But we always socialized with the lieutenants of Fox Company. Paul Federico lived a few doors down from O'Brien in base housing. Mary was his wife.

Lee Harvey Oberdorff's first and middle names were neither Lee nor Harvey. Shortly after he reported to the battalion he ran into Lieutenant

Tex, the anti-armor platoon commander. Tex took one look at him and shouted, "Lee Harvey Oswald!" And that was all it took.

Ian Campbell was tall and quiet, and took a lot of pride in his Scottish ancestry.

As I came up Federico threw his arms around me, nearly upsetting my beverage. "Here he is!" he announced. "My hero."

"How so?" I asked, the embrace having pinned my beer can against my ear.

"Private Dove," said Federico. "I've been trying to get rid of that worthless piece of shit for months, and now he's gone. The only way you could have done me a bigger favor was if you'd shot him."

"Anything for a pal," I said.

Federico released me. "Here's your reward," he said, offering me an angry looking green pepper. It was no gag; he ate those jalapeños like gumdrops.

"No thanks," I said, plunging my non-beer hand into the box of pretzels Lee Harvey was holding. "I prefer not to cry like a little girl during my morning bowel movement."

"The dreaded red eye," said Milburn.

"What the hell happened last night?" Nichols demanded. "I heard you had to go hand-to-hand with the guy."

In an infantry battalion, gossip moved literally at the speed of light. And Jim always made sure he was the first one to know everything.

So I had to tell the tale of my duty.

"Good sea story," Milburn said after I finished.

"Read the logbook," I retorted. They say the difference between a fairy tale and a sea story is that a fairy tale begins with, "Once upon a time...." while a sea story starts off with, "Now this is no shit...."

"Did you call the XO?" O'Brien asked me.

"Yes, Dad."

"What did he say?"

"He said, "all right," and hung up."

"That means you did good," said Federico. "If he thought you'd fucked up, he'd have melted your earwax over the phone. Then he'd probably get dressed, come down to the CP, and do it again in person."

O'Brien said, "You know, I can't decide whether you're an unlucky son of a bitch for all the shit that's gone down on your watch, or the luckiest son of a bitch in the Corps because Dudley's gone before he could toast you on your fitness report."

Captain Dudley had seriously disliked me. The man was a total careerist who ran his company according to the zero-defect system.

I should explain. The senior officers in the military were like the Queen of Hearts in *Alice in Wonderland*. If anything upset them they screamed, "Off with their heads!" Except that careers were chopped off instead of heads. So a certain percentage of officers felt that the best way to make general was to never make a mistake. It was called zero-defects, and it was the way the military really worked as opposed to its popular image. And there were two, and only two, guaranteed ways to never make a mistake. The first was to do absolutely nothing. The second was to arrange for someone else to take the blame when the inevitable happened.

Dudley practiced both, but mainly the first. We'd had an adverse chemical reaction from the moment we first met, and after that he'd done nothing but throw fastballs at my head.

It really started when, on my second week in the company, he had me command a detachment to the rifle range. The first thing I did was ask O'Brien where the rife range was. During practice shooting Captain Dudley told me his rifle wasn't any good. Following the Company Gunnery Sergeant's advice I'd brought a number of spare M-16's in case someone had a breakage. So I got the Captain a new one. The sights weren't right. He kept it up; it was total neurosis. He didn't need an armorer, he needed a sport's psychologist. Finally I had to tell him he'd exhausted all the spares; we'd have to pick a Marine and take his rifle away. I'm afraid I didn't word it much more diplomatically than that.

Then the games began. He had me sign out classified material so he could take it home and read it, and if the dog ate it I'd go to jail. Totally illegal, but your career was just as over if you reported it.

I hadn't given him an excuse to relieve me, but it was no mystery what my first fitness report would have looked like. And now he was gone.

"That's what happens when you get commissioned on a Friday the 13th," I said.

"No shit?" said Federico.

"No shit," I replied. My Irish mother was horrified, but it was last day of OCS and they didn't change the training schedule for things like that.

We very gingerly got around to talking about the grenade accident. O'Brien said, "If I ever see that fucking weasel Gudtfreund again, he's a dead man." A lot of people might use those words, but I wouldn't want to bump into Jack after hurting some of his Marines.

Having their husbands in the field from Monday to Friday didn't leave the women wanting to hear about the Marine Corps all weekend. They told us we'd have to obey the no-shoptalk rule before they let us back into the house for dinner.

"But we've got the chicken," Lee Harvey mentioned in protest.

"It's only too obvious," Federico told him, "that you, my friend, are not married."

After dinner we were all helping move the dishes into the kitchen, and I just happened to look out the back window onto the yard. It was getting on dusk. Unlike many of the units in the warren of company-grade housing, O'Brien's backed up onto a wooded treeline. There was movement all over the grass, and I stuck my nose to the window to get a better look.

"Lynn," I said, "there's something like twenty rabbits on your lawn."

"I know," she said. "They're out there every night."

"And unless I miss my guess," I said, "they're all having sex." I could hardly believe my eyes. The rabbits were paired off and humping away like there was no tomorrow. Every single one of them. "I'm not lying. Look for yourself."

It had to be a regular occurrence, because Lynn wasn't surprised. "This place is fertility central—just ask me."

I turned away from the window to look at her, and she was smiling at me. "That's right, I'm pregnant again," she said.

I gave her another big hug. "When's the date?"

"Just when you're thinking, Mike. When you guys are on deployment."

"Oh, Jeez," I moaned.

"I know, Mike, I know. No planning at all. We're just going to have to suck it up."

Hearing the Marine-ism come out of her mouth made me smile. But man, what a hard thing for each of them to deal with on their own.

I liked all the wives, but Lynn was my favorite. Officers' wives could be even more careerist than their husbands, and lieutenants' wives had to walk as softly as lieutenants did. But Lynn broke the mold by being cheerfully blunt and unpretentious. She took crap from no one, especially her husband.

Back in the living room I sat down next to O'Brien and said quietly, "Congratulations on being a second-award Dad."

"Lynn told you?"

"No, Jim did. Who the hell do you think told me?"

"Jesus, it's totally out of hand. Seems like all I have to do is look at her and she gets pregnant."

"Actually, it's a bit more complicated than that. But we'll have that little talk later."

"Thanks."

Lynn brought out the Trivial Pursuit board along with ice cream and cake, which of course we drank beer with.

"I'll sit this one out," I told her.

"Trivial Pursuit against your religion?" she demanded.

"No, I've just got this weird total recall for odd facts. Makes me a nightmare to play Trivial Pursuit with. I guarantee you'll want to lynch me."

"There's only one solution for that," Lynn replied. "You'll be my partner."

I was right—everyone wanted to lynch us before the game was over. We beat them like a drum, then Lynn left to give Bonnie her bath.

"Mike, is it true you went to Princeton?" Mary Federico asked.

She obviously didn't realize that a lot of Ivy Leaguers sucked at Trivial Pursuit. But the word had gotten around. In the movies military men are always saying, "Hey, buddy, where you from?" The truth is that no one really gives a shit, unless you happened to have grown up at the Playboy Mansion. But they do want to know where you went to college.

The first time I mentioned it there was auspicious silence, which was understandable. At OCS, Frank from Harvard and I were occasionally pointed out as if we were exotic animals.

When I was introduced to the battalion at a social function known as a 'hail and farewell,' Colonel Sweatman our battalion commander had called me up in front of everyone and began, Colonel-like, "Mike Galway has been with Echo Company these past three weeks. He's a graduate of Princeton, a history major, so he'll probably be taking notes on us for his master's thesis."

Everyone had laughed a little too hard at the boss's rapier wit. I stood there like a dick, battling to keep my smile from turning into a grimace.

Pleased with himself, the Colonel had continued with, "He's...." Then he halted abruptly and examined the paper in his hand closely, brow wrinkling in confusion. He let off a nervous little chuckle. "Lieutenant Galway is actually of Russian, not Irish extraction. He is a chess grandmaster and a highly ranked polo player. He enjoys fine wines, hunting big game in Africa, and collecting abstract art."

It wasn't hard to find the suspects. O'Brien and Milburn were doubled over laughing. Everyone else had been understandably puzzled.

The Colonel had smiled tolerantly and refolded the paper. "I wouldn't necessarily take that as gospel. I suspect Lieutenants O'Brien and Milburn got their hands on this biographical information before it reached my desk. But I'm sure you'll join me in welcoming Lieutenant Galway to the battalion."

They gave me a round of applause, the lieutenants barking out Marine Corps oo-rah's. I went along with my new image by giving my public a series of graciously dignified Queen of England waves. These are done with the elbow pressed tight to the body and a hand motion akin to unscrewing an upside-down mayonnaise jar. One day I would have my revenge.

"So what brought you here?" Mary Federico asked me.

"Didn't like 9-5. Couldn't stand working in an office." I wasn't about to tell anyone I'd made a choice between taking the test for my broker's license and going to OCS, determined not to reach 50 and realize that I'd never really gone anywhere or done anything except take the kids to Disney World every year, because I didn't have the balls.

"What does your Dad do?" Milburn asked. They were still trying to get a handle on that Ivy League thing.

"Construction," I said.

"You mean like he owns a construction company?" said Nichols.

"No, I mean like he works construction."

O'Brien was grinning at me.

"No shit?" said Milburn.

"No shit," I replied.

After Federico had a few drinks it didn't take much for O'Brien to get him going. Everyone needs a hobby, and Paul's was the compilation of a list that he called *The 100 Metaphors For Masturbation,* which unlike most things in this world was exactly what it sounded like. He'd explained his project to me when we first met, inviting my participation.

Which was the great thing about the military. You never knew what was coming next, and you'd never, ever, be able to say, "Now I've heard everything." At the time I'd asked, "How far along are you?"

"The count is forty-eight," he'd replied.

"Spanking the monkey?" I said off the top of my head.

"Please." I'd obviously given him the masturbatory equivalent of See Spot Run.

I took another shot, for pride. "Squeezing the cheese?"

"I like it," he'd said, beaming. "Forty-nine."

While his wife rubbed her temples as if a migraine was coming on, Paul closed his eyes and began reciting. It was like watching the high priest of some onanistic cult chanting his liturgy: "Beating the weasel; spanking the monkey; choking the chicken; flogging the dummy; ramming the musket; buffing the flagpole; waxing the surfboard; polishing the silver...."

It might not be to everyone's taste, but who knows? Maybe one day *The 100 Metaphors for Masturbation* will take its place alongside such classics as *Njal's Saga, The Epic of Gilgamesh, The Song of Roland,* or *Poem of the Cid.*

Before he was finished, Bonnie charged out of the hallway in her jammies. "Great," O'Brien groaned. "You'd think we washed her in liquid amphetamine." And then the usual, "Lynn, please do something about your daughter."

Bonnie bounded around the room and ended up in front of me. I put down my beer and lifted her up into my lap. Momentarily at a loss, the only thing that popped into my head was to play the toe game. You know, "this little piggy went to market; this little piggy stayed home…."

After the last little piggy went wee wee weeing all the way home I was fresh out of material, so I jumped back into the grownup conversation. And while I was talking I think I was absentmindedly rubbing Bonnie's feet, because Lynn brought the talk to a halt by saying, "Oh my God."

Lynn was looking at me, I looked down, and Bonnie was sound asleep with her mouth open. Lynn directed me with hand-and-arm signals, opened doors and led the way. Carrying Bonnie like an unexploded bomb, I set her down in her crib.

We gingerly shut the bedroom door and tip-toed out into the living room. Lynn said, "Mike, I'll be expecting you this time every night."

"And you can drive over to my house after you're done here," said Mary Federico.

I guess you never knew when some hidden talent was going to emerge. Evidently I was the Baby Whisperer. "You'll find my rates on my web site."

O'Brien, Milburn, and Federico began chanting, "The pipes, the pipes." And Ian Campbell opened his case and began assembling his bagpipes somewhat unsteadily. I told you he was a Scot.

"Did we or did we not just put the baby to bed?" I asked Lynn. She gave me a resigned shrug.

If you're looking for an instrument to play while intoxicated, the bagpipes are the way to go. Mainly because it takes an aficionado to tell the difference between good bagpipe playing and mediocre bagpipe playing. Ian puffed up the bag and tore into *Scotland the Brave*. He sounded good to me, which was always good when you were hearing bagpipes at a range of less than ten feet. The next tune, of course, was *The Campbells are Coming*.

Ian finished to a wild round of applause. Out of air and with a face the color of a ripe raspberry, he slumped back onto the couch. And we all called out, in bad Scottish accents, "A piper is down, a piper is down."

"He's just pissed," Federico said, completing the dialogue from the movie *So I Married an Axe Murderer.*

Lynn went in to check on Bonnie. She came back out and reported, "She slept like a rock through the whole thing."

"Unbelievable," I said.

Lynn shook her head again. "If a door squeaks she'll probably be up and running again."

A few minutes later Milburn nudged me and gestured to O'Brien. Jack was sitting upright, his chin on his chest, fast asleep.

"I didn't touch him," I said. "I swear to God."

"This is SOP," said Jimmy Nichols.

"It's not that he isn't a stud," said Milburn. "It's a straight body-mass issue. When Jack checks off the net, that's my signal to stop drinking."

Which sounded like good advice. Lynn grabbed Jack by the arm, and he actually got up and moved. He wasn't out but he wasn't conscious. It was like some kind of zombie state.

Jimmy Nichols had given up alcohol as an enlisted man, after a couple of problems. He and Tracy left. Mary Federico poured her husband, Ian, and Lee Harvey into their minivan.

Milburn and I decided we weren't quite ready to drive. A DUI or DWI was an automatic career-ender for a Marine Officer, so we usually ended up on the O'Brien couch. Even though we always tried to be gone early, Lynn occasionally came out in the morning to find her living room carpeted with bodies. She was the world's best sport about it.

Frank and I policed the living room for her—Marines were the perfect house guests—and then bucked up for the couch. I got it, the first time that had ever happened.

And I woke up in the wee hours of the morning. Sometimes it happened with two snoring dachshunds lying on me. But this time it was Bonnie staring at me eye-to-eye—which was more than a little disconcerting. Milburn was gone.

"So, you broke out of the crib, huh, babyface?" I whispered to her. "Did you tie the bedding together, or did you free-climb?" She just grinned happily at me.

I picked her up and walked her around the living room for a while before taking her back to her crib. And then I beat feet out of there, checking my six in the rearview mirror to make sure she wasn't following me down the driveway.

CHAPTER FOUR

After every accident, especially fatal ones, there is an investigation. These were the findings.

The fuse of the M67 fragmentation hand grenade has a delay of 4 to 5 seconds. Even after pulling the pin, the grenade is safe as long as the thrower keeps a firm grip on the spoon, a thin spring-loaded metal lever running from the fuse down the length of the grenade. The spoon flies off when released or the grenade is thrown. This starts the fuse burning and 4-5 seconds later the grenade blows.

Four to five seconds is a long time when clearing a room. Long enough for someone to pick up the grenade and throw it back at you. So ordinarily the drill was for the thrower to flip off the spoon, let the fuse cook for 2 seconds, and then throw it.

But Captain Dudley refused to let us do that. Too dangerous. Ironic, isn't it? So the thrower was supposed to chuck it without releasing the spoon.

That's what happened on the range. But the grenade didn't go off. On a short throw the spoon might not have released. Or it could have been a dud for any number of reasons.

But it was a dud, and there were specific rules for dealing with them. The range had to go cold; that is, cease all firing. The range safety officer had to call Blackburn and request an explosive ordnance disposal team. Only when they cleared the dud could firing resume.

Sometimes EOD was busy, or it was the lunch hour, and they took a hell of a long time to show up.

Gudtfreund decided he didn't want to wait. Seeing the dud on the sand floor of the room, he decided to throw in another grenade so that its explosion would blow up the dud.

I have no idea where that bonehead idea came from. Explosives were funny things. Sometimes one charge would set off another a considerable distance away. Other times a blast an inch away did nothing. The only sure way to detonate one charge with another was to make sure they were in physical contact. I learned this in demolition training when we spent an hour meticulously policing up scattered chunks of plastic explosive after another lieutenant decided he didn't need to bother taping the bars together.

Corporal Anderson knew what was right. But, as he told us on the scene, Gudtfreund wouldn't listen to him. Anderson refused to throw in the second grenade, or allow any of his Marines to do it. So Gudtfreund threw it himself.

The second grenade didn't detonate the dud. The blast just kicked it up and over the wall of the grenade house. And probably jarred the jammed spoon loose, so when the grenade landed in the midst of Staff Sergeant Meadows debriefing Sergeant Palermo's squad, it blew up.

Unlike the Mark II pineapple of World War II, the M67 is shaped like a baseball, with a smooth steel body. The explosive charge is wrapped in steel wire, like piano wire, notched every fraction of an inch. This creates a uniform pattern of lethal fragments in a perfect circle. The wire and explosive are carefully designed so that everyone within 5 meters of the grenade becomes a casualty. But the fragments lose velocity quickly, so everyone progressively farther away is progressively safer.

Which was why Sergeant Palermo's squad suffered 100% casualties, while 20 yards away from the blast all I felt was the rush of hot air going by.

There would have been more dead except that the Marines had all been wearing helmets and flak jackets

Since it was a spectacular it made the news, even a few seconds on CNN.

We stood down from training during the investigation. If anyone needed a reminder on the nature of the profession we'd chosen and the price of mistakes, they got it.

Once everything quieted down the Chaplain timidly crept down to our office to see if anyone needed any grief counseling. O'Brien politely brushed him off.

I had no time for our Chaplain, a Baptist who'd joined the Navy because he couldn't hold a congregation. Other than battalion functions, we never saw him. He never once dropped by the company offices or the barracks to meet his flock, let alone go out to the field to get a feeling for the Marines and what they did. And the combination of a kind of shifty, squinty expression and a permanently pasted-on salesman's smile didn't do much for him.

So when he came to me I said, "Why should I be sad? None of *my* Marines got killed."

He looked like he'd just received an invitation to a black mass. His smile faded but didn't disappear, and the eye with the squint started twitching. For some reason he didn't ask anyone else if they needed grief counseling. He just left, kind of fast.

O'Brien's face slowly appeared from around his wall locker. "Oh, you fucker," he breathed. But he was smiling, so he knew I was just screwing with the padre, not disrespecting his dead.

"Fine work, Mike," Milburn said. "Who's going to look after our spiritual needs now?"

Eventually the Commanding General received the investigation report and made his determinations. Captain Dudley was relieved from command of Echo Company. Even if not physically present, officers are responsible for whatever happens or fails to happen in their commands. They can delegate their authority but never their responsibility. Dudley's Marine Corps career was over.

So was Gudtfreund's, and there might still be a court-martial in his future. We all felt it was negligent homicide. And in today's military it was much more likely for a measly 1st lieutenant to get hung for something like that than, say, the captain of a sub who killed a bunch of Japanese sailors.

We never saw Captain Dudley again. We heard that he tried to render fitness reports on all of us before he left, but Colonel Sweatman ripped them up right in front of him.

So we got a new company commander, Captain Charles Zimmerman. It was kind of surprising to find that name attached to a North Carolina redneck, but life was full of surprises.

The quarters were so close in his office that my armpits were sweating even though the air conditioning was roaring. I was breathing through my mouth to keep from gagging at the sickly sweet smell of all the chewing tobacco spit into empty soda cans. The sound was almost as bad; like cows being milked into metal pails. I think I was the only Marine infantry officer who didn't either drink coffee or dip snuff.

Everyone was sitting with notebooks open. What would be our ruler's will?

Our new XO was Dick Herkimer, a tall Nordic type who'd come over from Golf Company. When the blond guys cut their hair Marine Corps short it went vertical without the aid of gel.

Giddy from five days of being a company commander, Jim Nichols actually went to admin to have the command tour put into his record book. He'd also started a mustache. Meeting Captain Zimmerman for the first time, the Captain's eyes dropped to Jim's upper lip and he gave his first order in command. "Shave that fucking caterpillar off your face."

Just outside the room was the fallout from the Captain's second order upon assuming command. Two of Captain Dudley's three company clerks had been sent back to their respective platoons to be grunts again. The sole survivor, Corporal Cates, was tapping away at the computer keyboard, his days of lazing around the office smoking cigarettes, drinking coffee, and bossing the two junior clerks now only a memory.

Captain Zimmerman was swiveling around in his chair like a little kid waiting for his parents to get up on Christmas morning. Not every captain got a rifle company.

Contrary to all my previous experience with Marine Captains, he didn't begin by telling us how great he was and all the wonderful things we were going to do. He just stated his facts. "All right. I'll say one thing about the past. From now on no one in this company takes a safety shortcut without clearing it with me first. Everyone understand me?"

We all nodded.

"I don't have to tell you," the Captain said, "in exactly six months we go aboard ship and deploy to the Mediterranean."

Omen or not, that very same day we officially joined the 32nd Marine Expeditionary Unit (Special Operations Capable) as its ground combat element. It was pronounced Three-Two MEU, as in the sound a kitten makes.

Every year or so every Marine infantry battalion packed up and deployed overseas for a six month stretch. Either to Okinawa, where the 3rd Marine Division was made up of deploying East Coast, West Coast, and Hawaii-based battalions. Or aboard ship as part of a MEU.

Which was the Marine part of a 3-ship amphibious task force. There's always one afloat in the Mediterranean, and one in the Pacific. Commanded by a full colonel, a MEU was a Battalion Landing Team, an Air Combat Element, and a MEU Service Support Group.

We were the battalion landing team. With the addition of a tank platoon, an amphibious assault vehicle platoon, an artillery battery of 8 155mm towed howitzers, a combat engineer platoon, a ground reconnaissance platoon, and a light armored reconnaissance platoon of 7 six-wheeled light armored vehicles mounting 25mm cannon.

The Air Combat Element was a composite helicopter squadron with light, medium, and heavy transport helicopters, attack helicopters, and Harrier jump jets.

The MEU Service Support Group, or MSSG, kept it in the field with supply, engineer, motor transport, landing force support, communications, maintenance, and medical platoons.

A MEU was the tip of the spear, the first to arrive at any crisis. I think we all felt relieved to be rid of Captain Dudley before that happened.

Captain Zimmerman continued. "We have to get on top of conventional operations for the MCCRES. And as soon as we check that block we have to start worrying about the Special Operations Exercise. The way it usually works is we train to college level and convince ourselves we're PhD's. Well, I intend for this company to become PhD's in infantry tactics."

He held up a hand to signal a halt. "I know what you're thinking. New CO comes in all tanned, rested, and ready. To get himself noticed he runs the troops hard and hangs them up wet. Then he turns them over to the next eager beaver. To keep from doing that we're going to plan out every minute of training tighter than a gnat's ass. So from now on when we go to the field, except for classes we're tactical all the way. None of this camping out shit."

I looked over at O'Brien. One of his eyebrows was raised fractionally higher than the other.

"I want to get a handle on our individual load," he said. "We are flat out carrying too much shit to the field. Gunny?"

"Yes, sir?" said Gunny Harris, the Company Gunnery Sergeant. The Gunny was big, black, and ferocious looking. Easy to write off as a Marine Corps stereotype, but one night on a bivouac we'd spent a long time discussing military history, and I'd come away highly impressed.

The Captain said, "I want all the tents turned back in to supply."

Expressionless, the Gunny said, "The CP tent too, sir?" Captain Dudley had made the whole company take tents to the field. Ridiculous for infantrymen, who either slept in the fighting holes they'd dug or leaned against their packs on patrol. Picture unzipping yourself from a tent while the enemy was attacking. It was just so he could use his Command Post tent, with folding cot, field desk, and Coleman lantern.

"You can burn that motherfucker," the Captain retorted. "No, check fire on that. I'm signed for it. Just turn it all in."

Jim Nichols had his pen raised for a question.

"Yes, Lieutenant Nichols?" the Captain said.

"Sir, are we wearing the ballistic plates in the flak jackets, or not?"

If the Captain knew that the Gunny's and Nichols's questions were our way of testing him, he gave no sign. The Interceptor flak jacket weighed eight pounds, and stopped fragmentation and bullets up to the 9mm pistol round. Ceramic ballistic plates could be inserted into front and rear pockets to stop 7.62mm rifle bullets, but they brought the weight of the jacket up to sixteen pounds. Captain Dudley made every excuse not to wear the plates.

Captain Zimmerman said, "You just touched a sore point of mine, Jim. We wear flak jackets in the jungle, we wear them in the desert, we wear them humping in the North Carolina summer. No one cares about losing a squad to heat casualties, but if anything ever happened to one Marine who wasn't wearing his flak jacket the commanding officer would hang. So we never take the goddamned things off, regardless of the tactical situation."

He sighed. "That's what I think. But one of the first things I learned when I joined this gun club was that the people running it really don't give a shit about what I think." That made him smile. "Since I know y'all do, I'll tell you. If we go to war they're going to make us wear the jackets and the plates. So we might as well get used to them. Find out how far we can go, and how fast."

"Roger that, sir," said Nichols.

The Captain had a hell of a lot more guidance to pass. He'd probably been holding it in since he was a lieutenant. By the time he was finished I couldn't feel my ass anymore.

O'Brien said to me, "What do you think?"

"I like what I heard. What about you?"

Jack was equivocal. "Money talks and bullshit walks. He's a ball of fire now. We'll see if he sticks to it."

I was a little surprised, but I realized that this was his third company commander, and the previous two had been incompetent. Not to mention assholes.

CHAPTER FIVE

Before he took us to the field for the first time, Captain Zimmerman made a statement. An unannounced urinalysis. A commander could order everyone to pee in the bottle at any time. Captain Dudley hadn't. There were some zero-defects commanders who boasted about having no drug problems in their units. But no one was popping positive because no one was peeing in the bottle.

On our way to the head I told Jack O'Brien the story of my first Marine Corps piss test. We were screamingly awakened at OCS and put standing at attention in our skivvies in front of our racks.

My Sergeant Instructor, which is what they called a drill instructor at OCS, was Sergeant Louis. A short, stocky black man, a master of psychological warfare. The others were the stereotypical screaming hillbillies. They don't specifically screen for screaming hillbillies; Drill Instructor School is like acting school and they all come out like that. But Sergeant Louis was different. One day with him and Freud would have been found huddled in a corner sucking his thumb.

Sgt. Louis had walked down the line and handed us each a plastic bottle. But instead of being sent into the head, as we expected, we received the following series of orders. In true OCS style, first the preparatory command, then the command of execution.

"Unscrew the bottles. Do it."

"Pull out your little lizards. Do it."

"Fill up your bottles." But with a caveat. *"And if one drop hits the deck, you can all just stand the fuck by."*

"That's some old Corps shit," O'Brien said, impressed. "Talk about putting your career on the line."

It was all totally illegal, of course. Even using profanity in front of trainees was illegal. If word had ever gotten out the whole staff would have been fired. But no one ever talked. It might have been the Stockholm Syndrome, where we ended up sympathizing with our captors—I don't know. But I really think we all had too much admiration for Sgt. Louis' personal panache.

"But a piss test has to be administered by an officer," said O'Brien. "Someone went along with that?"

"He was a brand new second lieutenant. You know, one of those shitty jobs they give you if you're hanging around Quantico waiting for your Basic School class to start. He didn't know whether to shit or go blind." I chuckled. "He probably still thinks that's the way you do a piss test."

"And did anyone spill a drop?"

"No way. But the worst part was pinching it off and having to wait in line to turn in the bottle before you could run for the head and finish up."

"A classic," O'Brien said.

We cut to the head of the line and filled our bottles to show the troops that the officers really were doing it too.

Soon afterward Frank Milburn approached us with a problem. "I got one who says he can't piss," he said. "Valentine." Then, in a whiny voice, "I tried and I tried, sir, but I just can't go."

"He's stalling," said Nichols.

"No shit," Milburn replied. "He knows he's going to pop positive."

"He's probably just a little bashful," O'Brien protested mischievously. "He can't tinkle with people watching. And now you're going to pick on the poor kid."

"You're goddamned right I am," said Milburn.

"Where is he?" Nichols asked.

"Still in the head, with Corporal Kinder. And that's where he's staying until he goes."

"If it's ecstasy or meth," I said. "And he did it early enough in the weekend, he may think he can beat the test if he holds out until late afternoon."

"And he may be right," said Milburn. "I'd like to start squeezing his fucking skull, but that's against the law."

Then I had a very twisted idea. "You mind if I take a crack at it?"

Milburn was suspicious, but he couldn't resist. Neither could the others, who all followed me into the head. A skinny Marine was pacing back and forth, while a thoroughly disgusted corporal sat in a chair and watched him.

"Lance Corporal Valentine," I said, my voice oozing with concern. "I understand you can't urinate."

He stopped pacing and eyed me warily. "Yes, sir, I just don't know what's wrong."

"When was the last time you went?" I asked.

"Uh, last night, sir."

I turned to my fellow lieutenants. "It's serious."

O'Brien had to face the wall to keep from laughing.

"Your bladder could rupture at any time," I said. "We need to get you to sick bay for immediate catheterization."

Getting concerned, Valentine asked, "What's that, sir?"

"It's a pretty simple procedure," I said, illustrating with my hands. "They take a plastic tubing and push it into the hole in the head of your dick…."

Valentine and everyone else in the bathroom involuntarily grimaced. Major guy thing.

"They keep pushing the tube in until it hits your bladder," I continued. "Taps it like a beer keg. Drains all your piss into a bag, you don't have to do a thing." I paused, and we could all see the gears in Valentine's brain whirring to try and find a way out. "We have to move fast, though, your bladder could go at any time."

I turned to my fellow lieutenants for confirmation. They all nodded gravely.

"It'll be all right," I assured him. "It won't be *too* painful."

Valentine said, "Uh, sir, I think I should give it another try first."

"Well, make it quick. They're waiting for you in sickbay."

Valentine grabbed the bottle, turned to the nearest urinal, and filled it to the brim. The battalion Intelligence Officer, who also doubled as the Drug and Alcohol Officer, was called to maintain the chain of custody. The bottle was sealed, signed, and removed.

We left the head triumphant.

"You are one sick motherfucker," O'Brien told me.

I don't think I've ever received a finer compliment.

We always waited until the last minute to put on our gear for the field, for reasons that will be apparent.

First a fat nylon gas mask bag that rode on the left hip. Then the Interceptor flak jacket, now with plates. Rifle magazine, grenade, and utility pouches attached right to the flak jacket, as did a bayonet, two 1-quart canteens, and a first aid pouch. The utilities were binoculars, camouflage face paint, flashlight, AN/PVS-14 night vision monocular, and Precision Lightweight GPS receiver that we called a Plugger.

Instead of the large framed rucksack stuffed with Captain Dudley's unnecessary comfort items, the small patrol pack containing only a poncho, mosquito headnet, two pairs of socks, a razor and a toothbrush, and an entrenching tool. Then three pounds of Kevlar helmet wrapped in a cotton camouflage cover. And finally the M-16A2 rifle. Though not politically correct to say so, so sexy that you could tell the relative new-ness of a Marine by whether or not he'd finally stopped posing with it.

Our new load almost gave lie to why a Marine infantryman is always called a grunt, after the sound made lifting all his gear off the deck and onto his back. We left the office to join the company forming up in the parking lot.

The morning air was still fresh with dew, though it wouldn't be for long, and smelled of newly mown grass and CLP rifle oil.

A rifle platoon was supposed to be three 13-man squads plus a headquarters of a platoon commander, platoon sergeant, platoon guide, radio operator, and Navy medical corpsman.

I had a grand total of seventeen Marines. I don't know what anyone was expecting, but they were the American melting pot, exactly rep-resentative of their society. Except they were the working class part of the country that the college-bound part knows next to nothing about.

The only thing they all had in common was having successfully escaped from where they didn't want to be. The Marine Corps was the means, and the mechanism by which they could now portray themselves as tough motherfuckers, no matter what they really felt like inside.

The platoon had been previously commanded by Jimmy Nichols, and he'd been very popular. Which made me forever leery of officers trying to be popular with the troops, because I'd inherited an undisciplined mob. It seemed that Marines would absolutely love your ass if you only went easy on haircuts, physical training, inspections, and discipline.

I'd found this out my first company formation as I watched, with sinking disbelief, the Marines of 2nd platoon straggle out of their rooms, scratching their balls like F Troop, while the rest of the company was all lined up in front of the barracks. At first I thought they had to be fucking with the new lieutenant—they *couldn't* be that screwed up. But they were. And that was when I started being a dick.

Especially because I only had a grand total of three non-commissioned officers. Sergeant Harlin was filling in as platoon sergeant in the absence of a staff sergeant. He was the enlisted equivalent of Frank Milburn, a recruiting poster type. Looked squared away, seemed confident, appeared knowledgeable. But then why was the platoon so fucked up? And why had he been just standing around after the grenade accident?

Corporal Jones had 1st squad but was getting out of the Corps in less than a month. He'd dropped his pack miles back down the road.

And then there was Corporal Turner, the 2nd squad leader. A tall black corporal old enough to be a staff sergeant. Which, unfortunately, he had been. He'd even been a Platoon Sergeant at OCS, the senior member of the team with the sergeant instructor. OCS was a high stress job, 24/7 and the staff didn't even leave the barracks the first couple of weeks. Staff Sergeant Turner got into amphetamines to keep going, and popped a urinalysis. That knocked him down to sergeant, and then they were gunning for him. Ten minutes late for a court appearance and he was a corporal.

I'd regarded him as nothing but a massive potential leadership problem until Lance Corporal Reilly broke his hand. Reilly was one of my fire team leaders and prospective corporals, a black Irishman whose cherubic face was marred by a nose that had been broken more than once. Hit an Irishman in the nose enough times and eventually it looks like it's going to disappear back into his face.

"What happened to your arm, Reilly?" I'd asked.

"Slipped and fell on the wet deck…in the head…sir."

I didn't change expression. "No, how did you *really* break your hand?"

He was stumbling badly; it wasn't like I needed a polygraph. "Uh, that's how I really broke my hand, sir."

My tone was incredulous. "You want to stick with that story?"

"Uh, yes sir."

"All right," I'd said regretfully. "It's up to you."

Then I'd gone to Corporal Turner. "How did Lance Corporal Reilly break his hand?"

"He slipped on a wet deck, sir."

"Corporal Turner, do you know what time of day I was born?"

Totally mystified. "No, sir."

"The afternoon. But it wasn't *yesterday* afternoon."

Against his will, he let out a little bark of a laugh.

"How did Reilly break his hand?" I repeated.

He thought it over, and I think decided he couldn't afford to piss me off. "Sir, you know about that Army Ranger company that flew in to train on our Combat Town?"

I'd nodded.

"Well, sir, some of the platoon ran into some of those Rangers at the enlisted club. And one of those Rangers keeps yelling all this, "Rangers Lead the Way" hoo-ya shit, pissing everyone off. So after a while Reilly walks over, real nice, and tells them they don't want to play that shit in our house. The Ranger stands up, yells, "Fuck you, Jarhead, and fuck the Marine Corps!" and swings at Reilly. Sir, Reilly knocks him out cold with one punch." Corporal Turner was really animated. Like every Marine, he firmly believed that the only reason anyone joined the Army was because they didn't have the balls to be a Marine.

"Reilly had every Marine behind him, sir, and that Doggie was an Army of One. So much for all that Ranger shit. Those boys are all mouth and no hang. One punch, sir, you know how hard that is to do?" Suddenly aware that he might be prejudicing his client's case, Corporal

Turner got a grip on himself.

But I'd been thinking about my Uncle Michael, for whom I'm named. He ran a bar in South Boston, and those who know Southy bars know that expensive damage to the physical plant can erupt at any time and with very little warning. Uncle Mike attributed his professional success to his ability to put the rowdy to sleep with a single punch. Once demonstrated, it didn't have to be employed very often. In fact, it was the erosion of this skill that led him to turn over day-to-day operations to my cousin.

I remember him saying, "It's time, Michael. Before, I hit a guy it was lights out. Now when I hit 'em they stand there and do funny things. Pretty soon...."

I'd come out of that reverie when Corporal Turner said, "Sir, Reilly is one of the best Marines in the platoon."

And that was how Corporal Turner won me over. He could have played it safe and kept his mouth shut, which would have been the smart move with a new platoon commander and his precarious situation. But not knowing what I was going to do, he went out on a limb for Reilly.

Then he asked, "What are you going to do, sir?"

I knew how it would go over. The senior officers wanted Marines to be Little Lord Fauntleroy's in garrison and not cause any career-damaging incidents, and then somehow morph into aggressive fighting men when sent into combat.

For me there was only one decision. "Hell, Corporal Turner, if I'd burn a Marine for upholding the honor of the Corps, I ought to find myself another line of work."

That surprised him. "Aye, aye, sir."

"But this is the last time Reilly slips on the deck," I warned. "And no one better think I'm giving a free pass on thumping, on base or out in town."

"No, sir." And then he said, "Sir, about the platoon straggling out to formation. Lieutenant Nichols refused to send anyone to Office Hours. The troops do it because they think they can get away with it."

Because they had up until now. Office Hours was official but non-judicial punishment, dispensed by the Company Commander. He could impose restriction to the barracks, extra duty, and withholding of pay, not more than 14 days of each. Anything more severe had to go up to the Colonel or be referred to the more formal court-martial process. I could just picture Jimmy crowing about his perfect disciplinary record whenever one of the other platoon commanders sent a Marine in to be hammered by the Captain.

And now I knew why my NCO's had been slack. Why bother if the boss wasn't backing you up?

Captain Zimmerman appeared in front of the company with his pack on. And tied to his pack was a 60 millimeter mortar baseplate, a 14.5 pound aluminum disk that kept the mortar tube from being driven into the ground when it was fired.

We stepped off in a column of two's, each lieutenant and his radioman in front of each platoon, the platoon sergeant in the rear.

Unusually for a military that uses euphemisms for everything unpleasant, like killing, the official term for what we were doing was a "forced march." Appropriate because almost nothing in the Corps is optional. But Marines call it a hump. Grunts hump a continuous 3.5 to 4 mile an hour pace until the destination is reached, whether it's 10, 20, or 30 miles away. And anyone who can't wait for the ten minute break every hour is perfectly free to relieve themselves in their trousers.

Happy, sad, sick, well, hung-over, blistered, toenails falling out, an officer was expected to be the last one standing. If I ever fell out I could rest assured that I'd soon be behind a desk doing something useful like processing Congressional inquires until my term of service expired. But I actually liked humping—something I always kept to myself, because it would have freaked out even other Marines.

Quantico had been rolling hills, mixed hardwood forest, and red clay trails that turned to grease when it rained. Lejeune was as flat as a pancake, and from what I'd seen so far no trees but the lowly pine were able to survive the coastal North Carolina sand.

Once we broke free from the developed mainside it was all pine forest and asphalt roads paralleled by sand tank trails because armor and automobiles don't mix. We walked in the sand.

There was hardly a cloud to hinder the sun. The road was bleached almost white by it and the salt air, and reflected the light like a mirror. The flatness of the terrain could be demoralizing—I looked forward to the occasional pitiful little rise in the ground just to break up the monotony.

Every hump I'd ever been on, the officer in charge came blasting out of the gate and then slowed down when he got tired. Nobody could keep to a steady pace. Captain Dudley had been the worst, starting so fast he nearly put the whole company in the ditch and then finishing so slow that, like South American tree sloths, moss could have grown on us. Captain Zimmerman was much better, but the mortar baseplate was half leadership performance art, half acknowledgment that he needed something to weigh him down.

Pretty soon our uniform camouflage began to fade into monotone dark sweat stains. The heat rose off our bodies, collected under our helmets, and stayed trapped there in an evil little cloud under the Kevlar. Whenever I took it off on a break I could feel my brain temperature drop. And we all had identical angry inflamed spots on our chins from the rubbing of the chinstraps.

I sucked water from my Camelbak water bag and went off inside my own head. Mostly I just sang a favorite song to myself, over and over. I called it the humping song; I think everyone had one. Wish I could remember the name of it.

When we finished the platoon corpsman checked everyone's feet while I looked on. Doc Bob was short and slightly rotund, with a round face and an indiscernible chin. He always reminded me of a scholarly but sweet-tempered badger in some illustrated children's book.

A Navy medical corpsman is always called Doc, but never by his first name. However, the company stood a battalion commander's inspection just after my Doc reported in. Lieutenant Colonel Sweatman was trooping the line, and of course he stopped in front of the Doc, saying in that hearty Colonel way, "What's your name, Doc?"

The Colonel was expecting just one of two possible replies. "HN Wiley, sir." Or, "Doc Wiley, sir." And everyone else was terrified that a discipline-challenged sailor might screw up and call him "Colonel" instead of "Sir."

Well, the Doc looked all the way up at the Colonel, broke into the biggest shit-eating grin you ever saw in your life, and then, like they were best buds back on the block together, said, "Bob."

Colonel Sweatman didn't know whether to laugh out loud or tear the

Doc a new asshole, so he'd just walked on, mumbling to himself. The Sergeant Major and the Chief Corpsman were the ones who ripped the Doc a new one, and from that day forward he'd been Doc Bob. A damn fine corpsman, too.

The focus of that week's training was the brainchild of Major Thom, the battalion executive officer. The battalion would soon undergo the MCCRES, pronounced Mac-cress. Which stood for Marine Corps Combat Readiness Evaluation System. A multiple-day exercise, simulated combat against another battalion, where we'd be evaluated on all our skills.

Major Thom thought we should have an in-house platoon-level MCCRES, where every rifle platoon was evaluated on an attack scenario. It was the kind of thing executive officers thought up, and commanders went along with to keep them happy.

Captain Zimmerman gave his platoon commanders two days to work with their Marines on their own, something else Captain Dudley had never done. Separate platoon bivouacs, too. In keeping with the Captain's new policy, we dug fighting holes and sent out patrols when we weren't doing the scheduled training.

The Marine rifle squad was supposed to be led by a sergeant and consist of three 4-man fire teams: a team leader corporal armed with an M-203 40mm grenade launcher mounted under his M-16; a rifleman armed with an M-16; an automatic rifleman armed with the M-249 Squad Automatic Weapon or SAW, a light machine-gun firing the same 5.56mm round as the M-16 but from a 200-round linked ammo belt stored in a plastic box that snapped underneath the weapon; and an assistant automatic rifleman armed with an M-16 who carried the spare barrel for the SAW and extra ammo.

A very effective force, assuming everyone knew what the hell they were doing.

When I told them we'd start with basic movement there was a lot of eye rolling.

"What's the problem?" I asked.

"We know all that stuff, sir," said Corporal Jones.

"It's always squad in the attack," someone in back muttered.

"Fine," I said. "Show me you got game and we'll move on."

So much for assumptions. While moving in combat formation I suddenly changed direction and the Marines on flank security just continued on, oblivious. They couldn't even be bothered to look over at the main body.

All the individual palm-sized mini walkie-talkies we called the intrasquad radio were in the shop that week for tweaking. Just my luck. So it was hand and arm signals. I still couldn't shake the feeling that they had to be fucking with me—trained Marines just couldn't be that screwed up.

I guess I wasn't the only one feeling that way, because when his Marines wouldn't look back at him for signals, Corporal Turner started throwing rocks at their heads.

Instead of life and death, they were treating it the way they'd learned to treat school for the past twelve years, as something they were forced to do that had no relation to anything else. I realized I was going to have to be a dick. I called the platoon in and said, "I'll tell you what I really believe: if you do it half-assed in training it becomes habit, and in combat you'll fall back on habit and get someone killed. So from now on we're going to be doing it the right way every time. After we take a break for a change of pace." There was muttered approval—for the break, that is.

"Platoon!" I called out. "Atten-hut! Pushup position...move!" We all dropped down into the pushup position, placing our rifles on top of our hands to keep them off the ground. There were the expected groans of protest.

We did some pushups. Then some mountain climbers. Then some flutter kicks.

"All right," I said cheerfully. "Squad leaders, take five minutes and make sure everyone gets some water. Then we'll start again."

Corporal Jones hurried up to where I was sitting. "Sir," he said earnestly. "I've got to tell you it's against Marine Corps orders to make anyone do incentive PT."

I was touched by his concern for my welfare. From time immemorial in the Corps, when a Marine screwed up in a minor way it was handled quickly and simply. If he dropped his rifle a corporal dropped him for pushups. This was known as incentive PT, for physical training. If a

Marine wore his uniform like a tramp he stood inspection on Saturday morning when everyone else was on liberty.

Anything can be abused, but instead of hammering the abusers, the generals, true to form, declared all forms of incentive PT to be illegal, except at Boot Camp. Which meant that even though everyone still did it, in true zero-defect fashion *their* asses were covered.

In our battalion you needed the Colonel's permission to work on a weekend. Which he never gave. Because his ass was hanging out if a Marine died of heat stroke while some lieutenant was PT'ing him on Saturday.

With every informal means of discipline available to NCO's ripped away, the only alternative was Office Hours. And if the matter was relatively minor a company commander might refuse to hold it, and the offending Marine would be thumbing his nose at the NCO.

I said, "You're mistaken Corporal Jones. I did not hold incentive PT. I held platoon PT to enhance the physical readiness of all the Marines under my command. I don't allow incentive PT, and anyone who accuses me of violating an order had better be prepared to back it up. Anything else?"

"Oh, ah, no sir." He wilted and slunk off.

I took a walk to pee in the bushes and give Corporal Jones time to give everyone the good news. Everyone always knew their rights. They were just a little fuzzy on their responsibilities.

But when we got going again it was amazing how much sharper everyone was. It had to have been my motivational speech.

I was even more amazed when, heading back to the company bivouac, the point signaled "enemy ahead." Carefully moving up, I saw that they'd located 1st platoon's squad leaders. Corporal Anderson and Corporal Beausoleil were sprawled out in a clearing, gear off and shooting the shit.

Both arms outstretched in a "safe at home" motion was the signal for everyone to move up on line—so they could fire freely to their front without shooting each other.

As Corporal Turner and his squad came up I got his attention and signaled enemy ahead with my rifle. While I was still thinking about how to signal it, he was already taking his squad on a wide right arc to make a flanking maneuver.

We inched forward without a sound. No one was supposed to open fire until the leader did, unless they absolutely had to. Since we didn't have any blanks, I shouted, "Bam, bam!"

Pretty lame, but the platoon went along with it.

Caught with their pants down, Anderson and Beausoleil jumped up, fumbled with their gear, finally got ahold of it, and ran.

And they ran right into Corporal Turner's squad, who popped up and ambushed them at point-blank range.

Anderson and Beausoleil fell down, got up, swerved, and disappeared into the brush, trailed by all the abuse my platoon was shouting at them.

Now, if life were like a movie, this would have been the dramatic moment in the delicate relationship between me and the platoon when we began to turn the corner. No such luck.

The 1st platoon squad leaders had plotted their revenge; they were waiting in ambush as we returned to our bivouac site that evening. And my platoon just walked through it and did nothing, as if to say: fuck you, we're tired.

"One minute they're geniuses," I said to Jack O'Brien, who was watching the whole thing. "The next minute they're assholes. The problem is I have to act like a total prick to get them to be geniuses. The asshole part they do all on their own."

"They're used to doing things a certain way," he replied. "You got your work cut out for you."

It hadn't been a one-way street, not by any means. While we were tip-toeing around 1st platoon's bivouac after dark I had Lance Corporal Vincent turn the radio off so an incoming call wouldn't compromise us. I also told him to tell the company CP we'd be off the net for a while.

I didn't give it any more thought until, back at our bivouac, Captain Zimmerman and Gunny Harris appeared out of the darkness. The Captain didn't quite chew my ass, but he nibbled it really hard for having my radio off. The Gunny did the same for Sergeant Harlin. Vincent hadn't turned the radio back on because I hadn't told him to. And with all the barking I'd done all day he wasn't about to do *anything* I hadn't specifically told him to do.

The talking-to was nothing compared to the whipping I gave myself.

Especially after spending all day chewing the platoon out for screwing up. Poetic justice I'm sure the troops savored like a cold beer after work.

The next day was better, though I wasn't sure if my patience could take it.

The following morning the company was supposed to pack up and hump to the training area where the platoon MCCRES would be held. We'd move cross-country in combat formation, and 2nd platoon would be the point for the movement. What was called an advance to contact, and the way the Captain always wanted his company to move tactically. The only thing certain in war, he said, was that the enemy was never going to be where intelligence told you they were. So you had to be ready to bump into them at any time.

Since the Captain wanted to leave very early we'd already filled in our fighting holes. So instead of the usual 50% alert, Sergeant Harlin assigned Marines to 1-hour radio/security watches all night long. The last man had orders to wake the platoon. Sergeant Harlin and I set reveille early enough to give us plenty of time to eat and pack up before the scheduled start time for the hump.

Tired, hot, and disgusted, I put on my gloves and mosquito head net to keep the bugs at bay. The nighttime low temperature was probably about 80°.

I could not get over the state of my platoon. How lazy and self-absorbed they were; they got hysterical if chow was five minutes late but couldn't care less about what they might need to know to save their own lives.

But the situation wasn't totally grim. Corporal Turner really had his shit together, and the fire team leaders were trying hard even though they had no experience. I finally fell asleep.

And awoke to full sunlight. Wait a minute, that wasn't right. I looked at my watch, blinked the grit out of my eyes, and looked again. The company would be stepping off in fifteen minutes. Holy screaming shit!

I ripped off my head net and shook Sergeant Harlin, Corporal Turner, and Corporal Jones awake. "We've got fifteen minutes before the company steps off!" I shouted. "Get everyone moving, now!"

It took a second to register on them. Then they went berserk. And a few seconds later so did the whole platoon. The sheer amount of kicking and shouting and cursing can only be imagined. Dust was flying everywhere, gear was being jammed into packs. As the Marines finally lashed down their pack straps, the NCO's and I frantically scoured the pine needle-covered ground for any misplaced equipment.

Needless to say, I was not going to call the Captain on the radio and ask him to hold up the entire company because 2nd platoon had overslept.

We blew into the CP area at a dead run. The rest of the company were calmly sitting on their packs awaiting the order to move out. We double-timed into position literally as the clock ticked over to the scheduled time of departure.

It was that close. We'd made it, but I wouldn't want to know what my blood pressure was just then. The troops hadn't even gotten the chance to splash a little water on their faces, let alone have any chow. Hopefully they'd filled their canteens the night before. What an utter debacle.

Fortunately I'd planned my navigation the night before. Getting myself and the entire company lost on top of everything else was too nightmarish to even contemplate.

The GPS hit the tank trail intersection that marked the MCCRES course starting line right on the nose. Two of the battalion staff were waiting for us. The Air Officer, a helicopter pilot dragooned to a year of duty with the grunts. And the S-3A, or Assistant Operations Officer. Both captains.

After a short consultation with Captain Zimmerman, the word came back that the platoons would run the course in regular order: 1,2,3.

O'Brien stepped off with 1st platoon and the Air Officer as an evaluator. Every other company in the battalion had already run the course.

Finally the S-3A called me over to his terrain model and gave me a formal operation order. A machine-gun squad, two guns, was attached to my platoon.

There would be a simulated artillery barrage hitting the objective at a designated time. So I couldn't attack before or during it, and I couldn't wait too long after it ended. It was an artificial constraint to put me under time pressure. Fire missions were turned on and off by radio.

The navigation was easy. I pulled out my map and protractor to plot good old-fashioned compass bearings and distances, just to back up the GPS.

After all the orders I'd given and received in training, always under time pressure, I could do this in my sleep. With the past couple of days fresh in my mind, I went into more detail in the execution paragraph than I would have normally.

Then I watched, with bated breath, as the squad leaders briefed their squads. Corporal Turner was immaculate. Hell, he'd probably taught officer candidates to do it. Corporal Jones was shakier, but still pulled it off all right. That was another class I'd have to teach to the whole platoon.

We crossed the line of departure right on time. And then, right on time, I had to pee. It always happened. Not a whisper of an urge before. All I had to do was cross the line of departure for an attack. Nothing to do but hold it in.

Corporal Turner's squad was in the lead, and I walked just behind him. Lance Corporal Vincent was behind me, close enough to hand me the radio handset. The S-3A was beside me as the evaluator.

We were paralleling a tank trail, but I'd laid out my course to take us farther into the woods. The underbrush on base was particularly thick beside the trails.

I halted the platoon just short of our first checkpoint. We were supposed to make a short security halt to see how smoothly the platoon could transition from a movement formation to a hasty 360° security perimeter.

Corporal Turner's point man halted, and the rest of the squad fanned out to form a semicircle. Then Corporal Jones brought his squad up to complete the circle. No hesitation, no switching places, no gaps in the perimeter, no screwups. I breathed a sigh of relief.

The S-3A said, "This is the smoothest movement so far."

Instead of grinning like an idiot I should have recognized the evil omen. As soon as we got moving again and crossed the tank trail my

GPS died. I showed it to the S-3A and he shook his head in sympathy.
I held up a hand to halt the platoon and moved up to Corporal Turner.

"The GPS is dead," I whispered to him. "I'll get on the compass and
start bearing toward the tank trail we're running alongside. Tell your
flank man to let you know when he sees it. He'll guide on the tank trail,
and we'll all guide on him. Everything clear?"

"Roger, sir," he replied briskly.

I gave him a few seconds to run over and brief his flank man. I let the
now-useless GPS dangle from the strap beneath my armpit, and flipped
open my compass. Sometimes a low battery gave a GPS hiccups, but
I'd never had one just die on me before.

We moved out again without having wasted much time. The terrain
was so flat that trying to compare the contours of the ground to the
contours on a map was useless. A half degree off my compass bearing
and we'd walk right by the objective. So the flank man would follow
the tank trail, keeping just out of sight in the brush. And we would
follow him.

Finally Corporal Turner signaled and I turned the navigation over to
him. But I'd still keep an eye on the compass.

I'd been calculating the distance traveled by counting my paces.
We'd deploy just short of another intersecting trail, cross it, and assault
the objective—which was at the junction of the two tank trails.

O'Brien and his platoon, having completed their attack, would be
the aggressors for us.

The point stopped. Corporal Turner moved up, looking agitated. I
glanced at my watch; we were running out of time.

Now I moved up too. And stared in disbelief at the huge cleared
area, blackened by forest fire, that was blocking our way. We hadn't
been guiding on the tank trail after all. It was between us and the trail.
And we didn't have time to go around it. Son of a bitch!

Corporal Turner looked like he wanted to shoot himself. I wanted to
shoot him.

I ran over to the machine-gun squad leader. "Set up your guns to
cover our move across the clearing." From Field Marshal Erwin Rommel's classic book *Infantry Attacks*. Never make an uncovered move.

He looked at me as if I was speaking Mongolian. I time to neither explain nor strike him with the butt of my rifle.

I ran back to Corporal Jones. "Come up to the edge of the clearing and cover our move. When I signal come across on line at the double time and bring the machine-guns with you."

"Aye, aye, sir," he replied.

Second squad and I sprinted across the clearing. Then I signaled for 1st Squad to follow. We went back into column and had to move fast to get where we were supposed to be in the first place. Hopefully we hadn't lost anyone, or Sergeant Harlin in the rear had been able to round them up. It was as if we were crawling and the time racing by.

Without a second to spare, but still not late, I finally brought the platoon on line and signaled the assault. I actually thought we were going to make it.

We started fire and movement. You begin on your belly, get up and make a short rush forward to the next cover, then fire to cover your teammates making their rushes. Then we ran into a wall of wait-a-minute thorn bushes. And instead of crashing through and resuming fire and movement the platoon stayed on their feet and continued the assault standing up, as if they were going over the top in World War I. Sergeant Harlin, the squad leaders, and yours truly were all yelling, "Fire and move! FIRE AND MOVE!!" at the top of our lungs, but were totally ignored.

While I was still reeling from this, Corporal Jones and 1st squad swerved to the left, broke away from the rest of us, and vanished from sight. I was running after the platoon shouting, "Jones, shift right! Get back with the platoon! Jones!" To no avail.

All this happened right before the eyes of Colonel Sweatman, Major Thom, and Captain Zimmerman. It must have been a sight to behold, a lieutenant chasing vainly after his platoon, yelling his lungs out.

Then it was over. Corporal Turner came up to me. "Sir…"

"We'll talk about this later," I said evenly. It's amazing, just when you're sure you've exhausted all your self-control, you find a little more. "Put your squad in the defense, 3rd platoon should be showing up soon." I pointed out the line I wanted. And then, "Sergeant Harlin?"

He looked exactly the way anyone would if they had a block of TNT with a burning fuse super-glued to their hand, and were waiting for it to go off. "Yes sir?"

"See if you can find Corporal Jones and 1ˢᵗ squad."

A few seconds later Corporal Jones came running up with his squad. Out of breath, but he had his spin ready to go. "I don't know how we did it, sir, but we took the objective."

To this day he probably has no idea how close he came to getting his lights punched out. I had to jam my hands into my pockets. "Corporal Jones, if you know what's good for you, you won't say another fucking word right now. Just get away from me and go tie in with Corporal Turner." Then I couldn't help it, I shouted, "And stay tied in this time!"

Humiliation doesn't even begin to describe it. My face felt like it was on fire. Hemingway said that a man could be destroyed but not defeated. Well, I wasn't destroyed, but I sure as hell was defeated.

It wasn't going to get any easier, so I marched over to the senior officers to take my medicine.

Colonel Sweatman said, "Hey, Lieutenant Galway, there'll be attacks like these. Go back to your platoon."

"Aye, aye, sir," I said.

Then Captain Zimmerman took me off to one side. I prepared myself for the mother of all ass-chewings, and maybe even getting fired. Instead he said very calmly, "The Marines bagged out on you; you can't let them get away with that. After this last attack is over, I want you to run it again and keep making them do it until they get it right."

All I could manage was, "Aye, aye, sir." You never knew.

Once Milburn was done I double-timed the platoon down the tank trail and cut back into the woods. The first thing I did was make them practice guiding on a road the right way. I think this wounded Corporal Turner's pride more than if I'd publicly ripped his ass. But you couldn't just decide to ignore orders and designate yourself the unit's human compass. Or if you did you'd better not screw it up.

I made them fire and move through those wait-a-minute thorn bushes five times. By the time they were done the bushes were beaten down to the ground, and the Marines were as red and ripped as I was after the first attack.

Then the word crackled over the radio that the trucks had arrived, and I ran them all the way back down that sand tank trail to the original line of departure.

While the platoon was loading themselves aboard the trucks, I happened to overhear a piece of a casual conversation between two of Milburn's NCO's near the front of the vehicles.

One said, "Yeah, I heard the lieutenant screaming from all the way up here...."

A slap to the face would have been easier to take.

The truck ride back to mainside gave me a lot of time to think. In his classic of military theory, *On War,* Clausewitz wrote that everything is simple in war, but even the very simplest thing is difficult. He used the word "friction" to illustrate the abrasive effects of terrain, weather, and human nature upon events.

I got it. I was *raw* from all the friction.

Nothing but doubts. I'd watched a lot of my fellow officers learn what they were taught and act like that was all they ever had to learn. While I made it my mission to read everything on infantry tactics I could get my hands on. Was I one of those guys who excelled at the theoretical and sucked at the practical?

One thing I did know—I was a major part of the problem. I was running around like a chicken with its head cut off, blowing my stack every other second, trying so hard to do everything perfectly that the anxiety was leaching its way into everything I did.

But I wasn't prepared to take all the blame. The case could be made that my Marines were fucking hopeless, and that it was time to concentrate on just getting by and looking good. An attitude that I suspected was at the root of all my problems. But I didn't get paid to look good, I got paid to prepare my platoon to survive in combat. And I wasn't going to watch them die because doing it right was too hard.

So I made a resolution sitting in the cab of that truck. I was going to do it right. I wasn't going to give up, and I was never going to lose my cool again.

Waiting back at headquarters was another surprise. My new platoon sergeant, Staff Sergeant Albert Frederick.

It was an interesting introduction, him pressed and starched; me funky from the field, face still streaked with green and brown war paint. We were both guarded initially, not sure of what we had in each other.

Staff Sergeant Frederick was black, medium height, and built like a greyhound—0% body fat. He was coming over from the School of Infantry, where he'd been an instructor. He'd also done Desert Storm as a new troop, and Somalia as an NCO.

He was one self-contained Marine. Not cold, but not about to use two words if he could get by with one. He really had presence, though.

And he cut right to the heart of the matter by asking bluntly, "What do you want from your platoon sergeant, sir?"

I didn't have to think very hard about that. "I want to know everything that's going on, not just what you think I ought to. Whatever it is, I can take it. I want the benefit of your experience all the time, even if I forget to ask for it or look like I don't want it. If I'm about to do something stupid I want you to let me know, not let it happen. I also want you to know that I'm going to give your opinion a hell of a lot of weight, but the final call is still mine."

"I understand, sir." And to let me know he approved, he stuck out his hand and we shook on it.

"Now, what do you want from your platoon commander?"

"To work through me to the platoon, and not around me, sir. And just tell me *what* you want done, not how to do it."

So we knew who was verbose, and who wasn't. "You got it," I said, and we shook again. "Okay, first thing. I want you to help me unfuck this platoon."

"Problems, sir?"

"Well, I've been in command for less than a month, and I'm pretty sure they're the worst rifle platoon in the entire Marine Corps."

I didn't miss the minuscule hint of condescension that escaped from his poker face. Young lieutenants were like divas, they had a tendency to be so dramatic. And staff sergeants were like the calm, efficient, experienced stage managers who kept them from flying off the handle.

I took him through a thumbnail sketch of my experiences to date, ending with, "I'll let you make up your own mind, but there are two moves I'm going to make right now. And I promise these are the last ones without your input."

That pleased him. We walked over to the barracks and I introduced him to the NCO's and team leaders. Sergeant Harlin was now bumped down to 1st squad leader. Normally Corporal Jones would become a team leader, displacing one of the lance corporals. But instead I made him platoon guide.

This was an extra NCO, a platoon sergeant or squad leader in waiting, who otherwise handled supply and logistics. So Jones could run Staff Sergeant Frederick's errands and walk around with his short timer's attitude and his thumb up his ass until his discharge.

I presented Staff Sergeant Frederick to 2nd platoon and left them to get acquainted. I didn't see him again until late afternoon. He reappeared looking grim.

I said innocently, "So, what do you think?"

"I apologize, sir. I thought you were…exaggerating."

"No, you thought I was full of shit, and I don't blame you. Didn't take them long to change your mind, did it?"

"No sir, you gave me the straight gouge. No two shits about it, they're a real SWAT team."

Sometimes you just knew when something was going to be good. "SWAT team?"

"Shitheads, Weasels, Assholes, and Turds!" he announced.

I can't remember a laugh quite so cathartic. At least I wasn't on my own anymore.

Then we talked tactics. A commander and second in command usually adopted Jekyll and Hyde personas. If the commander was a nice guy his deputy acted like the hammer. And vice versa. I'd already had to start off as the dick, so he would have to be Dad to the platoon.

"A really pissed-off, hard-to-please Dad until we get them straightened out," he said.

My motivation renewed, I said, "Okay, let's put our heads together. What about an equipment inspection?"

"It's a place to start, sir."

So I was going to be the enthusiast, and he the realist.

CHAPTER SIX

That Friday the battalion held a memorial service for our dead from the grenade accident. The whole unit in the base gym in forest green Service Alpha dress uniform instead of our usual cammies.

The Corps lives by uniformity—in the spring the whole base rolls up their cammie sleeves on the designated day, and in the fall they come down. But the pair of lieutenants assigned to escort each family were in Dress Blues. I'm sure you can guess who was one of them.

Blues are the world's most spectacular uniform, but the only way they could be more uncomfortable was if they came with a popsicle stick to ram up your ass to make you stand straighter. To keep from leaving a trail of heat casualties in the summertime we wore lightweight white trousers instead of the usual sky blue wool with the red blood stripe.

Staff Sergeant Frederick came to the service with an attractive black lady in her early thirties. I walked up to introduce myself, and the Staff Sergeant said, "Lieutenant Galway, I'd like you to meet my wife, Annette."

I shook her hand lightly but firmly. "It's a real pleasure."

"Mine too," she said. "Albert's told me all about you."

Staff Sergeant Frederick didn't look too pleased at having that information revealed. Of course I couldn't let him off the hook. "You'd better not tell me," I whispered loudly. "I don't think we're ready to share our feelings just yet."

That brought her hand up to her mouth. "Just kidding," I said quickly, and she let out a nervous little laugh. "It's very good of you to be here."

"Actually," she said, "I'm down from Newark for a visit."

Since no one offered I wasn't about to ask why she was living in Jersey. I introduced her to the Captain and the other lieutenants.

It was a rainy day, so they held the service in the base gym. And it was a little incongruous to have Marines in full dress uniform performing a solemn ceremony on a basketball court. Not that it took anything away from it. The military reserves its greatest formality for the cemetery: taps, firing party, the folding and presentation of the flag. This was more like a testimonial to the dead, with the whole battalion in attendance.

When it was all over Dave Peters, the battalion adjutant, and I drove Lance Corporal Barlow's family to the Wilmington airport. They were nice people. I didn't mention their son's bizarre habit, which he'd exhibited on three separate occasions. Barlow had gone out in town on liberty, gotten zombie drunk, then returned to the barracks and broken into Sergeant Palermo's room. Where he proceeded to take a shit in his squad leader's rack. He then curled up on the floor and fell asleep, only to wind up sporting a couple of black eyes after Sergeant Palermo returned home.

But hypocrisy was expected. The dead are always the honored dead, no matter how much of a pain they were in life.

As when Mr. Barlow asked me if I'd known their son. "Just by sight, sir," I said, leaning over the seat to make eye contact.

Mr. Barlow smiled a little. He was a truck driver who wore his sport jacket, slacks, and tie like a prisoner in a set of chains. "My son was handful in High School, I don't mind telling you. Whenever he was out I was always afraid the phone was going to ring and he was going to be calling me from jail. When he told me he was joining the Marines I was relieved."

That started Mrs. Barlow snuffling into her handkerchief. The little brother was stone-faced adolescent boredom. The little sister was grade school best dress and ribbons, looking out the window at the unfamiliar sights.

Mr. Barlow went on, forcing that same strained smile on me, anything to keep silence away from the inside of that van. "We went down to Parris Island for his Boot Camp graduation. Seeing him in his uniform, standing so straight." Then, the amazement still in his voice, "He even called me sir." At that the voice cracked, "My son called me sir." He broke down, sobbing into his hands.

There's nothing worse than a grown man crying. Dave Peters drove with his face locked on the windshield. I reached over the seat and squeezed Mr. Barlow's shoulder, then turned back around, knowing he'd be even more humiliated if I watched him too long. We'd cut the kid's hair, taught him to stand up straight and call his father sir. Then we sent him back to them in a box.

When they went down the jetway to their plane the two lieutenants breathed a simultaneous sigh of relief. It was after dark. I said, "Am I the only one who needs a drink?"

"Fuck no," Dave replied. And then, "You know, it'd be a shame to waste a Friday night in Wilmington in our Blues."

Dave was a great guy. Black, a senior first lieutenant, and chairman emeritus of the Lieutenant's Protective Association. Which is an informal organization that exists in every unit, lieutenants banding together to assist each other in the face of a hostile world.

If he was going to lead, I was prepared to follow. "You're on."

The town outside the gates of Camp Lejeune, Jacksonville North Carolina, had a population of 873 when the base was established in 1942. Now the civilians numbered over 30,000, all of them feeding off the military in one way or another. They all loved to complain about living under the iron thumb of the Corps, but if there were no Marines, Jacksonville would just be another blink twice and you're through rural farming hamlet like the others in the area, with the aroma of chicken and pig shit hanging heavily in the air.

It was a fine town for fast food, car dealerships, pawnshops, tattoo parlors, and adult entertainment. In such matters the Bible Belt yields to commerce.

But when you added some 40,000 Marines, the vast majority of them male, to the civilian population you ended up with a seriously skewed male: female ratio. This left the women just as snotty as men would have been with the situation reversed.

And no officer worth his salt would frequent any entertainment establishment where he was going to bump into his troops. The only real solution to this monastic atmosphere was to commute down to Wilmington.

Where Dress Blues turned out to be magic. The first nightclub we tried the doormen practically threw people out of the way to usher us in. Dave and I both gave each other that look of: oh, yeah.

It was the only time in my life I didn't have to push my way through a club. The waters just parted before us.

Dave grabbed a table and I went to the bar to get the first round. As I was leaning in to give the bartender our order I felt a hand lightly touch the fabric of my sleeve. I used my peripheral vision to make sure it was a woman. It was. A sweet looking brunette with big, soft, intelligent brown eyes. She made every other woman in the place look like they were wearing three coats of varnish. And wearing a summer dress. Ah, those girls in their summer dresses.

"It's irresistible, isn't it?" I asked her.

The hand shot off and she looked like she'd been caught shoplifting.

"Go ahead," I said, smiling and offering her my sleeve.

At first I thought she was going to bolt, but then she let out a little giggle and touched it again. "It's so heavy, isn't it hot?"

"It's not cool," I said. "But why shouldn't men have to wear uncomfortable clothes for a change?"

Her eyebrows twitched up, as if she hadn't expected to hear that and was reappraising me.

"Mike Galway," I said, offering her my hand instead of my sleeve.

"Jenny Warfield."

Her touch gave me that little tickle of abdominal electricity. Don't blow this, I told myself. "It's nice to meet you, Jenny. Aren't you going to ask me who I work for?"

She laughed. "No, I don't think so."

"Okay, then what about you?"

"I teach at UNC-Wilmington."

"Full professor?"

"No, associate."

"What do you teach?" Please God, no psychologists.

"English."

Thank you, God. My B.A. is in History, but I could have gotten another in English if I hadn't been too goddamned lazy to do the requirements. "What's your area of specialty?"

"Shakespeare," she said, as if she expected *me* to start running.

The girl next to her, who'd been eyeing me harshly, said, "Jenny, we really have to go."

Great, the helpful friend who was going to save her from the killer Marine. So I said, "I prithee, pretty youth, let me be better acquainted with thee."

She couldn't have been more startled if I'd goosed her. "Tell me what play that's from."

"*As You Like It.*" So much for knuckle-dragging Marines. I have amazing recall for things I'm interested in, unfortunately none of them likely to make me any money.

"And I suppose your favorite is *Henry V?*"

"No, the two *Henry IV's.* Hal lost me when he dumped Falstaff."

"Jenny…," the girlfriend said insistently.

"You can go if you want," Jenny said.

Yes, the anchor was *dropped.* I restrained myself from doing a triumphal double fist pump.

Tired of waiting for his drink, Dave Peters reached over me to get it off the bar, winking as he retired.

"Is he with you?" Jenny asked.

"What makes you say that?"

She smiled. "You know, I've never met a man who wore white gloves before."

They were sitting on the bar atop my white barracks cover, or should I say hat.

"Part of the uniform. You have to carry them even if you don't wear them."

"That serious?"

"Well, otherwise the ensemble would be ruined."

It was so easy; I'd never made that kind of connection at first meeting. We started talking, and of course she got around to giving me the modern dating Rorschach Test. "What's your favorite movie of all time?"

"Seven Samurai." The eyebrows went up as if I'd goosed her again. "And yours?"

I was expecting *The Piano,* but she said, *"His Girl Friday."*

Well, what did you know? Not the woman as a mute victim, the woman as the wisecracking superior of all the guys.

If I was just someone who could quote Shakespeare she'd be interested. But a Marine in dress blues who could quote Shakespeare fascinated her. Every question she asked me had an unspoken subtext: how could a smart guy be a Marine? My unspoken reply was: who the hell would want to be a bond trader?

We got so into it I can't even remember the number of drinks we had, but it wasn't many. It turned out that neither of us liked talking about ourselves. We talked about everything else, mostly books. And not getting the answers we were expecting only ramped up the electricity.

I lost track of time until I received a tap on the shoulder. Dave said, "I'm thinking of rolling."

"Go ahead," I said.

"You going to get back all right?" he asked, the senior man taking care of the boot.

"Not a problem."

"Okay, later."

Jenny said, "Was he your ride?"

"He was," I said.

"You passed it up to stay here with me?"

"Didn't even have to think about it."

It was hard to tell in that light, but I could have sworn she blushed. There's the kind of person who expects everyone to be attracted to them, and then there are those always amazed when someone is attracted to them. I was the second, and I think Jenny was, too.

"I guess that makes me responsible for you," she said.

"I'll try not to be too much trouble."

We closed the club. I was starving, and she took me to a diner she knew. She just had coffee, but I finally got her to talk about her work. Associate professors were the infantry of academia, just one small step above grad students. All the work with none of the pay, job security, or respect.

I tried not to talk too much about my work, because I knew the hard time she was having putting me together with it. Jenny kept stealing glances at my chest while I was eating.

"Go ahead," I said, opening my left arm.

She fingered the silver wreathed crossed rifles and pistols of my shooting badges. "Rifle Expert, 2nd award."

"Just targets," I said. It was amusing to watch. She didn't like the idea of it at all, but she really thought the badges were pretty.

I had to fight her for the check, which was also kind of amusing.

"Would you like to take a drive by the beach?" she asked.

"Being your slave, what should I do but tend upon the hours and times of your desires?"

"I'll take that as a yes," she said, her tone letting me know she wasn't buying it but I was still doing okay.

Just as well, because that was it for my repertoire of romantic Shakespearean quotes. Never much cared for *Romeo and Juliet*.

"What do you think?" she said, parking the car. "I'd never walk on the beach at night, but I am with a Marine."

I wasn't about to say no to anything she suggested—I just hoped we wouldn't run into anyone who might turn that into an epitaph.

My contribution to the eternal boxers—briefs debate is that you can walk down a beach at night in dark-colored boxers without fear of arrest. Finally something was going right; I hoped the magic wouldn't disappear once I took the Blues off.

"You're crazy," Jenny said as I stripped down.

Maybe so, but not enough to go walking in the sand in a $500 dress uniform. Especially one that hard to get out of.

She gave me her hand as we walked. The sand was still warm under my feet. The surf was beating in my ears. The sky was just beginning to purple at the edge of the horizon. The way the ocean breeze molded her dress against her body sent the tightness in my stomach up into my windpipe. Not kissing her would have been a crime.

Her thigh was pressed against my groin, and it was no secret how my body felt about that. One hand's fingers were spread in the hair at the back of her head, the other's were following the valley of her spine. The touch of her bare arm alongside my neck, and the thumb hooked over the waistband of my boxer's were enough to make me lose my reason. She wore her perfume so lightly that this was the first time I truly appreciated its full effect.

"We really shouldn't," she said after the kiss broke.

Just the kind of statement that leads men to doubt what women say, since I had in fact been invited out to the beach in my underwear. Her tongue in my ear might also have had something to do with it. "Aren't all the best experiences when you do what you shouldn't?"

I was kissing her neck, and had slipped off one of the dress straps that had gotten in the way, when my leg was swept and I landed on my back on the sand. Nice takedown. What made a summer dress the world's most erotic piece of clothing was the way the top came down and the bottom came up. I was trying to use my hands to best effect, tasting the salt on her skin, her hair teasing my collarbone as she kissed me, the fear of discovery making it even better and longer.

Say what you will about those English teachers. There's a volcano bubbling away underneath.

CHAPTER SEVEN

Jenny drove me back to Jacksonville on Sunday night.

Whenever the 3-5 date rule is broken, it's incumbent on the guy to either provide reassurance or change his phone number. I had flowers sent to Jenny's office first thing Monday morning.

But before the florist even opened for business, Jim Nichols was at my desk. "Hey, I heard you missed the van back from Wilmington."

"Yup."

"Have a good time?"

I hate talking about my sex life, which I guess makes me un-American. I also knew that whatever I told Jim would be all over the battalion by lunch. Even more reason for keeping your mouth shut. "Yup."

Jim gave up, and then there was Staff Sergeant Frederick. He didn't want to talk about my weekend. "Sir," he said. "I've just been watching the squad and team leaders laying out the Marines' gear for inspection."

At first that sailed right over my head. Then I said, "Wait a minute...."

"That's right, sir. The Marines know that the NCO's and team leaders really care about looking good for inspection. So they wait until time gets short and just dump their shit out and shrug their shoulders like it was the best they could do, knowing the leaders'll have to jump in and do all the work to make it look good for display."

The thought of U.S. Marines even contemplating doing something like that, let alone actually doing it, put me in danger of having an aneurysm. The thought of *my* Marines doing it made me want to run over to the armory, sign out a weapon, and kill them all for the good of the Corps.

But Staff Sergeant Frederick was philosophical. "Sir, every platoon gets this way every now and again. It's only a disaster if they get away with it. Before all you had to do was take away a couple of their weekends and work 'em nonstop. Now we have to be a little more creative. But there's something else."

"Which is…?" I said.

"Lance Corporal Dean and Lance Corporal Hampton were an hour late coming back from the weekend. Car trouble," he added ironically.

On normal liberty weekends Marines weren't allowed to travel farther than a 200 mile radius from Camp Lejeune without special permission. This was to keep them from getting in a broken-down car and trying to make it to New York City or Miami and back over the course of a weekend. Not that they didn't give it a shot anyway.

I said, "UA is still a violation of the UCMJ, am I right?" UA was Unauthorized Absence, or what used to be called AWOL. The UCMJ was the Uniform Code of Military Justice, the military's criminal code.

"You're right, sir."

"Suggestions?"

"We run them up and disk them, sir. We have to. And not just them—everyone."

Heavy is the head that wears the crown. "Too bad Dean and Hampton had to fuck up just when we needed a couple of examples."

But I didn't hear much sympathy for the fellow enlisted. "Sir, this job just isn't that hard. *It is not that fucking hard.* Everyone knows the rules. When they don't follow them it means they were trying to get over. And that's what got this platoon into trouble, sir, the attitude that every rule is just something to try and get around. They know how to stand a good inspection. They know if their car blows a valve coming back from Myrtle Beach to call the duty NCO. If they won't follow the rules, then we have to teach them."

For a man of few words like my Staff Sergeant, that ranked up there with Hamlet's Soliloquy. And I got it: it was business, just apply the rules. We plotted and came to a meeting of minds. I got two charge sheets from the company clerk, filled them out, and gave them to the First Sergeant. Then I invited the Gunny back to our work space.

"Gunny," I began, "you know all about 2nd platoon."

"Only too well, sir," he replied.

"The way we see it, the Marines are acting like punks because they've been getting away with it. We have to send a message that life only gets easy when they act like Marines."

"I'm with you, sir," the Gunny said. "What do you have in mind?"

"Every working party," I said. "The police of the company area every day. Every detail, every shitty little job that comes up. Don't bother spreading them around or being fair, just give them to 2nd platoon. If there's anything you've wanted done but haven't gotten around to, we'll do it. And we'd rather do it after the company secures for the day."

The Gunny looked over at my platoon sergeant. Staff Sergeant Frederick nodded and said, "Penal platoon."

"You want it, sir?" the Gunny said. "You got it."

We wargamed with the Gunny, and then he left. I told the Staff Sergeant, "Platoon formation right after the inspection. I think I need to go off on them."

I'd said it so casually a faint smile crept onto his face. "Is that right, sir?"

"That's right," I replied. "Today I settle all the family business."

We didn't spend much time on the inspection. It was what's known as a junk-on-the-bunk, where all field gear is arranged in a uniform display on a Marine's bunk. A good way to check for cleanliness, serviceability, and missing equipment. The Staff Sergeant and I went through like a hurricane, and except for the NCO's and team leaders we turned it into a junk-on-the-floor.

When we were done the Staff Sergeant called the formation to attention and turned it over to me. I'd been working on my motivation ever since the walk over to the barracks, and I left them standing at attention. It's a misconception that Marines are always addressed using the Boot Camp scream. That's only for Boot Camp or OCS. I spoke just loud enough for everyone to hear me.

"The platoon sergeant, squad leaders, team leaders, and I have been taking it for granted that you were Marines and men," I told them. "We were wrong. Because whatever Marines do, they take pride in being the best. And men do their jobs. You obviously don't feel this way. You even think the NCO's and team leaders should do your jobs for you, because *they're* Marines and men. But it's all right. If you want to act like children, we'll treat you like children. Since you can't get to formation on time, we'll hold a special 2nd platoon formation earlier, and anyone who's late for that is UA. Then you can all wait around for the rest of the company to show up on time. And now you're going to be doing a lot more work than the rest of the company. But what do you expect? They're Marines and men, and you're not. Just so we're clear, this is going to keep on until you decide to get with the program. I guarantee you, you'll get tired of it long before we do. Enjoy it—you *asked* for it."

I turned the platoon back to the Staff Sergeant and walked away. To cool down I went to get the weekly haircut. On my way back I ran into O'Brien returning from supply.

Going down the hallway of the battalion CP I heard Jim Nichols's voice say, quite distinctly, "That never happened when I was in command." Then Captain Zimmerman going up the other stairway and Nichols outside the office door.

O'Brien stalked by him without a word or a look. I got right up in Nichols's face and said, "Listen, Jim, next time you better strap on your kneepads, crawl into the Captain's office, and shut the door behind you, 'cause if I ever hear anything like that again I'll take you out back and kick your little punk ass."

I pushed the door open so hard it crashed against the opposite wall. On the other side of the office the Gunny exclaimed, "Jesus, sir." Nichols didn't follow me in.

Since I didn't inherit the genes of the Fraternal Order of Hibernian Wall Punchers, I didn't put my fist through a locker. That's not my way. Instead I started calling Nichols "Jimmy," and pretty soon so did every officer in the battalion. At the right moments I'd throw out a remark like, "Better sit with your back to the wall around Jimmy." Or, "Careful what you say, you don't know where Jimmy'll be taking it." Usually when he was in the room, and of course he didn't do anything about it. Pretty soon that was the image of him in the battalion. He shouldn't have started it. He was an ambitious and malicious child, playing his little games, but I was the one with the instinct for the jugular.

After lunch Staff Sergeant Frederick and I were waiting around for Office Hours to begin when Corporal Turner came to see us.

"Sir," he said. "I got to the bottom of missing reveille out in the field. Lance Corporal Moeller fell asleep on radio watch. Since he didn't wake his relief, no reveille."

"Okay, I'm listening," I said.

"If he fell asleep in combat he could have gotten us all killed," Corporal Turner said.

"I'm still listening," I told them.

The Staff Sergeant said, "Let's not go for another charge sheet, sir. Moeller can stand duty all weekend."

I could tell Corporal Turner disagreed, but he didn't contradict the Platoon Sergeant.

"Fine with me," I said.

After lunch a dazed Lance Corporal Dean and Lance Corporal Hampton were marched into the Captain's office. And they marched out under 14 days restriction, 14 days extra duty, and forfeiture of 7 days pay.

Staff Sergeant Frederick and I regarded the proceedings with some satisfaction. "It'll take about a heartbeat for the word of this to get around," he predicted.

""To encourage the others,"" I quoted.

"Sir?"

"In 1756 a British admiral named Sir John Byng got his ass kicked by a French fleet off Minorca in the Mediterranean, and the Brits lost control of the island. The government of the day made him the scapegoat. The next year he was court-martialed and shot by firing squad."

"That's some harsh shit, sir," said the Staff Sergeant.

"The French writer Voltaire wrote, "In England it is thought a good thing to shoot an admiral, from time to time, to encourage the others.""

The Staff Sergeant liked that so much he had me say it again so he could write it down in his notebook.

It worked. The next couple of weeks went just as Staff Sergeant Frederick predicted. The platoon quickly got sick and tired of doing all the shitty jobs for the whole company. And out in the field every single time something was done wrong we stopped, taught the right way, and did it again. Over and over and over again. And if it was done wrong because someone was too lazy to do it right we did platoon PT. Say what you will about collective punishment, it swung the peer pressure from in favor of the screw-ups to against them as everyone got tired of doing pushups.

It paid off when, after the usual long hump into the training area, Captain Zimmerman had us issue MILES gear.

Which stood for Multiple Integrated Laser Engagement System, the military's version of laser tag. A laser transmitter box that snapped onto a weapon, and receiver buttons on a harness and helmet band. When a blank round was fired the box sent a pulse of eye-safe laser light downrange. The receiver unit chirped at a near miss, while a hit was an annoying continuous squeal.

With MILES playing war was almost real. No more arguments about who killed whom, and if you were lazy or careless and exposed yourself you got shot.

Captain Zimmerman didn't offer any instruction. He picked a spot among the pines and had a machine-gun crew dig their gun in. "Each squad attacks the gun," he ordered. "Any way the squad leader wants. The other squad leaders and team leaders can watch."

My platoon must have made a real impression on him during the platoon MCCRES. I could see what he was doing, and it was brilliant. Marine squad leaders didn't like to look stupid. They liked it even less if it happened in front of other squad leaders.

Milburn's platoon went first. The first squad fired and moved pretty well, but when they got close to the gun they stood up and assaulted. A few short bursts and the air was filled with squealing MILES receivers. The whole squad died. Every one of them.

After the second squad got massacred the others began to slip away to do a little practicing before their turn.

Ordinarily we'd only have enough blank ammo for each squad to do one attack, and any lessons learned would have to remain theoretical.

But the new fiscal quarter began next week, and since Captain Dudley hadn't done much training we had a lot of ammo left. It had to be used up, since any left over at the end of a quarter didn't roll over to the next. It just vanished.

The squads kept getting better but were still taking heavy losses. I pulled my squad leaders aside. "Look, you can't maneuver in front of machine-guns without fire superiority. Try using two teams as a base of fire to keep their heads down while you maneuver around and assault their flank with only one. And don't be in such a goddamned hurry to jump up in the open and get your head blown off. Use cover and crawl up on your belly if you have to."

Sergeant Harlin decided to do it his way, by the book. He was picked off by the first burst and got to be a bystander to his squad's destruction.

Then Corporal Turner took my advice and made the first successful attack with only one casualty. Captain Zimmerman exclaimed, "Now that's the way to do it!"

The new Lieutenant Galway decided that if looking stupid in front of the whole company didn't teach Sergeant Harlin anything, nothing I could say would. And I knew Corporal Turner would be rubbing it in anyway. He was junior in rank but senior in time in service and experience. But rank was what counted, and it was a constant source of friction between them—and their squads.

As we watched the action, O'Brien remarked, "Did you ever see such a bunch of low-crawling, fire-and-moving sons of bitches in your life?"

"Un-fucking-believable," said Milburn.

"I tried to pound the same thing into their heads over three whole days," I said. "It was like pissing into the wind. And the Captain's got them all snapped in over a period of, what, one morning?"

"For these fucking idiots, it's a miracle," said Milburn.

O'Brien and I both checked to see if he was serious. Contempt for my Marines? No way, not even when they were driving me crazy. I'd just had to realize that in so many ways they were still kids. Or maybe men-children was a better word for them.

It showed in their instinctive hostility toward authority, that of course went hand-in-hand with a tireless search for some authority to sub-mit themselves to—the schizophrenia that was like the badge of their immaturity. Or their behavior: acting up, doing stupid things, bickering with each other, constantly pushing at the boundaries, but also secretly hungry for praise and attention. It was why I couldn't let them get away with anything.

O'Brien glanced at me and I could see we were on the same frequency. But he changed the subject, saying, "They don't want to sit and listen to a class—they shut right down. They want to *do*." He paused. "Gents, I'm starting to think we got ourselves a company commander." Then, almost as an afterthought, "Captain Z's going to work out just fine."

I don't know if Captain Zimmerman ever had any idea where or when he got his nickname.

More humping took us to the western side of Camp Lejeune, which was actually split in two by the New River Inlet. We crossed the underpass beneath Interstate 17 to reach the Great Sandy Run area, and at the platoon fire and movement range we did the same squad attacks again, but with live ammunition and practice M-203 grenades that gave off a little puff of colored powder instead of blowing up.

When my squads took the range I felt like Vincent during the grenade accident. All I could do was stand there and watch for the two fire teams suppressing the objective to cease fire just as the third team attacked from the flank and swept right across their front. One second of inattention, one careless twitch of a trigger finger, one mindless piece of jacketed lead screaming downrange, and we'd be zipping some mother's son up in a body bag. But it didn't happen. And the point was that we had to risk zipping them up in body bags, over and over again, so we wouldn't be bagging up even more of them in real combat.

I'd never seen the troops so fired up. But of course shooting weapons and making things go bang was why they'd joined the Corps. That such a pathetically small part of their time was spent doing that made a fine case for deceptive advertising. Especially when two days of good training involved shooting off nearly four months worth of ammunition.

Gunny Harris dropped by right after we finished. "Sir, we've got some soldiers from Antigua training on base."

"Antigua?" I said. "I didn't even know they had an army."

"You and me both, sir. But they just showed up with a public affairs weenie who wants us to give their officers a quick class on the SAW and let them shoot a belt. The Captain tapped 2nd platoon for the dog and pony show." Which was the resentful term for any public relations demonstration.

"Nobody ever pre-plans anything around here, do they?" I said. "We always have to pull something out of our ass."

"You wouldn't be the first one to say that, sir."

I told the Staff Sergeant to keep everyone working, borrowed a squad automatic weapon from Lance Corporal Conahey, and went off to do it myself.

The Antiguans had a lot of fun shooting the SAW. And I thought nothing more of it.

Later the platoon and I were sitting in the shade cleaning our weapons. This was great, because after a little while the Marines forgot I was there. It was like hanging out with my college rugby team at age 19. If there's no women around, it's everyone razzing each other to see who can take it, who shows weakness, and who's going to be the top dog in the pack. Sexual boasting, whether or not you're really getting any, is the order of the day. And the homoerotic banter. All the "bitch," and "taking it up the ass." The sphincter-tightening fear of faggotry that's at the heart of all macho banter. I guess the same way the alpha wolf bluff-mounts the other males to demonstrate his dominance. Make no mistake, we're not that far from the wild. There's also an element of: we're so not gay that we can make jokes about being gay all the time. Not so surprising when you consider that most young men join the Marine Corps to prove to themselves that they really are a real man.

I discovered that my bottle of CLP, or Cleaner, Lubricant, and Preservative, was almost empty. "Corporal Turner, can I borrow some CLP?"

For some unknown reason this request caused my normally self-possessed Corporal to start stuttering. "Oh, ah, Reilly, give the Lieutenant some CLP."

"It's okay," I said, reaching over Corporal Turner's leg and grabbing his bottle. "I've got it."

I'd already poured some on my bolt before I noticed what was wrong. The liquid in the plastic squeeze bottle was much lighter in color than CLP. I cautiously sniffed it. "What is this? Sulfuric acid?"

Corporal Turner laughed nervously. "Ah, no sir."

"Well, what is it? Do I have to send it to the lab?"

Trapped, Corporal Turner sighed and said, "Half WD-40, sir. And half Hoppe's #9."

Only CLP was authorized for use on the M-16. It was made of high-speed light alloys, so light and high-speed that if you detail-cleaned it every day for a year, never firing it once, at the end of that time it would be worn out, unserviceable. As it was, most of the bluing around the barrels and magazine wells of our rifles was gone.

The platoon's normal chatter ceased. They were trying not to give me the E.F. Hutton stare, but I had their full attention. Would I explode and chew ass, or even write Corporal Turner up?

I wiped the bolt with my rag, and the carbon literally slid right off. Hmmm. WD-40 and Hoppe's #9 solvent. I made a show of examining the tips of my fingers very closely.

"Something wrong, sir?" Corporal Turner asked finally.

"No," I replied. "Just checking to see if my fingerprints are still there."

That got a laugh. Then Lance Corporal Asuego, one of the team leaders and my choice to make corporal next, said, "Can I have a word with you, sir?"

I reassembled my rifle and we walked farther into the woods. He looked very nervous, so I said, "Sit down, Asuego, and tell me what's on your mind."

"I think I'll stand, sir."

"Okay, in that case *I* better sit down." Which I did, cross-legged in the sand, waiting for him to come out with it.

"Sir, Conahey should have done the class and the shoot with the Antiguans, instead of you taking his SAW."

I'm embarrassed to say that my first reaction was a quick flash of anger. The insecurity that comes with any kind of serious authority— how dare you question me? Thankfully I didn't say anything before I engaged my brain and realized what an incredible thing it was for a

Lance Corporal fire team leader to be sticking up for his Marine and having the balls to come to me instead of bitching about it privately with the troops. It said even more about his expectations of me.

Lance Corporal Conahey was a Native American who was not called "Chief." A really good Marine and a damn fine SAW gunner, but so introverted I couldn't immediately recall ever hearing him say anything other than, "Yes, sir."

I said, "Sit down, Asuego." He did. "When I grabbed Conahey's SAW, all I was thinking was that it was a pain in the ass job, and rather than jam anyone in the platoon with it I'd take care of it myself. But you see how we've got a major misunderstanding? I think I'm doing Conahey a favor, and he thinks I don't have any confidence in him—or I'm trying to grab some glory."

Asuego nodded.

"This was my fault," I said. "I was wrong and it won't happen again. I appreciate you coming to talk to me like this—I know how hard it was to do. Okay, anything else?"

"No, sir." And even though Marines never salute in the field, he came to attention and threw me one that I stood up and returned.

He went back, and I walked over to the company CP to give them time to talk it over. I felt lighter than air, because the platoon and I had *really* turned the corner this time.

At the CP Captain Zimmerman had a question for me. "Mike, where did you get the idea to suppress with two teams and attack with only one?"

"Rommel, sir."

He broke into a big smile. "Good old *Infantry Attacks*. Everyone reads it, few get anything out of it."

Impulsively, I decided to strike while the iron was hot. "Sir, what about promoting Corporal Turner to sergeant?"

A frown followed by a long pause. "I've heard about his record."

I knew from whom. The First Sergeant didn't like Corporal Turner; didn't like anyone who'd been a drill instructor and fallen from grace. The First Sergeant hadn't just been a drill instructor. He'd been the one drill instructor in the Marine Corps picked for an exchange tour with the British Royal Marine Commandos. "If we judge him for fucking up, sir, we should give him extra credit for getting back on track. He deserves it, sir."

"I'll think about it."

"Thank you, sir."

I thought he'd moved on then, but from behind I received a clout in the back that nearly sent my glasses flying off. I guess I did good. An unfamiliar sensation.

CHAPTER EIGHT

Jenny took it well, but weekend duty was a little hard to explain to a civilian. Only a Marine would understand going out to the field from Monday to Friday, working effectively a 100-hour week, and then coming back in on Saturday and pulling a straight 24-hour shift.

I was relieving First Lieutenant Ské, the XO of Golf Company. As I rolled into headquarters on Saturday morning he greeted me with his usual, "Hey, motherfucker."

What would have been an invitation to single combat from anyone else was just a warm comradely salutation from Ské. He was another Mustang, and probably would have become the Sergeant Major of the Marine Corps if some stupid officer hadn't made him an officer. I say this for no other reason than old Ské was both a genuine Marine Corps idealist and an honest man. If things were fucked up he said they were fucked up. An officer had to be much more politic. And the only thing polished about Ské were his boots and his brass. He was Marine Corps crude, which was like having a black belt in crude. Pretty close to the perfect formula for rubbing your superiors the wrong way.

Ské was wearing the OD's pistol in a shoulder holster. Instead of handing it over he reached into the wall locker and gave me the OD warbelt, pistol included. Then he unloaded and cleared what turned out to be his own Beretta, securing it, the shoulder holster, and his own ammo in a Pelican hard case. He bade me farewell with a hearty, "Good luck, motherfucker."

"You too, motherfucker," I replied.

My Staff Duty was Staff Sergeant Cruz, the S-1 (Personnel) Chief.

"I don't get it," I said to him. "Does he think that if he caps someone and turns in a clean pistol and all his rounds, no one's going to figure out that he did it?"

"I think it's fair to say, sir," Staff Sergeant Cruz replied, "that Lieutenant Ské dances to the beat of his own drummer."

The day was uneventful, which gave me a lot of time to think about Sergeant Harlin. I'd reviewed his record on Friday, hoping it would give some clue to his difficulties.

It did. Sergeant Harlin had made it to corporal on his first enlistment and then his career stalled. He'd gotten out of the Corps and joined a Marine Reserve unit. He picked up sergeant in the Reserves and then came right back on active duty as a sergeant.

It explained how someone who looked so good in the abstract and so poor in the execution came to make sergeant. But I still didn't know what to do about him.

During my rounds I stopped off to visit Sergeant Turner, who had our company duty. That's right, sergeant. When Captain Zimmerman didn't want him promoted, that was when I stopped being a completely good boy. The popular perception of Marines is that we attack everything head-on, but we're actually pretty sneaky.

My first move was taking the battalion adjutant to lunch. And Dave Peters said, "Your Corporal must be able to make the cutting score."

Every month Marine Headquarters published a cutting score for every occupational specialty, PFC to sergeant. Every enlisted Marine had a composite score, which was a weird mathematical formula of the rifle qualification, physical fitness test, correspondence test scores, time in service, etc. If the composite score equaled or exceeded the cutting score, the Marine got promoted automatically unless he or she was specifically not recommended. Totally nonsensical, but that was the system.

"By about a thousand points," I replied.

"Okay, then they're using his disciplinary record to justify holding it up." He gave the matter some thought. "You need to go see the Career Planner."

"The Career Planner?" I said. Meaning is that the best you can do? He nodded. "Go see Staff Sergeant Clark."

And it turned out that Staff Sergeant Clark knew all about my predicament. "I was coming to see *you,* sir. If Corporal Turner isn't promoted to sergeant I have to send a message to Headquarters Marine Corps explaining why."

For once the automatic promotion system worked in a lieutenant's favor. Once Staff Sergeant Clark and I made sure battalion heard about it, and the possibility they might get in trouble with Headquarters, everything happened so fast we had a promotion formation after morning PT, with everyone still in T-shirts, shorts, and running shoes.

When we all gathered around to congratulate Sergeant Turner, Jimmy Nichols shook his hand and exclaimed, "Looks like all my hard work paid off."

Where he found his chutzpah I have no idea.

For me shaking Sergeant Turner's hand, seeing the look on his face, and hearing him say, "I'm back, sir," was one of the high points of my life, not just my career.

At about 2100 hours the phone rang. Staff Sergeant Cruz was looking at me—he'd heard about my last duty. I breathed an, "Oh, shit," and picked it up. "Officer of the Day, Lieutenant Galway speaking, may I help you sir?"

It was Frank Milburn. "Mike, I'm in trouble. I got picked up for DWI. You gotta help me."

Not good news. "Well, I'm standing duty, Frank." Meaning that just because I had a pistol didn't mean I'd be busting him out of jail. "What can I do?"

"Call Jack. He'll figure something out."

"Okay Frank, take it easy." I hung up the phone with an inkling that a hosing was in progress. Otherwise Milburn would have called O'Brien directly.

I called O'Brien, who sounded like he had a few beers in him. As I described the situation at least two other phones clicked on. Milburn, Herkimer, Nichols, and O'Brien all began making the whirring sounds of a hooked fish taking out line. There was a lot of cackling, I told them all to go fuck themselves, they wished me good luck, and we hung up.

I counted my blessings. At least they weren't running around trying to stage some kind of phony incident.

So when the phone rang again at 2200 I thought it was another prank call. It seemed too early for a real emergency.

But the real voice of the Golf Company Duty NCO said, "Sir, three Marines just beat up a pizza delivery man."

Jeez. "Three Golf Marines just beat up a pizza delivery guy," I told Staff Sergeant Cruz. "Call the MP's and have them get someone over to the barracks fast."

"Shit hot, this is great," he said happily. Admin Marines were usually somewhat bookish types; they tended not to run amok the way grunts did.

Yeah, great, I said to myself as I sprinted over to the barracks.

I stuck my head in the Duty NCO office. The pizza guy was sitting down, bent over and holding his head.

"What room?" I said. There was no answer. "What room!" I shouted.

"Three seventeen, three seventeen," he moaned.

I charged up the stairs, the Beretta in my hand. I turned the corner onto the third floor walkway just as three Marines were leaving a room in a really big hurry.

"FREEZE!" I shouted. I advanced on them fast, pistol out in front, barking out orders. "Get on the ground! Get on the ground! Face down! Hands behind your head!"

When they did the last it was all over. The trick was to move fast, achieve control, and make them think they were going to get shot if they didn't do exactly what the crazy son of bitch with the pistol was yelling at them. By the time they realized that wasn't such a good idea it was too late.

Keeping them covered with the pistol, I shouted, "Firewatch!" If they were stupid enough to assault a pizza delivery man, they were stupid enough to try to get up and run, leaving me with the choice of shooting them or losing them. Once again the Colonel would be really pissed if either happened. "Firewatch!"

One of them moved his head to whisper something to the other, and I was all over him. "Shut up. Shut the fuck up. You so much as twitch and I'll put one in your spine and you can roll around in a wheelchair for the rest of your life." That quieted them down.

The firewatch finally ran up. "Yes, sir."

"Go below and keep an eye out for the MP's," I ordered. "Bring them up here. Make sure they know the guy with the pistol is the OD."

"Yes, sir." He pounded down the stairs.

That would be all I'd need, getting shot by a couple of trigger-happy MP's.

I didn't have long to wait. The firewatch returned with first one MP, then another, who put the bracelets on my prisoners and hauled them away.

Then, as always, it was a matter of reconstructing the incident and getting it down on paper.

The three Marines in question had been hanging out watching TV, dead broke and hungry. Then the brains of the group got the idea to order a pizza and give the number of the empty room next door. Funny thing about teenagers and groups. With two a dopey idea only had a fair chance of being adopted. Three or more and stupidity was a done deal.

When the pizza delivery man showed up with their pie, the three sprang out of the darkness and tried to relieve him of it. He fought back, and they thumped him pretty good. For the *pièce de resistance* someone grabbed his wallet.

Then they proceeded to set the stupid bar a couple of pegs higher. Yes, this was possible. Leaving the delivery guy stunned on the walkway, they actually took the pizza into their room and started to chow down on it. Then someone finally grasped the fact that they'd committed enough crime to get themselves into Leavenworth and maybe they ought to blow town. Which was when I showed up.

When I got back to the headquarters building Staff Sergeant Cruz was beside himself. "This is so fucking great," he kept repeating. "This is really great."

I called Major Thom and, as usual, had to talk to the XO's wife first. Why couldn't these bastards put the phone on their side of the bed? No one was going to be calling their wives at zero dark thirty in the morning.

His first words to me were, "What happened this time?" Which struck me as more than a little unfair, as if I was the mastermind behind these incidents.

I told him; all he wanted to know was that it had been handled. I told him it was handled; he hung up. I managed to get some sleep, and dreamed of my Friday the 13th luck.

CHAPTER NINE

I've got a pretty good idea how they must feel on Super Bowl Sunday, because everyone's nerves were pretty tight on MCCRES Monday. We were stepping off at 1500, so we had the whole morning and most of the afternoon to deal with the tension.

Every element of the battalion from platoon on up would have an evaluator tagging along, all the counterpart officers from the 1st battalion of our regiment armed with identifying white tape around their covers, the MCCRES standards, and very sharp pencils to note every one we didn't meet. So my evaluator would be the 2nd platoon commander of Alpha Company. The same battalion would be the aggressor force against us, led by their executive officers and Staff NCO's.

No one was puking in their wastebasket, but punting a MCCRES didn't exactly enhance an officer's career prospects.

The day didn't start off well. At morning formation I noticed a couple of missing faces. "Where's Peterson?" I asked Staff Sergeant Frederick.

"UA, sir."

"Terrific." Though if I'd been thinking clearly I would have concluded that not having Lance Corporal Peterson around for the MCCRES was a definite plus. He was the platoon problem child, always in trouble. And everything you did to try and reform him only made it worse. It was amazing how many little kids in this world only got attention when they acted up. By the time they were teenagers their behavior was fixed.

"What about Westgate?" Sergeant Harlin's 1st squad was missing its third fire team leader.

My question brought the Staff Sergeant up short. "I don't know, sir." And he didn't like not knowing.

Sergeant Harlin wasn't going on the MCCRES because the company had been granted an incredible three school slots and I'd gotten two because I had fewer school-trained NCO's than the other platoons. Also attending was Sergeant Eberhardt, who'd just reported in. Now-Corporal Asuego was leading 1st squad and Lance Corporal Reilly 3rd squad. I wasn't happy about having two inexperienced squad leaders for a MCCRES, but I couldn't pass up the school billets.

Sergeant Harlin hadn't left for the day's classes yet, so the Staff Sergeant and I made a beeline for him. "Where's Lance Corporal West-gate?" I asked.

"I excused him from formation, sir."

My radar warning system started warbling. "I didn't ask you that. I asked you where he was. Fair warning, Sergeant Harlin—jerking me around is just going to make me angry."

"Listen to the Lieutenant, Crazy," Staff Sergeant Frederick advised. He called all the Marines "Crazy." Except me. So far.

Sergeant Harlin quickly weighed his options, took a deep breath, and said, "He's in his room, sir."

Westgate was lying on his rack, in his civilian clothes, smelling like he'd been rolled home inside a beer keg. I shook him but there was no response. I swear at first I thought he was dead. I grabbed his wrist but there was a pulse. "Get Doc Bob in here, fast," I ordered. Westgate wasn't just unconscious, he was almost comatose.

Doc Bob ran in with his Unit-1 bag. He flashed his light in West-gate's pupils, which fortunately were equal and reactive. "I'll go for a stretcher, sir. We need to get him to sickbay and have Doctor Patel check him out."

The Doc rushed off. Staff Sergeant Frederick stayed with Westgate, and I took Sergeant Harlin outside.

"How did he get back here?" I said.

"Someone in a car dumped him out, sir."

"And you didn't tell anyone about this?"

"No, sir."

"You were covering for him because you didn't want him to get in trouble, maybe lose his fire team?"

"Yes, sir."

"Just taking care of your troops. Let me ask you something, Sergeant Harlin. What if, while Westgate was lying there unconscious, he puked, choked on his vomit, and died?"

A look of surprise flashed across his face.

"Didn't think of that, did you?" I said. "Is that what you'd tell his parents? "Sorry, I didn't think about that?" You know what, Sergeant Harlin? I'm going to have that tattooed across your chest. I DIDN'T FUCKING THINK!" I threw up both hands. "Go away, Sergeant Harlin. Go to Squad Leader's School. Try to learn something."

They took Westgate to sickbay and plugged an IV into him. Doc Patcl, the battalion surgeon, told me he had never seen a human being that intoxicated. Neither had I for that matter, and I thought my experience in that field was pretty comprehensive. Westgate was still out of it, but otherwise all right. They'd keep him under observation.

Every lieutenant absolutely hates having to go in and tell his company commander something negative about his platoon. Captain Z was no Captain Dudley, but I still caught myself trying to read his face to see where I stood. And I felt ashamed when he calmly told me to keep him informed.

Peterson turned up around mid-morning. He was escorted to the office by Staff Sergeant Frederick and ordered to lock himself up at the position of attention in front of my desk.

"All right, Peterson," I said. "Let's hear it." I didn't chew ass without hearing the Marine's story first. And I gave points for a good one, even if it was total bullshit.

But Peterson didn't explain to me why he was absent without authorization. Instead he said, "I'm being picked on, sir. It's not fair. Everyone else gets breaks but me."

Peterson was the catalyst behind my theory that your attitude is always inversely proportional to your capabilities. "You're right, Peterson, we pick on you. Why? Because you don't do anything unless we pick on you. You're right, we don't give you breaks. What have you ever done to rate one? Have you ever done your job without being made to, let alone help anyone else do theirs? Have you ever contributed anything besides a lot of bitching and backtalk? You need breaks because you're always in trouble. Guess what? You don't get breaks because you're always in trouble."

"I don't get any breaks because I'm African-American, sir."

I glanced over at Staff Sergeant Frederick. He was about to blow. But the irony was so rich that, rather than be enraged or outraged, I was just curious as to what I might hear next. "So it's racial bias?"

"Yes, sir."

"Now you've got me confused, Peterson. Your fire team leader is African-American. So is your squad leader. And the platoon sergeant. They're the ones who keep bringing you in here." Then my inner Grinch compelled me to say, "So what are they—Uncle Tom's working for The Man?"

I think Peterson finally woke up and caught the explosive vibe coming off Staff Sergeant Frederick, because he didn't say anything. But we both could tell what he was thinking, and as they say in the Marine Corps silence is consent.

"Congratulations, Peterson," I said. "Great work destroying what little goodwill you had left around here. Here's a little tip for you. If one person calls you an asshole, it might be racism. If *everyone* thinks you're an asshole—you're an asshole. Dismissed."

He left the office with Staff Sergeant Frederick so hard on his heels they were practically riding piggyback.

After lunch I sought out Doc Bob. "Is someone going to stay back with Westgate?" I knew the whole medical section would be going out on the MCCRES.

"No, sir."

"Is he still unconscious?"

"Yes, sir."

That brought me right over to sickbay to see Doc Patel. He was a Navy lieutenant, same rank as a Marine captain. But unlike a Marine captain, a doctor was handed the rank like the charm in a box of Crackerjacks. "Excuse me, sir," I said. "With everyone in the battalion going to the field, doesn't Westgate need to go to the Naval Hospital?"

He was very abrupt; they were rushing about packing their equipment into the Humvees. "That will not be necessary."

"But he's unconscious, sir."

"Lieutenant Galway, I have examined him, and I am telling you that he will be all right. Now, we are very busy."

"I'm sure he's *going* to be all right, sir. But I'm worried about what might happen. Suppose he vomited and aspirated it?"

"That will not happen. Now, if you will excuse me."

"I'm sorry, sir. I'm sure you're right. But if something did happen to Westgate while he was all alone here, or in his room, we'd both be responsible. And I think we'd both have a hard time living with that."

"Now, listen to me please, Lieutenant...."

"I'm sorry, sir, but I can't leave knowing we made the wrong decision."

"You mean you're not going to leave."

"No, sir."

"All right, all right." He turned to one of the corpsmen who were busy packing but had stayed close enough to hear everything. "Take him to the hospital in the ambulance." One of the Humvee ambulances was parked outside. "I will call to have him admitted." He turned back to me with a gesture of, are we done now?

"Thank you very much, sir."

Every MCCRES began with a 40 kilometer or 24 mile hump that had to be made in under eight hours with no more than 3% of the troops falling out. Since Captain Zimmerman took over Echo Company we'd been training hard and realistic. Humping the same way too, a realistic combat equipment load and increased distance each time.

Which didn't mean squat when Marines were still arriving to fill out the unit. We lost one of my new PFC's, named Thomas, but he was thoughtful enough to go down from the heat just as we rolled into a break. Doc Bob stripped off Thomas's gear and blouse, grabbed a jerrican of water from the company Humvee, and emptied it over the kid's head to bring down his body temperature.

Thomas was moist with sweat and, though disoriented, still conscious. Doc Bob had the situation well in hand, so I shot some photos with the disposable camera I'd started carrying around.

"That's fucked up, sir," I heard from behind me.

The rest of the platoon showed zero sympathy. A heat casualty was regarded as a self-inflicted wound.

"I told the stupid shit to keep drinking, sir," said Lance Corporal Reilly.

"You want us to piss on his head, sir?" a couple of Marines asked, cracking everyone else up. It was the last resort if you didn't have water to spare. A heat casualty's temperature was always over 100°, while urine was 98.6°.

"Yeah, sir, it'll make a great picture."

"That's even more fucked up," I said. "Save it for the next one, in case we run out of water."

The break ended with Thomas left for the trucks following the column. Someone said, "Welcome to the FMF, boot." The Fleet Marine Force being the operational part of the Corps.

Enlisted Marines didn't hump to 24 mile MCCRES standard before they got to an infantry battalion. They did Hollywood humps with minimal equipment in Boot Camp, and the longest one in the School of Infantry was a ridiculously short 12-miler. My cynical guess was that otherwise a lot more privates would flunk out and the numbers wouldn't look so good.

It was a shame. Kids who didn't have what it took ought to be sent home during Boot Camp, not get broken at their first duty station. But natural selection seemed to be the Marine Corps way.

We only had two other drops for the whole company, putting us well under the limit.

On one of the rest stops when I was at the front of the column, Captain Z said, "Doc Patel came to see me."

I braced myself for an ass-chewing. "Yes, sir."

"He said you were right, and he was wrong. He said you were calm, respectful, and professional, and you wouldn't turn loose of him until he gave in."

Well, what do you know about that? "Just trying to keep us all from having to send out our resumes, sir. Or maybe even sharing the same cell block at Leavenworth."

"That's what you get paid for, Mike. Taking care of your Marines and keeping my ass out of jail."

We arrived at Landing Zone Albatross tired but in good form just prior to 2230 hours. Which was where we met our evaluators. Captain Z knew his. Not unusual; it was a small Marine Corps, less than 20,000 officers. Mine was 2nd lieutenant who'd been in the class before mine at Quantico. He'd also been to Army Ranger School, which I mention only because he dropped that into the conversation at the earliest opportunity. The Army sent every one of their infantry officers there, but the only Marines who attended as a matter of course were those assigned to the Reconnaissance Battalions and Force Reconnaissance Companies. Occasionally a school billet fell from the skies like manna and everyone fought for it like wild dogs. And sometimes an Infantry Officer Course class got one Ranger School spot. Mine hadn't. My evaluator's had, and he had to let me know he'd been the one chosen to go. I really sympathized with all the troops who didn't like officers.

We'd be doing a lot less walking for the next two days. As the ground combat element of a Marine Expeditionary Unit, one company was the helicopter company; another the boat company with Zodiac rubber boats and fiberglass Rigid Raiders; and another the mechanized company. We were the mech company.

The mech were AAVP-7's, which stood for Amphibious Assault Vehicle, Personnel, Model 7. Marines always called them amtracs or tracks. With a crew of three and twenty or so Marines in the back, it could do 30 miles an hour on land and 9 knots in the ocean on water jets, but was really neither fish nor fowl. Too big and high to be a good armored personnel carrier on land, and too slow to be a good landing craft on the ocean. But it was the only thing around that could do both.

We linked up with our amtracs at LZ Albatross. There was no amphibious shipping available, as usual, so the battalion would be simulating a landing. In the morning we'd climb aboard the amtracs, drive into the ocean, turn around, and come back in to hit the beach. All the other units would be released from Albatross in what would be their normal landing order by either helicopter or landing craft.

The amtracs drove us to the beach. Not the part we were landing on; we'd bivouac for the night farther up. The wind was whipping off the water, and it felt much colder than September. It was going to be a frosty night even with the dunes between us and the ocean.

A 24-mile hump is no joke, and we were just settling down for some much-needed rack time when a summons from battalion came in over the radio. And all the officers trudged down to the beach road and sat shivering until a truck showed up to take us back to LZ Albatross. Where in classic military hurry-up-and-wait fashion we sat around some more before being ushered into a tent to watch infrared video imagery of our landing beach, taken by an unmanned drone.

An hour and a half later we were in the truck heading back to the beach.

"Well that was about a waste of fucking time," Captain Zimmerman grumbled.

"Who would have guessed there'd be enemy on the landing force objective?" I said.

"I know I'll sleep better knowing we've got all these high-speed recon systems," said O'Brien.

"Oh, me too," said Milburn. "Minus the three hours we missed going to that worthless fucking briefing."

It was really cold now. We rolled up in our ponchos and burrowed into the sand to try and hold in our body heat.

And it was still dark when reveille passed among us in whispers. We packed up, shouldered our gear, and filed over the dunes to the tracks.

I put the platoon inside our vehicles so they could eat chow out of the cold. Dawn was just about to break. The marshy beach smell clashed with the chemical vapors from MRE heater packs that had to be activated outside otherwise they'd gas everyone out of the back of an amtrac. My face was raw from the wind, and everyone was walking around with their hands in their pockets—an un-military act forbidden in garrison but permitted to Marines in the field. It wasn't as great as making love on the beach, but it was pretty good.

I climbed up the side of my track, opened the commander's turret hatch, and stuck my face in, saying, "How are you this fine Marine Corps morning, Sergeant Bean?"

"Good to go, sir. Ready to kick some ass and take some names."

"You sound like you had your Wheaties this morning."

"As a matter of fact, sir, I did." Grinning, he held up an individual serving box of cereal. "You want one?"

"Only if you brought enough for everyone."

"Sorry, sir."

"Thanks anyway, then."

I shut the hatch and climbed down, smiling and shaking my head. Amtracers took everything to the field, including ice chests and Coleman stoves. I heard our evaluator saying to Captain Z, "My God, I never heard a company wake up and move that quietly. I was packing my gear, I looked up, and everyone was gone. I never heard a thing. We almost got left behind."

Then he demanded to know how Captain Z had trained the company to do it. I couldn't see Captain Z's face, but I know he was satisfied. It was the payoff for making us do it night after night in the field until we trained ourselves to be quiet and not unpack anything except a poncho.

When it was time the amtracs fired up their engines and churned down the beach slope. The impact with the water was like hitting a sapling: a sharp jolt, then release as the ocean yielded to it. A few seconds later a sickening lurch as the treads grudgingly left the sand and the AAV turned into a boat, leaving you wondering if it was going to float. It did. Plumes of spray kicked up behind us when the water jets were exposed by the waves. I could see everything through the bulletproof glass vision blocks in my cupola, but the troops in back had only each other and light green walls to look at. An amtrac had all the sailing characteristics of a slightly-pointed brick, rocking forward and back with the waves while also rolling side to side. Not too good on the stomach.

When we were far enough out the amtracs turned south for a bit, and then headed for the beach. I'd been worried about the wind but it had died down and the Atlantic was fairly calm. No one in back had puked yet, always a good sign.

As we approached the beach four Harrier jets flashed across our front making simulated bombing runs. All it needed was background music. I twisted in my seat, ducked down, and signaled the troops that we were about to land.

The amtracs hit the beach on line. As soon as the treads bit back into the sand the drivers raced for the cover of the dunes. The warning horns blared, the rear ramps dropped and the Marines charged out, splitting right and left to come around each side of the vehicle.

The machine-guns and rocket launchers set up atop the dunes, and we fired and moved across the sand through the scrub trees. Two Cobra attack helicopters screamed overhead, chasing after the aggressors. We pushed them off the beach; they piled into *their* amtracs and bugged out across the Intracoastal Waterway.

While we finished clearing the beach our attached engineer squad checked the sand road for mines. The command and control Huey helicopter with Colonel Sweatman, Major Jonesy, and the helo squadron commander passed over along with the CH-46 and CH-53 medium and heavy transport helicopters taking Golf Company to do their air assault.

As soon as the engineers told us the road was clear we piled back into the tracks and crossed the Intracoastal Waterway. The method was to drive down the bank, stop, look both ways for oncoming civilian boat traffic, splash and hope all the drain plugs were still screwed in tightly, then up the opposite bank and onward.

We linked up with our platoon of four M1A1 tanks, who ordinarily would have followed us ashore in a big high-speed hovercraft called an LCAC, pronounced el-cack, or Landing Craft Air Cushion.

We also paused to receive and give the order for the next attack, on LZ Dove. Really a formality for the evaluators, since it was a repeat of our rehearsal the week before.

We headed north until we ran into Route 172, the hard surface road that cut across the training area, crossing on one of the thick concrete pads built into the asphalt to keep heavy tracked vehicles from tearing it up.

Then the whole column stopped. Over the radio we heard that one of Frank Milburn's vehicles had gotten too close to the trailside embankment and thrown a track. It was going to take a while to fix that, so Milburn crammed his whole platoon and all their gear into one amtrac. We left the busted vehicle and its crew sitting on the trail. I kept repeating to myself: no omen, no omen.

The 60mm mortar section, with two tanks, continued up the tank trail that led to LZ Dove. The rest of the company, the other two tanks in the lead, made a hard left to head west and then east, following the boundary of the training area with the intention of coming in behind LZ Dove.

Captain Z was gambling that the most we'd run into, and that only if the aggressors were on the ball, was an anti-armor team with a couple of Humvee-mounted TOW anti-tank missile launchers. He was prepared to lose the lead tank and roll right over them, no stopping so we could be into the attack before a radioed warning would do any good.

Much more naïve, I couldn't believe that the aggressor commander wouldn't have a more substantial force blocking a major avenue of approach into his flank and rear.

I was wrong. Just a four-man observation post that demonstrated why there had to be leaders to hold Marines' feet to the fire. They were way behind the lines, nothing was happening, so they were stretched out on a bank in full view of the tank trail, just fucking off. When we showed up they were so surprised they almost fell into the trail and got run over, then compounded the sin by firing their rifles at a column of armored vehicles passing broadside, announcing their presence even if by some slim chance we hadn't seen them.

Now we had to move fast. We were behind enemy lines, we were compromised, and every second was more time for the enemy to get ready for us. All we had in our favor was the sometimes amazingly long time it took information to work its way up the chain of command and then back down to the right place. Friction of course.

We exited the amtracs, leaving a Stinger missile team to protect them from air attack. We had to cross another asphalt road, Marines Road, to arrive at the rear of LZ Dove. The road was where I expected to be engaged.

We were spread out and ready to fire as the point sprinted across. Nothing happened. They signaled all clear and the platoon went across.

As we were picking our way very quietly through some boggy ground laced with thick growth, the point radioed all clear again, which meant we'd walked right through the back door into the LZ.

We emerged from the brush with a sand bank in front of us. I signaled the platoon to get on line, then shucked off my helmet and stuck one eye above the bank.

Under the trees on the edge of the LZ, less than fifty meters away, were the four aggressor M-1 tanks. Like the German Tigers of World

War II their only vulnerability to most infantry anti-tank weapons was a shot in the rear, where the armor was thinnest. And there I was looking up the asses of four M-1's.

The whole aggressor company was facing the other way, and we were sitting undetected behind them.

In my mind I kept chanting: don't fuck up, don't fuck up, as if it was my mantra. I took the radio handset from Lance Corporal Vincent and got ahold of Captain Z. "Echo-2 in position, over." Only the battalion radio net was encrypted, so we had to be careful about people listening in.

"You see them?" said Captain Z, meaning the enemy tanks.

"All right in front of me," I replied.

"Understood," he said, and I could hear the excitement in his voice. "Echo-1 isn't in position yet, over."

"Roger, out." O'Brien was still maneuvering on the other side of the tank trail. But I had priority of fires, so I got back on the radio. "Echo-4, this is Echo-2, over."

Sergeant Lenoir, the mortar section leader, came up on the net. "This is Echo-4, over."

I could hear the tanks and tracks that were with him gunning their engines. They'd driven up the road sounding like the full mech company, then stopped short. And while the mortars were setting up the vehicles kept making noise, fixing the aggressors' attention on the expected direction of attack.

The movies would have you believe that all you need do was whisper into a microphone and moments later artillery would be falling on the landscape like raindrops. It was actually an involved process, since getting them to land in the right spot was critical.

I said into the radio, "Fire mission, adjust fire, grid, over."

Sergeant Lenoir responded, "Fire mission, adjust fire, grid, out."

"Grid 858308, over." The spot on the map I wanted to hit.

"Grid 858308, out." Sergeant Lenoir read it back to confirm he'd heard right. One missed digit and the first round might land right on top of my platoon.

"Company in the defense; Danger Close; HE-VT last round Willie Pete; at my command, over."

He read it back again. Danger Close mean that we were less than 400 meters from the target. A Variable Time fuse explodes a High Explosive mortar shell in the air overhead. Very effective against troops in fighting holes. The last round fired from each of the three tubes would be White Phosphorus, always called Willie Pete. These would blanket the area with white smoke, and let me know for sure that there were no more incoming mortar rounds still in the air as I began my assault. Of course nothing would be fired for real, but we were also being evaluated on our calls for fire.

The aggressors might be monitoring our intra-squad net, so I crawled down the line to tell each Marine with an anti-tank weapon which tank I wanted him to shoot at. Some of the platoon were carrying the AT-4 84mm one-shot disposable anti-tank rocket launcher. And there were the two SMAW rocket teams from the weapons platoon assault section with their 83mm bazooka-like weapons.

Before I was done Sergeant Lenoir reported, "Guns up," and Captain Z told me that 1st platoon was in position.

I pressed down the transmit button, "Fire, over."

"Fire, out." And a few seconds later, "Shot, over."

"Shot, out," I said. Sergeant Lenoir was letting me know that the single spotting round was in the air, and I should watch for its fall.

About thirty seconds later, "Splash, over."

The round had hit. "Splash, out." And then I gave an imaginary adjustment. "Direction three two zero six. Left fifty, drop fifty, fire for effect, over."

When the imaginary rounds were in the air, I said over the intra-squad radio, "AT-4's and SMAW's only; fire at will."

They popped up over the bank. I got my feet under me, ready to signal the assault, when to my total disbelief Corporal Maple, sighting over his AT-4, began shouting at the top of his lungs, "Tank! Direct Front! Fifty met…."

"Shut up and fire, goddammit!" I yelled.

Infantry operations always walk a razor's edge, and I thought we'd just sliced our feet off. I couldn't signal the assault until our mortars were done firing. All I could do was squat there and wait for the tank crews to swing their turrets around in our direction.

But it didn't happen. Our luck held; no one paid any attention to all the yelling going on behind them. Sergeant Lenoir radioed, "Mission complete." I signaled the assault, and the platoon poured over the bank.

Despite Maple's outburst we got right on top of the tanks before anyone inside woke up to our presence. As we swept by, one of the tank commanders was screaming hysterically, "Keep your fucking hands off my tank! Keep your fucking hands off my tank!"

We reached the edge of the LZ and threw ourselves down, looking out over the open sand. First and 3rd squads fired across the LZ at the aggressor positions on the other side, while Sergeant Turner and 2nd squad began working their way around the edge. Over the intra-squad radio I called my two machine-gun teams, who were firing back up on the bank. "Gun team one, keep your fire on the far side of the LZ. Team two, stay in front of 2nd squad."

I'd learned to direct instead of control. There's a big difference. And the more training we'd done together, the more mutual confidence we'd gained, the easier it was.

Once Sergeant Turner worked his way around the LZ I sent 1st squad behind him. Then a radio call from me and two of our tanks raced into the LZ, turbines screaming, making white smoke. Which I thought was a nice dramatic touch.

That ended it. The evaluators jumped in to separate the two sides because the aggressors were very upset. I heard one wailing plaintively, "I can't believe they did that to us!"

They climbed into their amtracs and left. Ours came into the LZ. And I stayed busy. "Corporal Asuego, take your squad back up to that bank as security. Don't fall asleep; they might try to sneak in a counterattack. Make sure you push out an observation post with eyes on the road—and that means just being able to see the road, not sitting in the middle of the fucking thing....What's that, Reilly? Your Marines get three MRE's a day, I don't care when they eat them....No, I don't know when we're moving again, but don't take off your clothes and start working on your suntan."

Then there was Corporal Maple. "Can I talk to you, sir?"

"Just what I had in mind," I said.

We moved away from the platoon and he began by telling me, in a lecturing tone, "Sir, you're supposed to give a fire command before you shoot, so if you miss everyone knows the range you were using."

It was the shock of surprise as much as anything that made it hard to maintain your cool. Such as Corporal Maple, after nearly blowing the MCCRES for us, seriously trying to match Corporal Asuego's achievement in getting me to admit that I was wrong. I'd found that the best way to keep my mental health was to cultivate a sense of detachment. Just a way of dealing with the fact that, no matter how much hard work and preparation you'd done, in the final execution something absurd or nonsensical was bound to happen. You had to find some emotional distance and treat it like an unavoidable natural disaster. The tornado wiped out the town? Okay, let's clean up the mess.

My reply to Maple took the form of a question. "And do you think that was a good idea in this particular situation?"

"You're supposed to give a fire command before you shoot the AT-4, sir."

"Corporal Maple, let me lay out a scenario for you. Your platoon has just sneaked up behind four enemy tanks, achieving total tactical surprise. Now, at that point is it a good idea to start screaming at the top of your fucking lungs, wake up the tankers, have them swing their turrets around, and turn us all into strawberry jam? Or is it a dumbass idea?"

"But, sir…"

"Look, it's one thing to have a brain fart and then tell me you learned your lesson and you won't ever do it again. But don't tell me your brain fart was justified because you had it by the book. If you don't understand that, I'm going to start worrying about you. Now, before you piss me off any more I want you to go away and think it over."

In case you hadn't guessed, Marines weren't all that great at grasping situational behavior. It was either a fire command every time or no fire command at all. I couldn't afford to let Maple keep believing, deep down, that he was right. So I went to his squad leader, Sergeant Turner.

"Maple doesn't think he fucked up," I said. "He needs to hear it from someone beside me."

Sergeant Turner couldn't believe it. "Doesn't think he fucked up, sir? Oh, he'll hear it from me." And he set off muttering, "Doesn't think he fucked up...."

Then Sergeant Bean jogged over from the amtracs. "Sir, terrorists just attacked New York and Washington. They crashed jets into the World Trade Center and the Pentagon."

I just looked at him and said, "Are you sure about that?"

"Yes, sir. One of my guys was listening to his radio."

He obviously believed it. "Okay, look, go talk to all your people and tell them to keep their mouths shut about this, at least for now. We're in the middle of a MCCRES, and the last thing we need is to get everyone all freaked out and then have no way of doing anything about it."

"Roger that, sir." And he sprinted back to the tracks.

I immediately told Captain Z, convinced that something probably had happened but that the magnitude, as always, had been inflated in the telling.

But he set me straight. "It's true, Mike. It's all over the radio net. Paralyzed the battalion staff for about a half hour, trying to decide what to do. But the word is that the MCCRES continues."

"The amtracers know about it, sir. I told them to keep their mouths shut, but I'm not holding my breath. I'm worried that if we don't say something to the troops then rumor control is going to get totally out of hand."

That was the way it was supposed to be. I gave the commander my information, I gave him my opinion, and then I walked off to let him process it and make his decision. And whatever he decided, I'd make it happen.

Captain Zimmerman called the whole company and all the attachments into the center of the LZ. "From what we've heard terrorists hijacked four jetliners this morning. They crashed one into the Pentagon, one into each of the World Trade Center towers in New York. The fourth went down in a field in Pennsylvania. That's all we know right now, and probably all we will know for some time. Except one thing. We're at war, and we are warriors. I'd like to send you all back to mainside to call your families. I've got a brother in law who works at the Pentagon. But today and tomorrow our job is to get ready for war. We may be going for real very soon." He paused. "Does anyone have any questions, or want to say anything?"

No one did.

Captain Zimmerman said, "Then let's take a minute of silence for everyone who lost their lives today."

When the minute was over Captain Z brought the lieutenants together. "We need to get moving and get everyone's heads back in the game." He unfolded his map. We kneeled around it, and he pointed to the next major tank trail intersection to the north. "Mike, I want you to go up on foot and make sure there aren't any surprises waiting for us there. Take the Javelin squad with you. The rest of us will be mounted up and ready to move. If you make contact we'll be right there. You understand?"

"Yes, sir," I replied.

"Outstanding. Move out as fast as you can."

I gave the squad leaders the order. It was only then I realized we were missing someone. "Staff Sergeant, see if you can find our evaluator." And he put Lance Corporal Conahey on the job.

I wanted to listen to Asuego and Reilly giving their orders, since this was something we hadn't rehearsed. Conahey waited for them to finish. "Sir, the evaluator's asleep in the back of one of the tracks."

Some Ranger. "Go wake his ass up and tell him we're moving out."

I went through the usual process of radio checks to make sure all the intra-squad radios were up and functioning. Vincent let me know he had good comm with the company headquarters. The squads were in formation ready to step off. I snapped, "Conahey, where the hell is the evaluator?"

"I told him we were moving out, sir."

Screw him, then. I gave the signal to move out.

The intersection was less than a kilometer up the tank trail. I knew the terrain. It was wooded all the way up on the left side of the trail. The right opened onto a cleared area, Drop Zone Plover. No way was I going to cross that. So I'd go up the left and make a wide arc to arrive on the flank. Staff Sergeant Frederick would take the two machine-gun teams and the Javelin anti-tank guided missile squad and set up a base of fire in the trees on the edge of the field. Having no idea what we might run into, I kept all three rifle squads and the SMAW rocket launchers with me.

The problem with sending a point fire team far enough out ahead that you didn't make first contact with your whole platoon was that the team leader either concentrated so hard on his navigation that he missed the enemy, or concentrated so hard on the enemy that he led you off course. I'd solved this by buying my own civilian GPS unit and tying it to the team leader with the admonition, "You don't want to be losing or breaking the Lieutenant's GPS."

It was the best investment I ever made, especially comparing the 5.5 ounce unit to my obsolete 2.75 pound battery-eating military Plugger, officially and laughably known as the Precision Lightweight GPS Receiver. In all fairness it actually was state of the art—when first issued 10 years ago. I'd already replaced my 2.25 pound issue Steiner binoculars with an 8 ounce pocket pair.

Once they saw it in action all the squad leaders went out and bought their own GPS. Marines always had to pay out of pocket for gear they should have been issued. I really think the leadership preferred it that way. Just think of all the money we save if the dumb, dedicated bastards pay for gear themselves.

When my Plugger told me we were just about there I got on the radio and told the point fire team to halt. We moved up to them and the platoon got on line. I made another call to Staff Sergeant Frederick and took the risk of ordering the machine-guns to open fire. It would give away our presence in the neighborhood, but.... The guns opened up, and so did the aggressors at the intersection right in front of us.

Now that we knew where they were I shifted our line obliquely to the right so Lance Corporal Reilly's center squad was even with the enemy. We were almost to the intersection when one of our Marines saw them, opened fire, and began the assault. Vincent was calling in a contact report on the radio, so I didn't have to worry about that. We broke out of the underbrush just in time to see the aggressors bolting into their two amtracs. Reilly's squad had the most contact, so Sergeant Turner and Corporal Asuego's squads on the left and right both sort of naturally bent around and cut the aggressors off from both sides. Not my idea, but good things usually happened if you let people do their jobs.

I saw Lance Corporal Conahey dash forward to the nearest amtrac and, grinning, fire his Squad Automatic Weapon into the open troop compartment.

That gave me an idea. I yelled, "Conahey, jump on that ramp and don't get off until I tell you!"

Corporal Asuego heard me and threw two Marines in front of the amtrac. Ahead of the curve as always, Sergeant Turner had done the same to the other track.

The amtrac commander nearest me was gunning the engine and jiggling the rear ramp, trying to knock Conahey off so he could close up and drive off. I tore open my flak jacket and stuck a thumb under my collar, flashing my bar like a badge. "Shut this vehicle down!" I yelled. "You injure someone down here and I'll see you in the brig." The engine shut off.

An angry little Staff Sergeant jumped down from the troop commander hatch and said, "Sir, you can't do this."

I held up one hand, though I didn't tell him to talk to it. "Keep your people inside the tracks. The evaluators will be here in a minute and they'll decide everything."

I took the handset from Vincent. "Echo-6, we are at the checkpoint. Be advised we've captured two amtracs and one aggressor platoon, over."

Captain Z's voice was wobbling over the sound of his amtrac's engine. "You what?"

"That's affirmative, Echo-6. We're holding them here at the checkpoint. Recommend you move up ASAP, over."

I couldn't believe these idiots had parked their amtracs right at their ambush site. A fifty meter run down the road and we'd never have caught them. But we had, and it was a major feather in our cap. Well, better to be a military genius by accident than a dickhead on purpose.

O'Brien showed up first. He took in the scene from his cupola, then climbed down shaking his head at the luck that fools sometimes enjoyed. Captain Z dismounted with his evaluator, who was immediately set upon by the aggressor platoon sergeant. But his side of the story had to wait, because the evaluator had to follow Captain Z over to me.

The Captain eyed the two amtracs filled with very pissed off aggressors. He produced a can of Copenhagen, banged it on his hand, packed a massive dip under his gum, and grinned like a chipmunk with a cheek full of nuts. "Okay, Mike, tell us what happened."

I did, ending with, "As soon as they broke to mount up their vehicles, sir, they were dead. They would have had to kill my whole platoon first, which they didn't."

At that point the evaluator pulled away to talk to the aggressor platoon sergeant.

Captain Z said, "Great work, Mike, but why in hell did you go off without your evaluator?"

"He was asleep in the back of an amtrac, sir. I sent one of my men to wake his ass up and tell him we were moving out, but he didn't show. The whole platoon was standing by ready to move out. I couldn't hold them up waiting for him to get his shit together."

He nodded. "Don't leave him behind again."

"I won't, sir. But I've got a pretty full plate here, and this fucker's only job is to follow me around."

Captain Z cocked his head in the direction of the company evaluator having some heated words with his lieutenant. "I've got a hunch that's what he's hearing right now."

A lot of talk about our prisoners was flying back and forth over the battalion radio net. Captain Z sent Milburn to block our open flank.

When the ass chewing was over I was my evaluator's next stop. "Man, why did you take off without me?"

"Are you telling me Lance Corporal Conahey didn't let you know we were moving out?"

"Yeah, but I thought we were going on the tracks."

He knew how weak that was. He should have been awake and listening to me give my order. I just stared at him until he walked away.

Which was when the Javelin squad leader appeared on my other side and said, "Sir, I wanted you to know that I killed those tanks in the trees."

I had been a little distracted, but now he had my full attention. "What tanks in the trees?"

He casually waved an arm toward the other side of the intersection.

"The four tanks back in those trees, sir. They're really well camouflaged, but we picked them up on our thermal sights."

I counted down from ten again, and said calmly, "You know, Sergeant, that information would have been really helpful before we went into the attack. Or during it. Or even after it."

"Sorry, sir."

"Look, I'm glad you killed them. But next time don't be shy about getting on the radio and letting me know."

"Yes, sir."

"Okay. Go on over there, knock on the hatch, and tell them they're dead."

A big smile at that. "Yes, sir."

I might have stopped losing my temper with my Marines, but that didn't include me. If I could have physically slapped myself without raising questions in a lot of people's minds, I would have. How could I have been so stupid to assume the whole area was clear of enemy without sweeping it? I'd been too busy gloating over my score. Another hard lesson.

And when Frank Milburn returned he made sure he told me about driving past the trees and having all the enemy tankers waving at him.

Battalion and the evaluators eventually decided that my prisoners really were prisoners. We'd hang onto them and practice POW handling procedures, something that was rarely done. O'Brien's platoon got the job of initially searching and segregating them. Battalion sent a couple of trucks and a security team to take them to the rear.

MILES gear would have settled who killed whom, not to mention made us realistically practice what Marine units also skimmed over—casualty evacuation. But no battalion commander would ever volunteer to use MILES during a MCCRES. In the zero-defects career stakes looking good took priority over being good. Even the best felt they couldn't afford to do otherwise.

The next part of the MCCRES extravaganza had the aggressor battalion moving to the other side of the base, across the New River inlet. Some went by helicopter. The amtracs swam the inlet. And the tanks went over on an old LCU landing craft, which was manned by an Army crew—go figure that. None of this was typical for a MCCRES, but then

Major Jones wasn't your typical operations officer.

If heroes didn't have tragic flaws, there would be no drama. Captain Zimmerman's was not knowing when to grab his chips and step away from the table. It always happened on a winning streak, when excitement overcame judgment. And we always knew when it was about to take place, because it was the only time he refused to listen to our input.

We knew that look well, and all resistance was futile. Like amphibious training in Little Creek, Virginia, when he insisted on the company running the Navy SEAL obstacle course (which is like Mount Everest compared to the standard Marine Corps obstacle course—we could have used ladders). They didn't all end in disaster, but the margin was always so close that it didn't make much difference to your central nervous system.

Reports began coming in from our reconnaissance assets. The aggressors and their amtracs were parked in a group up on the riverbank across the inlet, administratively as opposed to tactically.

Captain Z decided that he wanted to cross the river, land and pull a quick raid, shoot the enemy up, and return to our side. Apparently violating them twice wasn't enough, he wanted to go for three.

My Irish mother would have had something to say about things happening in threes.

After Captain Z gave his order, of course it was Jack O'Brien who spit some tobacco juice onto the sand and said, "A daylight raid, sir? You sure you want to do that? I can think of about ten things that could go wrong, for not much payoff on the mission."

I was eyeing my map. "Sir, it looks like there's only enough room at Town Point for one track at a time to land. And high banks on both sides."

"They could see us coming with more than enough time to get ready," Milburn added.

But the Captain was determined. And much to our surprise he got permission from battalion to do it. Another argument in favor of MILES gear—it would have made everyone think twice about pulling a wild-ass stunt like that.

I was the lead platoon again. I hadn't suspected my company commander of being superstitious, but I guessed he was going to stay with me as long as I was hot. We splashed into the Inlet for about a 4000 meter angled swim across.

And ran into trouble right away. The tide was coming in almost faster than the water speed of our amtracs. I stayed off the intercom because the crew had their hands full.

The current caused us to turn out of the main channel too late, and the column of tracks swept right past our landing at Town Point. So we had to turn around and head back.

Shit. We came around the point like a fleet of Civil War ironclads. The only thing in our favor was just one aggressor track up on the bank able to shoot at us.

As soon as my amtrac hit dry land I ordered everyone out. With banks on both sides we could only rush up the landing trail. It was an impossible tactical situation, which I'm sure happens more often than not in real war, with the only option to put your head down, assault hard, and hope most of your platoon was still standing when it was over.

At least the aggressors were surprised again and spazzing out. All but one. A Humvee raced down the tank trail and stopped in front of us, blocking the landing. The Staff Sergeant inside shut down and smiled triumphantly at me.

The smile was what did it. Lance Corporal Reilly was right next to me, leading the point squad. "Reilly!" I ordered. "If he doesn't back this vehicle off the trail in five seconds, drag his ass out and move it yourself."

The words weren't even out of my mouth when I said to myself: what the fuck did you just do? And it would have to be Reilly I'd give the order to.

What I'd done was what every leader of Marines knew not to. Because Marines obeyed orders, instantly, whether or not they thought those orders were fucked up or made no sense. And if you left any ambiguity in your orders, they'd usually be obeyed in exactly the way you didn't want.

Which is what I expected just then. But before Reilly could finish counting, lay hands on the Staff Sergeant, and speed me on my way to a court-martial, the Staff Sergeant correctly decided that he wasn't being bluffed and gunned the Humvee back up the trail.

The rest of the amtracs were able to land. We swept through the area, hopped back in our vehicles, and headed back to our original side of the river. We were lucky, very lucky.

Our next mission was a night crossing of the inlet to take up blocking positions around LZ Parrot, sealing it off so Fox Company could do a night attack.

Except for one big complication. On the way back from refueling Frank Milburn's one remaining amtrac went down. If Milburn stayed behind we wouldn't have enough forces to accomplish our mission. The ensuing conference came up with only one solution. Stuff Milburn's platoon in with my platoon on my amtracs. I'd drop him off at his objective, then continue on to mine. It had to be me; O'Brien had a different landing point and route to his objective.

"I don't have a problem with it," I said. "But what about the safety question of putting tracks into the water with that many Marines aboard?"

Everyone turned to Lieutenant Houseman, the track platoon commander. "They'll float," he said. "But if there's a problem I don't know about anyone getting out." He let out a breath. "I'm willing to do it." Working with Captain Z seemed to have turned his nerves to asbestos.

Captain Z didn't even hesitate. "We'll do it." Another gutsy call. If anything happened he was toast. Most captains would have given lip service to training the way they'd fight.

Milburn and I did a couple of rehearsals, to see if we really could cram everyone inside. Their packs too; we couldn't hang them outside the vehicles while swimming. It was tight, so tight that 3rd platoon couldn't sit down. Or even bend over.

Milburn would be back in the troop compartment too. "Just don't fuck around getting to my intersection," he said.

"What if I have to pee?" I asked. "Or I see a 7-11 and really need a Slurpee?"

"Just keep talking. You're not stuck in back."

"It's a great chance to get close to your men, Frank." Just then I happened to notice the grenade sticking out from one of his pouches. It was shaped like a soda can but colored gray, not green like a run-of-the-mill smoke.

"Funny," I said, "I don't remember CS being authorized for the MCCRES." CS was a very potent tear gas.

"Been saving it for the right occasion."

"Do me a favor? Try not to let the pin snag on anything inside the track."

"That would be totally unsat, wouldn't it?"

We waited until the absolute last moment to board the vehicles. How tight was it? The crewmen inside the troop compartments had to inch the rear ramps closed to make sure no fingers or noses got nipped off.

The red night lights were on inside to keep everyone from losing their night vision. The scene was appropriately hellish even without them. It didn't seem as if there was any unused air back there, let alone space. Just a solid block of Marines. Amid the usual chorus of bitching, I heard the voice of Lance Corporal Turpin saying, "Anyone pops a rod, I'm dropping a dime on them." To which someone of course replied, "Better keep that sweet ass puckered up, Turpin."

Sergeant Bean said over the intercom, "It looks like field trip day at Clown College, sir."

"I'm just glad someone else said that," I replied.

I was praying pretty hard when we hit the water, but we stayed afloat. It was eerie looking though my night vision goggle as we chugged along, seemingly inches above the water, the tips of the waves flashing like green sparks.

When we landed on the other side I said over the intercom, "Let's go before someone loses it back there."

Sergeant Bean replied calmly, "Don't worry sir; there's no room back there to lose it in."

I was counting off intersections as we raced down the tank trails. "Okay, next one."

The drivers stood on the brakes. The ramps dropped and it was as if the two amtracs vomited 3rd platoon out. As soon as they were clear the ramps went up and we were off. Just after we disappeared down the road, and before they had a chance to shake off the effects of their cramped journey and get organized, Milburn was attacked by two aggressor amtracs charging into the intersection from the opposite direction.

Deciding that the right occasion had in fact arrived, Milburn yanked out his CS grenade, pulled the pin, and chucked it in front of the onrushing amtracs.

The effect was miraculous. The gas was sucked into the vehicle air intakes and settled in the troop compartments. The ramps and hatches all flew open. The aggressors stumbled out, coughing, wheezing, eyes on fire, mucus jetting from their noses, fumbling to get their gas masks on. Which gave Milburn and his boys enough time to shoot them up and fade back into the trees.

After reaching my objective I set up my ambush and positioned the two amtracs behind us to block the tank trail.

Then it was just a matter of waiting. A couple of hours later, after midnight, we heard firing from the direction of LZ Parrot as Fox Company went in with their night attack.

Five minutes later a Humvee sped down the tank trail heading right for us, and I do mean speeding. I barely had time to open fire and initiate the ambush.

The Humvee didn't even slow down, roaring though the intersection straight for my amtrac roadblock. I jumped up and ran out into the trail, positive that the stupid bastard was going to crash right into the amtracs.

The Humvee slowed down as he saw them, but didn't stop. The driver actually tried to run up the embankment bordering the tank trail. He would have made it but he hit the bank too fast and cut the wheel too hard—two wheels on top and two on the slope. Rolling a Humvee wasn't easy but he pulled it off, sliding down the slope upside down.

I could just picture the accident investigation gigging me for not hanging safety lights on my tactical roadblock. Over the intra-squad radio I ordered, "Doc Bob, out on the road. Everyone else stand fast."

By the time the Doc and I reached the Humvee, the driver had crawled out and was sitting dazed on the side of the bank. It was the Staff Sergeant whom I'd almost allowed Reilly to punch out. As they say in the Corps: good initiative—poor judgment.

Doc Bob made him lie down and checked him out. The amtrac crews were standing by with their extinguishers. Sergeant Bean appeared next to me in the darkness, saying, "Glad I'm not signed for that vehicle, sir."

"You and me both," I said.

Doc Bob came over to report. "No broken bones, sir. No skull or spinal injuries, and no signs of internal bleeding."

"No medevac?" I said, surprised.

"I don't think so, sir. Instead of trying to get an ambulance in here at this time of night I'd rather watch him for signs of a concussion or a stiff belly."

"Okay," I said. "Good work, Doc." And then to the patient. "Hey, Staff Sergeant, what say you don't cap off a full night by trying to overpower my Doc and escape? Deal?"

"Deal, sir, deal," he moaned.

Sergeant Bean said, "Sir, I think we can roll that Humvee back right side up. You want me to try?"

"No, leave it be. They're going to need photos and measurements for the investigation."

That was the end of the action. The rest of the night was the hard boring part of training—not slacking off when you're tired and nothing's going on. Troops on an ambush are linked by a parachute cord tug line for silent communication. And I did a lot of tugging to keep everyone awake.

The MCCRES ended that morning. I dozed in the cupola while Sergeant Bean navigated us to the final assembly area where the Battalion Landing Team broke up and went home to see what had happened to the world in our absence.

Part Two

"Apparently they can learn nothing save through suffering, remember nothing save when underlined in blood-'"

William Faulkner, ***The Bear***

CHAPTER TEN

I think everyone in the country tried to call someone. Nothing northbound was getting past New York, so I sent my folks an e-mail.

There was a message from Jenny on my desk when we got back. As soon as the company was secured I drove down to Wilmington.

Jenny didn't want to go out to eat; she didn't want to go out at all. She just wanted to be held, and to talk. I don't think she was alone in the country in feeling that way either.

We were lying in bed, and I was saying, "If we hadn't been in the field I probably wouldn't be here. Locking the barn after the horse is out is a military specialty. By the time we came in everyone was guarding something. All that was left was the base swimming pools."

"You shouldn't kid. Not about this."

"I wasn't kidding. Just because it's absurd doesn't mean it's not true."

"All I heard around campus was how this was all our fault."

"That sounds like my school days. Dictators, tyrants, and murderers always get a free pass. And it's always our fault."

"You know, Michael, there are legitimate grievances against us in the Arab World."

"Sure. There were legitimate grievances in Russia in 1917. And the Bolsheviks didn't address them, they exploited them to seize power. It's not about grievances, or us being Rome. It's the same old story of a clever psychopath and his accomplices who want to rule the world, or in this case be the Caliph of the Islamic World."

"They always think it would be a perfect world if only fill-in-the-blank was dead, don't they?"

"Sure, and Bin Laden wouldn't be the first to think that God wanted him to do it, or send the true believers out to die while he stayed home. You won't see him or his lieutenants flying any planes into buildings."

"I suppose everyone in the military is blaming Bill Clinton?"

"He *is* widely regarded as a gutless bastard. But there's plenty of blame to go around. The Iranians take over our embassy in Teheran. The Iranians and Syrians blow up our embassy and Marine barracks in Lebanon. They take Americans hostage in Lebanon—Ollie North sends them missiles. Al Qaeda blows up a base in Saudi Arabia, two embassies in Africa, and an Aegis destroyer in Yemen. And we don't do diddly squat in each case. Carter, Reagan, Bush, Clinton, Bush—all the same. Terrorism always worked."

"I hate to think restraint only egged these people on."

"Showing weakness always does. If you give them reason to think they can take you, they'll try. You either have to destroy them or they'll destroy you."

"I don't even want to think about that."

"I know you don't. That's why you have people like me to destroy them for you."

Jenny hugged me tighter. "I don't want to think about that, either."

"That's why you're worth defending."

CHAPTER ELEVEN

When I walked into the company office I could have sworn there was an adult male chimpanzee sitting at the XO's desk.

You were never quite sure what was going to happen in an infantry battalion. I sometimes wondered what other people's Monday mornings were like.

No, it was a human being after all. He'd taken a real beating, not the Hollywood kind where the victim shows up in the next scene with a little black eye. This guy's face was pushed out to about twice normal size by all the swelling and edema.

Eventually I realized who it was. Captain Carbonelli, not that it should have been a surprise. One of my early junior lieutenant jobs was visiting the company's incarcerated in the brig. Whenever a unit had a Marine in stir, an officer had to drop by and check on the jailbird once a week.

Captain Carbonelli was actually Private Carbonelli, but he'd won his nickname the day he decided to see how the other half lived. Buying some captain's bars at the PX, he pinned them on and toured the base grandly accepting and returning salutes from the lowly enlisted. The only flaw in his plan was that he was what the Marine Corps calls a shitbird lance corporal. His cammies were a mess, his boots looked like they'd been shined with a Hershey bar, and no matter how hard he scrubbed—not that he scrubbed all that hard—there would always be dirt under his fingernails. Eventually an MP asked to see his ID card, which everyone including captains were required to produce on demand.

Ten seconds after we met at the brig Captain Carbonelli began whining about his misfortunes. Apparently in reply to some lip the brig MP's had moved him to a cell with a concrete slab instead of a mattress and a bucket in lieu of a toilet. And he wanted my help in getting his mattress and potty back.

"You want your privileges restored?" I said. "Stop running your mouth." After that I think he decided not to bother asking me to bring him some smokes the next time.

The lieutenants were, as usual, congregated around Jack O'Brien's desk. I joined them and said, "That *is* Captain Carbonelli, isn't it?"

"Himself," said Frank Milburn.

"So what do you think?" O'Brien asked me.

"What do I think? If they keep making *Planet of the Apes* movies, I see a chance to make some real money."

Once they stopped laughing, O'Brien said, "Wait until you hear this one," turning the floor over to Jimmy Nichols, Captain Carbonelli's platoon commander.

"You know Corporal Cushing?" Nichols asked me.

I shook my head no.

"In the assault section," said Nichols. "Great kid. He and his wife— major love story. He writes her a love poem every day; she hides little notes in his gear so he finds them out in the field. Well, she's out of town with a sick mother or something, and misses their anniversary. So she sends him flowers, and sends them to the barracks so they don't sit on the doorstep all day long. But he's gone when the flowers get delivered. And guess who signs for them?"

"Okay," I said, "I may be coming out of left field on this one. Captain Carbonelli?"

"That's affirmative," said Nichols. "And Captain Carbonelli doesn't give the flowers to Cushing. He makes off with them and gives them to some hosebag out in town."

The dramatic arc of the story was beginning to make itself clear to me.

"It really pissed the platoon off," Nichols continued. "Last night the duty NCO and firewatch were both from the mortar section. You know where they're doing landscaping out by the barracks, with the wood lathe fencing around it?"

I nodded.

"The firewatch spots Carbonelli coming back to the barracks. He calls the duty. They each rip a wooden lathe off the fence...."

"And they give Carbonelli a wood shampoo," I said, finishing the sentence. "Outstanding."

"Payback is a medevac," said Nichols.

"I can't believe you weren't the OD for this one," O'Brien said to me.

"Simple assault with a deadly weapon?" I scoffed. "Child's play."

"Just about what you'd expect from the mortar section," said Milburn. "They couldn't wait a day or two for Carbonelli to get court-martialed again for stealing the flowers."

"Didn't Carbonelli get six, six, and a kick for impersonating an officer in the first place?" O'Brien asked Nichols. He was referring to the standard special court-martial sentence of six months in the brig, six months forfeiture of pay, and a bad conduct discharge.

"Oh, yeah," Nichols replied. "He got the Big Chicken Dinner." The insider's term for a bad conduct discharge, or BCD. "He's just waiting around for it to come through."

"Not the sharpest knives in the drawer," said O'Brien.

"But they did a hell of a job on Carbonelli," said Dick Herkimer. "Good thing he doesn't have any brains either, or they'd have leaked out his ears after that ass-whipping."

The fire door banged at the other end of the office, and we all looked over to see Captain Zimmerman closely examining Captain Carbonelli.

"Uh, oh," said Herkimer.

"I can't wait to see what he does," said O'Brien.

The Captain having received one version of events from Captain Carbonelli, the First Sergeant followed him into his office to provide a more objective overview.

Then the First Sergeant called us into the Captain's office.

It was with great anticipation that we took our seats. Captain

Zimmerman looked out at Captain Carbonelli through the open door and motioned for the First Sergeant to close it. He turned back to us, shook his head sadly, and said, "They beat that boy like a redheaded stepchild."

Whenever the Captain favored us with one of his Southernisms, the four Yankees would crack up while Milburn rolled his eyes at being among the heathen.

Back out in the main office Staff Sergeant Frederick and Staff Sergeant White of 3rd platoon were sitting at our desk. No matter how many times I told my platoon sergeant not to, he always vacated the chair behind the desk when I showed up.

I'd given up fussing over it. "What's up?" I asked, sitting down.

"We were just passing around some pictures of the wives and kids, sir," Staff Sergeant White said, handing me a few.

"A handsome family," I told him, even though they were as plain as he. I was pretty sure Staff Sergeant Frederick didn't have any children, but suddenly I was holding a photo of Staff Sergeant Frederick, a young oriental lady, and two little children who were obviously theirs. "And the same here," I said. And then, "Excuse me for a second."

I went to the head because I wasn't sure how long I could maintain. Okay, if I had already met his wife Annette from New Jersey, and this was his wife and kids....

I was so shaken I had to splash some water on my face. It made no difference if it was bigamy or just adultery, since both were crimes under the Uniform Code of Military Justice. What civilians shrugged at the military was deadly serious about—at least for everyone under the rank of general.

What now, lieutenant? Well, there was no way I was going to lose the best platoon sergeant in the battalion, if not the Marine Corps. So right then I vowed that I would never again ask Staff Sergeant Frederick a personal question. What I didn't know I couldn't testify to. So now I'd be starting each day with a short prayer that he'd be able to keep his personal life from blowing up in all our faces. I never imagined how much of being a platoon commander would involve turning a blind eye.

When I returned from the head Staff Sergeant Frederick said, "PFC

Jenkins's wife is here, sir. She wants to see you."

"Me?" I said, in a much higher pitch than John Wayne would have used. "What does she want to see me about?"

He only shrugged.

It looked like one of those days that was only going to get worse. "It's either twenty grand in credit card debt, or he hit her," I predicted. I spent more time being a financial and family councilor than a platoon commander.

To the troops there were two kinds of officers, the ones you could talk to and the ones you couldn't. Since I'd admitted to Corporal Asuego I was wrong I'd been the first, and I was more than proud of that. But one thing was certain, no matter how open my door I only got the call after the Titanic had hit the iceberg. This wasn't going to be something I wanted to hear. "Don't run off. I've got a feeling I may need a witness."

PFC Jenkins had been Lance Corporal Jenkins, fire team leader, before he popped for marijuana on the same urinalysis I threatened Lance Corporal Valentine with catheterization. Incidentally, Valentine also popped. As predicted, his drug was Ecstasy.

Jenkins's wife was all dressed up to talk to me. Without him. The Staff Sergeant got her a chair, and we all sat down.

She launched right into it as if she'd over-rehearsed and was afraid any extraneous small talk would throw her off track. "My husband can't go on deployment."

I was right, I didn't want to hear this. "Why can't he go on deployment?"

"Because I need him."

Staff Sergeant Frederick's anger was hiding behind his poker face. "All the wives of Marines in this battalion need their husbands," I said. "How are you different?"

"Because I'm different. I'm not well, and I need my husband with me."

"I'm sorry to hear that. How are you not well?"

"My nerves. My nerves are very bad from stress."

"Your nerves?"

"Yes."

"Well, I'm very sorry about your nerves, but your husband made the decision to join the Marine Corps. He's a Marine, and he's going on deployment."

I got up and moved toward the door, so she really had no choice but to come along. I held it open and she went out. If she hadn't, I would have. On the way through she turned and said, very determined, "No he's not."

It took a lot to get Staff Sergeant Frederick excited, and right then he was totally ballistic. "Who the *fuck* does she think *she* is? Comes in here and says, I don't want him to go, like that's all it takes. I tell you what, sir, now I know what made Jenkins go pop that piss test."

"Well," I said. "Either nothing's going to happen next, or something is." I tried not to indulge my imagination about what that something might turn out to be.

Another fire team leader had to go down. Lance Corporal Westgate was now fully recovered from alcohol poisoning.

"You know why you're not a team leader any more?" I said.

"Because I fucked up, sir."

"Because you didn't set the example. What if I missed the MCCRES because I went out and got drunk off my ass the night before? You'd say, "Who is he to tell us how to act?" Right now that's you. I can't rely on you to show up sober for a major exercise, and you've got no credibility with the Marines in your fire team. They made the MCCRES—you didn't. You understand what I'm saying?"

"Yes, sir."

"You've got the next move. You can either start working your way back to being someone I can rely on all the time, and acts exactly the way he tells other Marines to act. Or not."

We had the MCCRES debrief, and as we suspected we'd kicked some serious ass. Got 100% on the beach assault, but were chastised for straying over a fire support boundary during our long end-around. Typical. But Golf company didn't fare as well, and Captain Chef got kicked upstairs to be the assistant operations officer.

We also replaced Golf as the helicopter company. We were stoked about that, even though grunts hated riding in helicopters. They crashed with depressing regularity. We knew that the top of the class in flight school got jets while the rest went to helos. We also knew that of the elements vital to safe helicopter operations—maintenance and spares, modern avionics, and enough flight time for pilots to be proficient let alone expert—the Marine Corps never fully funded all three.

But Afghanistan was landlocked, and everything was going to have to come in by helicopter. And we wanted to go in very badly.

We already had helicopter skills. We just needed to go up to the air base at Cherry Point to spend some time in the helo dunker, a mockup helicopter fuselage that was dropped into a pool to simulate a crash into the ocean. It was a lot of fun until they put blackout goggles on us and we had to get out by feel.

We also brushed up on fast-roping, which was how you left a helicopter that didn't have room to land. A nylon rope as thick as the ones you had to climb in gym class got kicked out, and wearing heavy gloves you slid down it like a fire pole, braking with the hands and feet. Now that was fun.

Helicopter raids and urban warfare were the main mission, so we went back to the MAC ranges and the grenade house.

And there Captain Zimmerman brought all the platoon commanders and platoon sergeants together and gave us a direct order that the troops were to let the grenades cook off before throwing them into the rooms. Just as we'd do in combat, and the responsibility all his.

When it was our turn I took Corporal Turner aside and said, "I want PFC Francois to throw a grenade."

The look on his face was worth paying money to see. Private First Class Francois was a young Marine with zero self-confidence. But it didn't make him withdrawn, quite the opposite. He was all insecure bravado. When walking around he liked to affect a pronounced inner city strut. It was never a secret when he was in the vicinity, because the air would be filled with outraged NCO bellows of, "FRAN-COIS! Don't you be diddy-boppin' through my fucking area!"

By general consensus a four-star pain in the ass, and sorely in need of a good ass-kicking. A court-martial offense I was afraid one of my NCO's would eventually provide.

It wasn't that I didn't think a little tune-up would do more than a few of my Marines a world of good. But I valued a good NCO's career more than the potential reform of some young pain in the ass. And that's how I made the case to them.

So in the absence of a thumping I'd decided that Francois needed something to give him some confidence.

But my solution rocked Sergeant Turner's world. "You want Francois to throw a *live* grenade, sir?"

"Your hearing is just fine, Sergeant Turner. I'd rather have him do it now than in combat for the first time."

He obviously felt the need to bring the lieutenant down from Utopia. "We may never get to combat, sir. But Francois could fuck up real bad in the next few minutes."

"I'll be the range safety officer, Sergeant Turner. And I'll be standing right behind Francois the whole time."

The Sergeant replied to that with a grudging smile and some typical grunt fatalism. "And we'll be behind you, sir. Maybe not *right* behind you, but we'll be behind you."

Francois's hand was trembling as he removed the grenade from his pouch. Something that could blow you into hamburger was a hell of a lot different from an otherwise identical blue practice grenade. I was locked onto that hand, war-gaming everything possible that could go wrong after he pulled the pin, and what I'd do in the time available. Like something as absurdly simple as him fumbling to get the spoon off and dropping it at our feet. Or "milking" the grenade, as we called it. That is, nervously squeezing and relaxing his grip on it, releasing the constant tension on the spoon and possibly starting the fuse burning even while he was still physically holding the spoon down.

That shaking hand, not to mention flashing back on what one grenade had done to a whole squad, was making me reconsider my master plan for boosting Francois's self-esteem.

But of course I had to go through with it. Gripping the grenade hard enough to crack the casing, Francois thumbed off the wire safety clip. Then he pulled the pin. You couldn't do it with your teeth; they'd come out before the pin did.

Now all Francois had to do was release the spoon, quickly count thousand-one, thousand-two, out loud just the way he'd been taught, and throw the grenade into the room.

His face screwed up in concentration, determined to do everything right, Francois flipped off the spoon and slowly and deliberately chanted, "One…thousand…and… one. One…"

The whole squad and I screamed, "THROW IT!!!"

I lunged for the grenade but Francois instinctively obeyed orders and whipped it into the room. It blew just as it passed through the doorway.

Everything went down way too fast for me to get scared right then. But I can't deny that once the dust settled my sphincter was so tight I couldn't have passed a piece of dental floss. I looked back into the blood-drained faces of the rest of the squad. The room clearers were frozen in place.

Francois's slow count had probably let that 4-5 second fuse burn for close to 4 seconds. Surprisingly, considering my past history, I didn't lose my cool.

I put my arm around Francois's shoulders and led him out of earshot. Praise in public and punish in private.

"Tell me what you did wrong," I said.

"I…I counted too slow, sir. I'm so sor…."

"Show me how to do it right," I said.

He walked through the whole procedure again, with the right count this time.

I walked outside, plucked one of the extra grenades from the case, removed it from the protective fiber canister, went back into the grenade house, and handed it to Francois under the disbelieving eyes of 2nd squad.

"Okay," I said. "You know what you did wrong, you learned from it, no one got hurt, and you'll never do it again. The only thing left is to do it right. You ready?"

He whispered, "Do I have to, sir?"

I wasn't going to give him permission to quit. "Yes, you do. You think I'd give you another grenade if I thought you couldn't do it?" I sure hoped I was right.

He let out his breath hard, and shuffled into position. While Francois was readying the second grenade, I looked back over my shoulder. The whole squad had subtly edged back a few feet to put themselves within diving distance of the nearest corner. I didn't say anything; it struck me as a prudent move, though one I couldn't take advantage of.

Francois thumbed off the safety clip and my stomach clenched as he wrestled with the pin. He got it out, and I went back to being totally focused on that grenade.

He flicked off the spoon and called out, "Thousand-one, thousand-two," threw it into the room, and then, "Frag out." It blew, and as the clearing team charged through the smoke to take down the targets, I grabbed Francois by both shoulders and gave him a hard "well done" shake. He looked back at me, and that formerly sullen-is-cool teenage baby face was lit up. My stomach hadn't quite fallen back down into its normal position yet, but that was all right.

Later we were sitting around eating MRE's and Francois was taking his due ration of shit from the platoon. After the razzing died down a bit, Corporal Crockett, one of Sergeant Harlin's team leaders, said, "Staff Sergeant?"

"What is it, Crazy?" Staff Sergeant Frederick replied.

Corporal Crockett was a tall kid from the Bronx, a basketball player. Not because he was black, because he loved basketball. He'd kicked ass in front of the meritorious corporal promotion board to make his rank, and was a natural leader with great personal force.

At first maybe a little too much force. Right after the promotion Lance Corporal Peterson came to me complaining that Crockett hit him. Fortunately there were no witnesses. I wouldn't trade ten Petersons for one Crockett.

When I had a talk with Crockett he guilelessly admitted everything. "You tell him to do something, sir, and he's got a million punk-ass reasons why he shouldn't have to. He's a little bitch, so I bitch-slapped him."

That really wasn't what I wanted to hear. "Corporal Crockett, a superior isn't allowed to bitch-slap his subordinates."

He squinted in disbelief, as if I'd just told him he had to wear a G-string under his uniform. "You mean I can't hit 'em, sir?"

"No," I said. "You can't hit 'em."

Staff Sergeant Frederick had been profoundly embarrassed, telling me it was all his fault. The Lance Corporal team leaders were used to inviting their fellow lance corporals outside to settle any problems. But once they became corporals it was an offense. He held NCO school starting that afternoon. Corporal was the toughest job in the Corps. I didn't get promoted one day and have to boss around my peers, dealing squarely with friends, enemies, and all the attendant jealousies.

I'd made Crockett one of Sergeant Harlin's team leaders because his qualities were those Sergeant Harlin wasn't overly endowed with. He'd also been one of the first to rush to the scene of the grenade accident.

His question for the Platoon Sergeant was delivered in such a serious tone I knew he had to be up to something. "Staff Sergeant, all those Medal of Honor citations hanging up in the hallway of the battalion CP? Most of them are Marines who jumped on incoming grenades and let themselves get blown up to save their buddies' lives."

"What about it?" Staff Sergeant Frederick asked.

"They're all PFC's," Corporal Crockett said. "What's that about, Staff Sergeant?"

Equally deadpan, and without missing a beat, my platoon sergeant said, "That's 'cause when a grenade comes in, the Staff Sergeant and the Lieutenant grab the nearest PFC and throw his ass on it."

I nearly choked on my MRE. The platoon fell over laughing, and there were cries of, "Francois, that coulda been you." Someone out of my sight line yelled, "I saw the Lieutenant behind you, Francois—he was ready."

We went aboard ship twice, the last for the Special Operations Exercise. Our part was a non-combatant evacuation with Fox Company, getting American and friendly civilians out of a war-torn country. Basically some role-players throwing rocks at us as hostile natives; dealing with the occasional sniper; and "diplomats" who refused to leave their poodles behind. The best were the girls who promised the Marines sex if they'd take them to America. The troops shrewdly demanded that the role-players strip to see if they were worth it. That was when the role playing stopped.

Captain Zimmerman hated working with Captain Lafrance of Fox Company. An early victim of male-pattern baldness, built like a small college lineman, his blustering earnestness had quickly won him the nickname Captain America. Pretty soon even the Chaplain was calling him that. As Captain Z said, "I wish Captain America would stop saying "God bless" when he really means "fuck you.""

CHAPTER TWELVE

My having the duty that weekend filled Jack O'Brien with joy. "Just reading about it isn't enough anymore," he said. "Maybe we can arrange some kind of live video feed?"

"Like *Cops* or something?" said Frank Milburn.

"Have your little fun," I replied. "But no matter what the crisis, the battalion will be safe in my capable hands."

"You hope," said Milburn.

"It has gotten worse each time," O'Brien pointed out.

"Sooner or later," I said, "the laws of probability *have* to kick in."

"You hope," said Milburn.

I had Sunday duty this time, which made me cautiously optimistic. I suspected that Saturday night might have been the root of all my previous problems.

My tour began with controversy right at 0800. I was relieving Lieutenant Daniels, the Weapons Company 81mm mortar platoon commander. And he got huffy when I removed the magazine of the Beretta and counted out the rounds.

Believing his honor to be in question, he demanded, "Don't you trust me?"

"Absolutely," I said. "Trust you with my life." But I kept counting rounds. With your career on the line it was much easier to be a moral coward than a physical one. If something happened to provoke an inventory, and I came up one round short of what I signed for because some previous OD had lost it and kept quiet, I was the one who got screwed.

My staff duty was Staff Sergeant Buck, from the Weapons Company antiarmor platoon. He was famous throughout the battalion for having taken the physically brutal Force Reconnaissance indoctrination test three times, and either passing out or succumbing to heat exhaustion all three times.

The Staff Sergeant confided that he'd accepted a few dollars from a fellow Staff NCO to take the duty with me. Evidently the word was that you saw too much action on my watch.

That pissed me off. "I'm the one who has to go out and handle all this shit," I said. "The Staff Duty just sits here and works the phones."

"That's what I thought, sir," said the Staff Sergeant. "But you know how stories get bigger the more people tell them."

The day was pretty uneventful, which according to past history meant nothing. When we hit the rack for the night Staff Sergeant Buck thought I was some kind of eccentric. "You don't take your boots off, sir?"

"Let's just say I've learned not to."

Sure enough the phone rang at 0200. "Sir, this is the Golf Company duty; someone just fired a rifle behind the barracks."

"I'll be right there," I said, whipping on my pistol belt. It was inevitable, of course; there would have to be a terrorist attack when I was on duty.

"Rifle fire behind the barracks," I told the Staff Sergeant. "Call the MP's and the reaction force."

"Yes, sir. Shouldn't you wait for them?"

That brought me up short, and I had to think it over. "I'm not going to go rushing into a firefight," I said. "But I have to see what's going on."

"Okay, sir." He said it with the resigned finality of a Staff NCO who'd performed his due diligence. The lieutenant was now free to step into the shit on his own.

It was the usual. Out the door at a dead run, pistol in my hand. Not that it would do much good if there really were rifles out there. I might get the chance to pop off a couple of rounds, just to demonstrate the

proper élan, before being shot full of holes. I tried to stay behind cover
as I came up.

Someone carrying a rifle flashed across my field of view and
disappeared into the middle of one of the barracks, where the stairwell
was.

There was no waiting around now. He was going into a barracks full
of Marines, and I was the only good guy who was armed.

I cut over to put the edge of the wall between it and me. On the
concrete walkway I dropped to one knee to peek around the corner. You
always expect a head to appear at head height. The stairwell was empty.
Around the corner, pistol out in front. I heard footsteps on the concrete.
My elbows were locked and I was looking over the sights, trying to
control my breathing.

A figure came around the corner, gripping the barrel of a rifle in one
hand. "Freeze!" I shouted, and in the enclosed space it sounded like the
voice of God.

The figure froze. "Golf Company duty, sir."

"Walk into the light," I ordered.

It was the Golf duty NCO, a sergeant I'd chatted with on an earlier
tour of the area. He was holding a civilian rifle.

"Everything's under control, sir," he said. "Here's the rifle, and I've
got the Marine in my office."

"Marine?" I said.

"Yes, sir. Dumb fuck was shooting off his own .22."

I holstered my pistol. Inside the office a very sheepish Lance Corporal was being guarded by the firewatch. I pulled the Article 31 card
out of my wallet and read him his rights, the military equivalent of the
Miranda Warning.

It was only then I realized what had slipped my mind. I dashed out
of the office, the duty, firewatch, and culprit all staring at me.

Onto the lawn in front of the barracks, then a complete stop. Unless
I missed my guess, a whole shitload of MP's and the base reaction force
were out in the darkness. All it would take was one Marine with an
itchy finger to fire one round, and it was going to look like the last five
minutes of *The Wild Bunch*.

"I'm the OD!" I shouted out into the darkness, keeping my arms away from my sides. "A Marine shot off his .22. He's in custody. Everything's all right." I didn't even want to think about how many rifles, shotguns, and machine-guns were aimed at me right then. If I'd been wearing night vision goggles I could have seen all the laser aiming dots dancing across my bod.

A spotlight snapped on and blinded me. Then a megaphone-amplified voice announced, "Everyone stand down."

A few seconds later the lawn was filled with people. Marines in cammies; MP's in the khaki and green Bravo uniform. Fortunately the MP platoon commander turned out to be my buddy Ernie. We'd gone to the Basic School together. He was a former staff sergeant who didn't get excited by much.

Which was just as well. The reaction force platoon commander, an infantry 2nd lieutenant even more junior than me, wanted to stay for the questioning of the suspect. For no other reason than they'd been sitting around on alert night after night. Now they were actually out in the air doing something, and none to anxious to have it end.

I would have just told the guy to get lost, but Ernie patiently explained the facts of life. "Look, there's no emergency. We," pointing to me, "have jurisdiction and you don't. And if you don't get back in your trucks and clear out it's going to get logged in. And then the Provost Marshal and Mike's battalion commander are going to call your battalion commander, and he's going to dance all over your balls."

That sold him. And then Ernie and I went inside to see what the story was. As I was writing down the particulars from the ID card of Lance Corporal Koch, the Marine in question, Ernie showed me a good trick. He took off his garrison cap, had Koch breath into it, then smelled it for alcohol. Have a drunk Marine in custody breath into your face, and you just might get it spit into.

Even though Ernie gave him his rights again, we still heard the story. Lance Corporal Koch was as bright about his right to silence he'd been with the rest of his activities.

Lance Corporal Koch had just bought a .22 rifle. Which was okay as long as the weapon was secured in the armory. Koch wanted to clean his rifle, so the duty armorer let him have it. Koch had yet to fire the rifle, and as he cleaned and played with it the siren call of that beautiful weapon became too much for him to bear. He also had an illegal box of .22 ammo in his room—this too should have been in the armory, and the armorer would never have let him have both rifle and ammo without permission. Koch took his rifle and ammo out to the narrow band of woods that separated our regimental area from the next, loaded a round, and squeezed the trigger.

At this point in his story, Lance Corporal Koch paused and said plaintively, "I didn't think it would be that loud."

Ernie and I almost lost it at that point, but we managed to hang on. You might ask yourself who could be stupid enough to test fire a rifle, at night, in the middle of a crowded barracks area, shortly after the most destructive terrorist attack in U.S. history. And the answer to that would be Lance Corporal Koch.

The consequences of his action dawning on him, Koch ran back to the barracks, rifle in hand, as fast as his legs could carry him.

Every firewatch on every barracks heard the shot. This was when I got the call. Staff Sergeant Buck fielded the next four after I left, as did the Regimental and 1st Battalion OD's in their respective offices.

Reaching the barracks, Koch ran into a brand new Private First Class, newly joined to the battalion. Keeping his streak of good judgment intact, he thrust his rifle into the PFC's hands with the words, "Hide this." The evidence now cleverly disposed of, Koch ducked into his room.

The bewildered PFC was still standing on the walkway holding the rifle when the duty NCO came outside. The Sergeant immediately took charge of the weapon and dragged Lance Corporal Koch from his room.

One squared away sergeant had left me with nothing to do but write it all up, or so I thought.

But Ernie got a call and had to leave, turning things over to his Gunny. And it was the same thing as the reaction force. I wanted to get some sleep, but the MP's were on the night shift and finally had something more interesting to do than write tickets and pick up Marines too drunk to walk.

They woke up every Marine in the next regimental area whose room faced the woods, just in case the round had gone through someone's window and plugged them.

Then they called for a couple of dogs and searched the woods for a body, in case Koch had been lying. I thought they were kidding. Who could make up a story like that?

Finally they decided they had to have the expended shell casing as evidence. They were actually going to get everyone on line, shoulder to shoulder, and sweep the woods to find a piece of brass not much bigger than a fingernail, in pine needles two inches deep, at 0300 in the morning.

Enough was enough. I was the only officer there, and it was time to exercise some goddamned authority. I called out, "All right, everyone just *stop!*"

Fortunately they'd brought Lance Corporal Koch back to the scene of the crime. I said, "Koch, get up here." Two MP's grudgingly released him. "Show me exactly where you were standing," I ordered. "Exactly."

He looked around, walked a ways into the woods, and stopped. I'd noticed that the .22 was a semi-automatic, which meant it ejected the empty case after each shot. And there was the little brass cylinder gleaming in the moonlight three feet to the right of where he was standing.

Without a word I handed it to the MP Gunny, and left.

On my way back I stopped at the Golf Company barracks to compliment the duty and firewatch on a job well done.

The sergeant shrugged it off. "This is my last duty, sir. I get out next week, and this is the reason why. I just can't put up with these stupid assholes any more."

I still told him I'd write him up an attaboy in the logbook.

After I told the tale to Staff Sergeant Buck, I had to wake up Major Thom once again. All he wanted to know was that it had been handled. I told him it was, and he hung up.

I was still on duty when everyone came in on Monday morning. O'Brien went right for the logbook and read my latest term paper. His smile kept getting bigger and bigger, and then he did a touchdown dance around the office.

"Yes!" he exulted. "I knew it, I knew it!" He stopped just as the ref was about to throw the flag for excessive celebration. "Hey, next time? Gunplay. I want gunplay. That's all you've got left."

"Don't…even…say…that," I told him. "Don't even think it."

Staff Sergeant Buck was really enjoying the show, which I knew would be grist for the Staff NCO gossip mill.

"We gotta go talk to Colonel Sweatman," O'Brien said. "There has to be some kind of rule—you have three duties like you've had and you don't have to stand any more."

"I'm up for that," I said. "Any time you want to start lobbying, feel free."

Captain Zimmerman came in and read the logbook, pleased because it hadn't happened to his company, and he wouldn't be the one tap-dancing in front of the Colonel's desk. "Mike, what is all this shit with you and duty?"

"I don't know, sir. You tell me. Was I born under an unlucky star because all this shit keeps going down on my watch? Or was I born under a lucky one because I've been able to handle everything so far?"

He gave me a little smile. "I've got a hunch it's lucky."

Maybe it was. The third time was the charm, because after that I had regular boring duty just like everyone else. Though it took me a while to stop flinching whenever the phone rang.

With everything packed up to go on deployment there was nothing to do but sit around or PT. Since Captain Z was our CO we PT'ed.

When we ran in formation, everyone was in step. The Captain in the lead, each lieutenant in front of his platoon, and the Gunny off to the side calling the "Jody," the cadence that kept us together. Usually he brought out the platoon sergeants or NCO's to sing a song. But for our last PT run at Camp Lejeune he called on the lieutenants.

Unfortunately we had to keep it clean within hearing distance of mainside, none of the old favorites like: *I don't know but I been told, Eskimo pussy mighty cold.*

O'Brien began with the saga of Jody himself, the slimy civilian who messed with your woman while you were away in the Corps. He sang the line and we repeated it, our left feet thudding into the pavement in unison with the verse:

"Ain't no sense in a-lookin' down,
Ain't no six-pack on the ground.

Ain't no sense in a-lookin' back,
Jody's got your Cadillac.
Ain't no sense in a-bein' blue,
Jody's got your girlfriend too."

Then I came out. After getting everyone back in step:

"My Marine Corps color is gold,
Shows the world that we are bold.
My Marine Corps color is green,
Shows the world that we are mean.
My Marine Corps color is blue,
Shows the world that we are true.
My Marine Corps color is red,
Red is for the blood we shed."

CHAPTER THIRTEEN

"This Marine's wife comes to see me," I told Jenny. "Her husband can't go on deployment. Why? Because she doesn't want him to. I say: sorry, but he's going. She says: he's not. Well, this week he shows up with his arm in a cast."

"Was it really broken?" Jenny asked.

"Oh, yeah. I asked him how it happened. He was working on his car; the jack slipped, and the car dropped on his arm."

"Ouch. What did you say?"

"I asked him how many times he had to drop the car on his arm before it broke."

"You didn't."

"It was the only question I really had."

"He could have killed himself."

"I've got to give her a lot of credit. She's hard-core. I ought to issue *her* some gear and take her on deployment."

"You don't seem too angry about it."

"Well, the Captain and I went to the battalion surgeon and got him a medical waiver. He's going on float after all."

"What if he breaks his legs this time."

"I bluffed my hand and told him I'd court-martial him. I don't even know if you can court-martial someone for messing themselves up these days, but he bought it."

"Maybe he and his wife will think of something else."

"If you knew him, you'd know it was all her idea. I'm sure she's up for it, but you get paid if you go on deployment, and you don't if you go to the brig."

"I think that's the most profoundly cynical thing I've ever heard."

"Jenny, this is a world where officers trying to impress their superiors chickenshit their Marines so bad that they're not even allowed to have trash in the wastebaskets in their rooms. They have to empty them each time they leave."

"That's a little hard for me to picture, but I may have read something about that. In Kafka."

"Then picture Marines getting married just to get out of the barracks, thinking that then they won't have to put up with any more chickenshit."

"That strikes me as a little overly optimistic. But typical of men. No offense."

"None taken. In that case picture a world in which women go out and get themselves pregnant just to keep from going on deployment. Or sometimes only a major exercise."

"Oh, my God. Why did you have to tell me that?"

"They're not who you hung out with in high school, or went to college with."

"But I can hear it in your voice when you tell me these stories how much you like them."

"You're right. I'm a little ambivalent about the Marine Corps, but I love Marines. It's been an education."

"Mike, I have to tell you something."

"No good news ever came from *that* tone of voice."

"My contract with UNC is up this year. I've got an offer from the University of Iowa. I'm going to take it."

And here I'd been worried about what was going to happen to our relationship while I was on ship for six months. "So you'll be in Iowa when I get back from deployment."

"That's right."

"You want to drop a car on my arm?"

"Someone will just get you a medical waiver."

I had two choices. I could play the guilt card and make her feel bad about taking a great opportunity. Or I could let her go, which was what was going to happen anyway. At least she told me straight up and didn't let me get on ship and then send me a dear Mike letter. I'll tell you, nobility sucks.

She read it all on my face, and before I could say anything, said, "Let's not part with any hard feelings. Who knows, we might run into each other again."

"I'm torn," I said. "I want you to do what's best for you, because I really care about you. But I don't want you to go for the same reason."

Jenny put her hand very gently on my cheek. "Men have died from time to time, and worms have eaten them, but not for love."

I have to admit I was taken aback by that. Maybe she and Shakespeare were just saying it was time to be a grownup. Maybe a summer dress was just something to project your fantasies upon. Like Dress Blues.

I suppose it was fitting, though. I'd met her with *As You Like It,* and lost her with *As You Like It.* Never really felt the same way about Shakespeare again.

CHAPTER FOURTEEN

The cold January day we shipped out was awful. Nothing to do but hang around waiting for our helo serials. Wives and kids clung to their Marines, grabbing every last second before six months of absence. And maybe more, maybe forever, because even if it hadn't been war accidents always happened. Wives crying. Older kids crying. Little kids not comprehending but still crying because it was bewildering. Just watching it was brutal. I could see it on the Marines' faces, hating to tear themselves away yet wanting to be on the ship so at least the agony of the farewell would be over. When we finally got aboard everyone was emotionally drained, almost shell-shocked.

Mother nature had a surprise in store once we cleared the continental shelf. Doing amphibious work-ups right off the coast had made me cocky. I wondered where all this seasickness bullshit came from.

Then I found out crossing the Atlantic in winter. The human body is not designed to have the platform it stands on rocking violently back and forth.

Now, the old salts will give you a few tips. You have to eat your chow, whether you feel like it or not. And you have to stay on your feet or sitting upright, no matter how much your churning stomach makes you want to lie down.

The problem I ran into is that you have to sleep sometime. Evidently most people get their sea legs before bedtime. Evidently I was the exception to this rule. Because right after I laid down I went from sick as a dog to about to hurl, which sent me sprinting for the head.

Which became my temporary duty station for the next two days. My roommates brought me back ginger ale and saltines from the wardroom. They wouldn't get the OD so he could shoot me, but they did fetch Doc Patel. He dropped by after I promised not to tell the AMA he'd made a house call, and cheerfully informed me that not only wasn't I alone in my extremity, but he couldn't do a goddamned thing to ease my suffering. Every tablet of Dramamine aboard ship had been expended in our battle with the Atlantic. Wonderful.

By the morning of our third day afloat I was able to make it down to the wardroom for breakfast. As I staggered in between O'Brien, Milburn, and Nichols, Captain Zimmerman looked up from his eggs and said, "Hey, Mike, where you been?"

"Talking to Ralph on the white phone, sir."

The Zooman, our motor transport officer, was sitting beside me. He'd been drinking a glass of milk, and made gurgling noises as it began to leak out his nose.

"Must have been a long conversation," said Captain Z.

"Yes, sir. We had a whole lot to talk about."

I was okay after that. But there were a few who needed to keep wearing the Scopolamine anti-seasickness patch behind their ears. Of course this was known as the pussy patch.

The wardroom was like a combination cafeteria and rec room. It cracked me up because it was more like high school with all the different cliques. The BLT officers at one table, the squadron at another. The Navy apart from the Marines. So much for the brotherhood of men at arms.

Ah, how to describe it. Or her, or whatever they call a ship. It was an LHD, for Landing Helicopter Dock. A brand new one, too, on her first float. The USS Inchon. The previous Inchon had been an old LPH helicopter carrier, turned into a mine warfare ship and recently scrapped.

Inchon was over 800 feet long; a straight flight deck to launch helicopters. And also a stern gate and flooding well deck to launch landing craft—the dock part of her name. Decks for vehicles and cargo; surgical facilities; extensive command and control. Just under a thousand sailors as crew and up to 1800 Marines could be crammed inside.

Everything was gray. It was like living inside a gray box. Not like a cruise—there were no portholes. You either lived inside a big box with a lot of people, like the whole company in one berthing space, or you lived inside a little box with a few people. O'Brien, Milburn, Nichols, and I lived in such a space. Four double-decker racks, a pair against each wall—or bulkhead in nautical-speak. Another wall of lockers, drawers, and fold-down desks. And a mirror and sink. You couldn't quite extend your arms and touch both walls, but it was close. Still, unspeakable luxury compared to the rows and rows of 4-stack vertical racks the troops slept in.

There were two other ships in the Phibron, or amphibious squadron. An LSD or Landing Ship Dock and LPD for Landing Platform Dock. Aboard the LPD was the MEU Service Support Group and Golf Company, the boat company. On the LSD were tanks, amtracs, the artillery battery, and Fox Company.

The Navy was a trip. A totally different culture, and despite our shared nautical language, to Marines a foreign one. The separate mess areas, kitchens, and food for sailors, chief petty officers, officers, and flag officers. Evidence of how, except for the abolition of flogging, naval leadership hadn't changed much since the age of sail. With a few notable exceptions their officers seemed to operate like passive-aggressives. Slack but hostile.

Our ship's captain had a Lazyboy mounted on the bridge in place of his captain's chair, and hardly moved from it while the ship was underway. He even slept there. So much for trusting your people.

We paid for our wardroom meals every month, and a favorite game when Marines came aboard was to cut down on the quantity and quality of the chow and when the deployment was over use the cash to buy luxuries. A few pilots started an underground newsletter that published odes to 3-shrimp gumbo and gave Colonel Sweatman the callsign "Tough Guy."

He went ballistic of course, but for some reason hard-ass Marine colonels turned into lapdogs around the Navy. Colonel Sweatman had even been on the verge of giving up Marines to scrape and paint until the company commanders revolted.

To Marines the only reason the ship existed in the first place was to transport us into battle. And when we went into combat we wouldn't be taking any of the crew along as extra riflemen. But we had to give up Marines to work in the mess, the laundry, the ship's store, and a hundred other jobs because their housekeeping concerns took priority over everything. It may be different on a destroyer, I don't know.

To the Navy we might as well have been overly-regimented vermin who did nothing but eat, sleep, PT, and infest their little world. They called us jarheads—we called them squids.

Shipboard routine quickly turned into, well, a routine. At 0600 the 1MC snapped on an instant before the bosun's whistle went into our ears like an ice pick. Then, *"Reveille, reveille. All hands heave out, trice up. Reveille."* This delivered in the pimply adolescent monotone the Navy must screen boatswain's mates for, because every watch was the same. To trice up was Navy-speak for making one's rack.

We then took turns at our room sink. When the military tells you to do things like conserve fresh water aboard ship, they don't just make the suggestion. If you took your hand off the sink tap it automatically shut off.

At 0615 on the way to the head to shower we heard, *"Muster restricted men."* Showering didn't take long, because only Navy showers were allowed. Despite what Marines felt about the Navy's personal habits, this was not just donning clean skivvies and deodorant. You stepped into the shower and turned the water on to wet yourself down, then turned it off. You lathered up with soap and/or shampoo, then turned the water on again to rinse yourself off. You ended up clean but dissatisfied, another fine metaphor for military life.

At 0615 on the way back down the passageway, *"Breakfast for the crew and embarked units. Meal passes are as follows: orange 0630-0700. Yellow 0700-0730. Green 0730-0800. Stragglers 0740-0800."*

After breakfast, down to the company office to see what was up. Something usually was. One aspect of being aboard ship was like the fulfillment of a dream for certain Marine officers. Now they could actually work themselves and their people seven days a week. Never did so many spend so much time thinking up so much make-work for everyone.

"Don't worry," Captain Z assured us. "They won't be able to keep this pace much longer."

"I don't know," Milburn said to me. "Looks like the married guys are rechanneling their sex drives into work."

"We'll be all right when they rediscover masturbation," I said confidently. "Skipper, Jack, Jim; you'll let us know when that happens, won't you?"

The First Sergeant experienced a fit of coughing.

"Shall I tell them to go fuck themselves, or will y'all?" the Captain asked.

"You *are* the company commander, sir," said O'Brien.

I'd PT the platoon either in the morning or afternoon, on the flight deck or the ship's fitness center. It all depended on whether helos were flying. When they were, it was classes on all the things we hadn't had time for yet.

After evening chow the Navy showed taped movies over the ship's cable system. Every berthing area had a TV, as did the wardroom. Taking the lessons of the workup to heart, I'd brought aboard a 13" TV that plugged right into the cable jack in our room. Milburn contributed the DVD player.

At 2000 or so came the command, *"Darken ship. Show no white lights topside."*

And at 2200, *"Taps, taps. Lights out."*

An action-packed existence, I'll tell you. It also took a little getting used to, particularly since our room was directly beneath the flight deck. It was HY-80 armored steel, but that only seemed to improve the harmonics. It felt like those helos were landing on your chest. But after a while you just rolled over and went back to sleep.

This was the routine. But I should explain something else about how being on deployment with a MEU worked. The Marine Corps is the nation's rapid reaction force, though the Army Airborne will argue that point. And the MEU's are the Marine Corps' rapid reaction force. Which was why we'd spent the previous six months training so intensely that we only came out of the field for the weekends. And were now as close to full strength as any military unit ever got.

While we were forward-deployed, we followed a normal sailing schedule with pre-arranged training exercises with friendly nations. But at any time, and in the amount of time it took for an operation order to spit from a printer, the peacetime schedule could be junked and we'd be sailing in harm's way. Or to a point just outside harm's way, where we'd sail around until the order came to go in.

This was why, one afternoon while we were lying in our racks—MORP'ing, which stood for Marine-Oriented Rack Posture—Frank Milburn said, "You know, I think we're fucked."

"That happens every day around here." O'Brien's voice replied from the rack above me. "You're gonna to have to be more specific."

On the first interoperability exercise O'Brien had informed me that the senior man got the bottom rack. I didn't care either way. Then one night of me sagging into the springs above his head changed his mind. Our brand new ship had been having teething problems, and among the rash of equipment failures were racks collapsing of their own accord. This may have led to nightmares of me squashing him like a bug. So the next morning he told me the senior man got the top rack. Fine, I said, but that had better be the last fucking time the senior man changed his mind.

"Two MEU's already in the Afghan theater," said Milburn. "You just know we're going to get stuck in the Med covering all the bullshit training exercises."

"We'll just have to see," said O'Brien. "If we stop in Spain to do our first scheduled Phiblex, we're screwed. If we keep going we may be all right."

All the speculation was necessary because we were absolutely the last people to be told anything. Well almost the last. But the troops compensated with a rumor mill that was totally out of control.

Living at close quarters, 24 hours a day, with the people you worked with could be very enlightening.

One night we bucked up to see who had to hike down to the wardroom to raid the popcorn machine. I lost. On my way back I bumped into Dave Peters coming out of the battalion office, and he asked me to drop a file off to one of the staff. The room was on my way.

When I knocked a suspicious voice said, "Who is it?" Which was not the usual response aboard ship.

"Mike Galway," I said, wondering what was going on.

The lock popped. "Come in."

The only light was from the TV, so it took a few seconds for my eyes to adjust. When they did I almost dropped my popcorn. Choking back laughter, I made my delivery and left.

Back in our room I announced, "My question has been answered. But at the cost of what may be some permanent psychological damage."

"How could we tell?" Milburn asked.

"I guess you don't want to hear," I said.

"Talk," O'Brien ordered.

I brought them to where I entered the room. "So there I am. Standing there holding four bags of popcorn. The room is full of captains and warrant officers. And this skanky fuck film is playing on the VCR. Well, I'm down with that. But everyone in the room is wearing their poncho."

"Get out," said Milburn.

"Like I could make something like that up," I retorted. "Sitting on the floor, wearing fucking ponchos. And I can't see anyone's hands."

"That is so unsat," said O'Brien. "I mean, they couldn't just watch the flick and go beat off in the head or something. I mean, ponchos or not, sitting there doing it in a room full of guys, it's, it's...."

"Fucked up," said Nichols. "I think that's what you're digging for."

"So what was the show?" Milburn asked me.

"Some amateur flick. I missed the credits."

"And the talent?"

"Oh, the girls next door," I said. "If you happen to live next door to a biker bar."

"Who was in the room?" said Nichols.

If Jimmy knew, the world would next. And then it would be quite clear to everyone who'd ratted them out. "Sorry Jim, I'm going to keep that on a need to know basis for now."

"Good call," said O'Brien. "With all the women aboard this ship, if word of stag night gets around the senior officers are bound to go into a major PC frenzy to cover their asses. We might have to tie our dicks in a knot."

It had been a pretty full week crossing the Atlantic. We docked at Rota, Spain, to do a turnover with the MEU we were relieving. There was some high-speed gear that the Marine Corps only had a few sets of, so they were passed from MEU to MEU. The outgoing commanders also passed information along to their opposite numbers. They were glad to be going home, but really pissed that they'd missed Afghanistan.

For our first liberty of the float we were restricted to base, and the ranks of private to sergeant allowed only Cinderella liberty. This meant they had to be back on the ship before midnight.

Ever since the birth of the Corps in 1775, appropriately at Tun Tavern in Philadelphia, Marines had been getting into trouble on liberty. No power on earth could prevent this.

They were teenagers, for crying out loud. Most of them away from home for the first time, living in an all-male environment, dedicated to immediate gratification—blind to long-term consequences; each with the sexual appetites of Caligula combined with just enough money in their pockets to get into trouble.

I wanted to look as good as the next officer, but there was no sense in getting all worked up over the inevitable. Realistically, all you could do was make sure everyone knew the rules and consequences, preach safety, and then dispense the appropriate justice afterward.

Full Colonels felt differently. Getting tapped to command a MEU meant you were a high flyer and they had their eye on you for general. So the only thing standing between you and a star was fucking something up. And liberty incidents, like accidents, loomed large in the zero-defects career stakes.

It hadn't quite reached the point where they could get away with locking all the troops aboard ship for six months, but Cinderella liberty was the next best thing. From my point of view anyone who thought Marines couldn't get into trouble before midnight needed their headgear checked out.

Nothing like preemptively punishing nearly a thousand troops just to make yourself look good.

I made sure I got back by midnight, and quickly discovered whose platoon had put themselves on the skyline with the first liberty incident of the float. Mine, of course.

All Cinderella liberty did was make everyone drink faster. At midnight Lance Corporal Conahey showed up in the berthing area in a condition 180° from normal, which was so withdrawn that strangers often mistook him for a mute. He proceeded to rip apart a line of racks and punch out his best friend, Lance Corporal Turpin, who tried to restrain him.

So I was back at work after a fast shower and changing into a set of cammies. I suppose I should mention that we always wore civilian clothes on liberty. The military stopped wearing uniforms off base during the Vietnam war, when all those civilians who now loved us tended to spit on us. We followed the same policy in foreign countries, even though our haircuts left little doubt who we were.

First stop was sickbay, where Turpin was holding an ice bag over a nicely swollen eye. As might be expected, he was quite put out about being beaten up by his best friend.

Then on to Captain Zimmerman. "Mike, the Navy's squawking about the damage to the berthing area," he said.

"Conahey's one of my best troops, sir. I'd hate to burn him too bad."

"You handle it the way you think best."

That was leadership. And not easy, either, because he'd have to absorb some big time heat with the mob baying for Conahey's head.

Conahey was in the company office, back to being his usual impassive self.

"Anything you want to tell me about this, or say in your own defense?" I asked.

"No, sir."

"Okay, you're restricted to the ship until further notice. You'll pay for all the damage you did, and you'll help the Navy do the repairs. You can either accept that or go see the Captain at Office Hours."

"I'll accept it, sir."

"I've got a couple more things to say. These aren't orders, just suggestions. If drinking made me go berserk and beat up my best friend, I'd give up drinking. If you feel you need help with that I'll get it for you, and it won't count against you career-wise. Second, you need to go to sickbay and talk to Turpin right now. You don't want to let pride cost you a good friend. I know you've got the guts to do it. Now get out of here. The First Sergeant will let you know how the money for the damage is going to work."

I watched as he left, and he was heading for sickbay. It was too bad. Conahey would have been next on my list for corporal, except that I wasn't quite sure if he'd be able to order his friends around.

Colonel Sweatman was so disturbed by the liberty incident that he decided to address our whole company. We assembled in the hanger deck. The aircraft elevators were folded up, sealing the big side openings into the deck. The air smelled of kerosene and grease, stifling one second and then a blast of cooler air whenever someone opened a hatch.

The company was in a horseshoe-shaped formation. The First Sergeant called everyone to attention, the staff sergeants out in front of the platoons. Then Captain Z took over the formation, the platoon sergeants posting to the rear and the lieutenants replacing them.

Colonel Sweatman was standing in the background, waiting for Captain Z to finish saying his piece about proper conduct on liberty. And Captain Z was trying to cover everything he thought Colonel Sweatman might say.

Something was going on in my peripheral vision. Frank Milburn was standing at parade rest like everyone else, except it was as if his feet were nailed to the deck and the rest of his body swaying around in ever increasing circles. He'd left the Rota officer's club with a Basic School buddy from the MEU we were relieving. I didn't know when he'd gotten in, but it looked like he'd had a bigger night than the rest of us.

Then Frank pitched forward and hit the steel deck face-first. A shiver went through the company, but Marines didn't break formation.

More perfectly timed than if we'd rehearsed it, O'Brien and I both stepped off, marched over to Milburn's prostrate form, each took a leg, and dragged him out of the formation. I threw him onto my back in a fireman's carry and took him up to the room, O'Brien clearing the way. We got lots of funny looks.

I dumped him in a chair and stuck his head between his knees. O'Brien wet a towel and draped it across his neck. We'd only resort to sickbay—which would make the incident official—if it looked like he was going to check out on us.

"I've never been so fucking embarrassed in my life," Jack said.

"How are we going to talk to the troops about liberty after this?" I said.

"Yeah, way to set the example. I don't know what was worse, going tits up in front of the troops or in front the Colonel—just as he's about to talk about liberty incidents."

Milburn recovered once we got some fluids in him. Then he went into Captain Z's stateroom for…a real ass chewing.

O'Brien couldn't believe it. When it was just he and I alone, he said, "We'd get special fitness reports for embarrassing the company in front of the Colonel. And he gets a good talking to."

"It's the Milburn gift," I said. "When you look like the template for a Marine infantry officer, you get the benefit of the doubt."

"How do *we* get some of that?" Jack said bitterly.

"We're talking massive plastic surgery," I replied.

We left Rota the next day, ahead of schedule, sailing through the Straits of Gibraltar with everyone on the flight deck taking pictures.

And to answer Milburn's question, we weren't fucked. Because we sailed right past our Spanish exercise area at Sierra de Retin and proceeded deeper into the Mediterranean.

And then it got serious, because the word went around that we were headed straight for the Suez Canal. Which may or may not have had something to do with what happened next.

It was around 2100. We were watching the nightly movie in the room when there came a knock on the door.

"Come in," O'Brien yelled.

The door opened part way and Corporal Asuego's head appeared.

"Come in," I said, swinging out of my rack. "What's up?"

"Sorry to bother you, sir, but Lance Corporal Thomas is down in the ship's library, acting really crazy."

I was already pulling my boots on. "Grab a chair and start at the beginning."

"Thomas's been acting kind of funny for a while, sir. Then tonight he's down in the library, just walking back and forth, back and forth. I think he's lost it, sir."

I was going to have to see this for myself. "Okay, I'll handle this. You can go back to the berthing area."

"You sure you won't need any help, sir?"

"With Thomas?"

"Okay, sir."

"Be careful out there," O'Brien said as I went out the door. Everyone else started chuckling.

After the heat exhaustion and other annoying little misadventures, I knew Thomas wasn't one of my brightest lights but I didn't think he was crazy. And as long as he wasn't armed I knew he wasn't dangerous.

Just as Corporal Asuego had reported, Thomas was in the library, pacing back and forth and muttering. And everyone else in there was doing their best to ignore him.

I walked up to him and said conversationally, "What's going on, Thomas?"

He started as if he hadn't seen me. His eyes were wide and wild. Then it came flowing out in a stream of consciousness. "I didn't do it sir they say I did but I didn't I know what I did but I didn't do that...."

"Didn't do what?" I asked.

But he switched to another track. "I could have been on TV instead of here I was better than everyone that got picked for *Moesha* they all lied to me Brandy would have liked me...."

I knew Thomas was from LA, but had no idea he'd chosen the Corps over an acting career. Which brought us to the heart of the matter. I'd seen a few Academy Award-winning performances in my time as a platoon commander. Now, a lot of officers got really hyper about Marines putting on an act. The only thing they hated more than being played was someone getting over on them.

I looked at it a little differently. If I couldn't tell whether Thomas was yellow or crazy, then good luck and Godspeed. At least he was out of my hair. And if it was real then he needed to see a mental health professional.

I said, "You'd better come with me, Thomas."

He did, Boot Camp discipline proving stronger than mental disturbance.

I sat him down in the sickbay, and out of earshot explained the situation to the duty corpsman, a First Class Petty Officer—the equivalent of a Marine Staff Sergeant.

"We'll check him out, sir," he said.

"Make sure you keep a close eye on him," I said.

"We know what we're doing, sir." Said in the self-important know-it-all way of certain corpsmen who'd picked up an attitude treating Navy doctors like golfing buddies.

"Whatever, Doc. He's all yours." I headed back down the passage-way, and who should appear at the other end but Major Thom, the bat-talion XO. The man was amazing. Whenever anything went down in the battalion, he turned up.

Just as I was about to open my mouth to brief him, from back in the sickbay I heard the First Class's startled voice exclaim, "Hey, come back here!"

And there was Thomas rounding the corner at a dead run, bent on escape. Which made me believe for the first time that he really was crazy. As he closed on us Major Thom exclaimed, equally startled, "Stop him!"

When the universe arranges itself in your favor you have to take advantage of it. I swung my right arm and caught Thomas with a forearm shiver to the head.

Contrary to the stories that went around, I did not hit him hard. But he landed on the deck like a sack of cement. As I bent down to put him in a wrist lock, from behind me I heard Major Thom's voice, filled with accusation. "What did you do?"

"Just following your orders, sir," I replied. He couldn't blame me for carrying them out.

I walked Thomas into the sickbay and kept his wrist in the come-along until they strapped him down in a bed. Of course I had to turn to the First Class and say, "You know what you're doing now, Doc?"

But Major Thom got his revenge. As we sailed past Sicily a CH-53 flew to the Naval Base at Sigonella to pick up mail and parts. I think we can all guess who went on that flight, with Thomas in a strait-jacket sitting between two corpsmen, to deliver him to the Naval Hospital.

Nothing like a long helicopter flight over the open ocean to put you in a good mood. At the Naval Hospital the attending physician took one look at poor, scrawny, mournful Thomas and snapped, "Get that strait-jacket off him."

"Right after you sign for him, sir," I said. "Then you can chase him around the hospital all day if you like."

Back at the ship, and back in the room, Milburn said, "Thanks for the mail, Mike. Nice trip?"

"Don't we all love helicopters?"

"You ought to be ashamed of yourself," said O'Brien. "So the kid's a little confused. And you dough-pop him, slap him in a strait-jacket, and send him to the loony bin."

"No, *you're* a little confused," I said. "*He's* as crazy as a shithouse rat."

I remember thinking, as weird as these first two weeks had been, what was it going to be like after six months?

CHAPTER FIFTEEN

As we sailed deeper into the eastern Mediterranean we became quite the item of interest. Ships, helicopters, and planes of all nations showed up to take a look at us. And, in the self-perpetuating process of intelligence, we did the same thing. The 1MC would order, "Away the Snoopy Detail," and the secret squirrels would dash topside with their cameras.

If the flight deck was open everyone would go up to see what the show was. On such an occasion I ran into Corporal Asuego. I had questions I wanted answered, and had already done my own intelligence gathering.

"Any idea what set Thomas off that night?" I asked.

"Not really, sir."

"Uh, huh. What happened in the woods back at Lejeune? I know there was drinking going on." Probably only lieutenant colonels and above believed that because Marines were underage, and it was against orders, they wouldn't drink.

Corporal Asuego was now in the awkward position of not knowing exactly what I knew, except that I knew too much. Which made withholding information a problem. "Some of the troops were out in the woods drinking, sir. Thomas was there. He passed out."

He stopped then, so I said, "And?"

More hesitation. "They pulled down his trou, sir, and took his picture."

Somehow I knew the high road hadn't been taken. "What happened after that?"

"Nothing, sir. But Thomas was being an asshole down in the berthing area, and someone told him they had a picture of him from that night sucking someone's dick when he was drunk. And Thomas went off."

"You mean he didn't say, fuck you, show me the picture?"

"No, sir, he just went nuts."

It was rough stuff, and I had some rough boys. But sometimes the pack separated out the weak on their own. I couldn't stop all of it unless I chained myself to everyone 24 hours a day. Just as Boot Camp didn't turn Marines into psychotics, Marines generally didn't have nervous breakdowns after being teased too hard.

We transited the Suez Canal with heavy machine-guns mounted on the catwalk around the flight deck and Egyptian military patrols on the shore.

One morning in the Red Sea our phone rang right after reveille. And right after breakfast we reported to the company office with our mission planning materials. Then all the Echo company officers walked down the passageway to a conference room with a guard outside.

An interesting group showed up. The Maritime Special Purpose Force commander, along with the Force Recon platoon commander and his Gunny. The two SEAL platoon officers. The helo squadron commander with his operations officer and the senior Cobra and '53 pilots. Colonel Sweatman, Major Woodman the new S-3, and Captain Farrow, the intelligence officer. And the MEU commander and his planning staff.

This had us all looking at each other. Something was up. Something different. Something big.

It *was* big. The briefing was long, but I'll provide the background because the S-2 gave us next to nothing. Before Osama Bin Laden found a home among the Taliban in Afghanistan he'd spread his wings in Sudan and Yemen.

Yemen was important. Although he'd grown up a Saudi, Bin Laden's family was of Yemenite origin. And the particular circumstances of the country made it very inviting for him.

Yemen had previously been two countries, the relatively Islamic military-run Yemen Arab Republic, or North Yemen, and the radical Marxist People's Democratic Republic of Yemen, or South Yemen. From the sixties onward South Yemen hosted terrorist training camps for the Palestinians, IRA, European Red Brigades, and Japanese Red Army. The two countries united in 1990 when the Soviet Union's collapse made being a People's Republic no longer profitable. A two month civil war in 1994 sealed the unification and sent the Marxists into retirement.

The radical Islamic fundamentalists gave the government a lot of help in making that happen, and their reward was an open door into the political, military, and educational establishments. And Bin Laden and his money came along on that ride. The weak central government's traditional lack of control over the remote tribal regions made it even easier.

Bin Laden also took a lot of his ideology from Yemen. The militant, puritanical, anti-Western Islam of the Yemeni Salafists made the Saudi Wahabis look like New England Episcopalians. They believed the world needed to be forcibly returned to exactly as it was at the time of the Prophet Muhammad 1,400 years ago—making exceptions for a few useful items like AK-47's, plastic explosives, and jet airliners.

Yemen was like the farm leagues of Islamic terrorism. The prospects from all over the world were screened in the religious schools, which usually offered electives in automatic weapons. The most radical, dedicated, and violent were sent off to the major leagues in Afghanistan. The Yemeni-trained Salafists were among the most feared fighters in Afghanistan, Algeria, Chechnya, and Kashmir.

Which brings us back to the briefing. Intelligence whose source we were not allowed to know had determined that around ten of the top Al Qaeda in Yemen, and maybe a couple who had escaped from Afghanistan, were meeting and hiding out in a remote village high up in the mountains near the Saudi border.

And we were given the mission of raiding the village and either capturing or killing them. We were moving on super short notice; these guys didn't hang around in one place very long. We launched right into our rapid planning process.

"Holy shit," O'Brien exclaimed when we finally took a break.

"Delta Force and the Rangers must be totally committed to Afghanistan, otherwise they never would have picked us over the glory boys."

"It has to be because we're in the right place at the right time," I said. "Only one day to plan before we execute."

"We're supposed to be able to do that," said Nichols.

"We all know that," said Milburn. "But this isn't like the Rangers parachuting onto a deserted airfield. It had to come from the Secretary of Defense."

I'll translate that. Their success in the military zero-defects system meant that our generals were almost temperamentally incapable of any kind of major risk taking. Which was why they'd had to be dragged kicking and screaming into Panama, Desert Storm, Haiti, and Kosovo by civilian politicians. It was also why the war on terrorism had so far emphasized low risk over mission effectiveness.

"We'd better pull this one off," said Captain Z. "Or we'll never be doing it again."

"Great intel," Nichols grumbled. "Situation, enemy: your guess is as good as ours. No wonder we got Pearl Harbored after spending 30 billion dollars a year."

"That one's easy," I said. "Everyone in town."

"What do you mean?" Milburn asked.

"In December the Yemeni military tried to pull a helo raid just like this to bag some Al Qaeda. Except they did it in daylight and got the shit shot out of them. Out in the boonies where we're going there's no law but tribal justice, tribal self defense. Everyone packs either an AK-47 or a rocket launcher. They kidnap tourists to get government services. The government keeps them quiet by holding the Sheiks' sons hostage. When you're a guest of the tribe, or paying them for protection, everyone in town is going to start shooting at anyone who flies in."

"Why didn't the S-2 mention that December raid?" said Nichols.

"You're kidding, right?" Milburn said to him.

"If we told the Yemeni government about this," I said, "we'd better plan on the terrorists either being long gone or locked and cocked and waiting for us to come off the birds."

"We will," said Captain Z.

We didn't really bother ourselves with whether the mission was a good idea or not. Pulling it off and bringing everyone home alive were all we had time for. And everyone knew the risks. I despise military memoirists who write as if the fact that people get killed, crippled, and maimed in war had somehow been kept a secret from them.

We had some advantages. The special operations guys tended to rely on surprise and their high-speed ninja skills to pull off a mission. Which worked great when everything went according to plan, less great when it didn't. Though not nearly as high-speed, we had an enormous amount of organic firepower available if the situation turned against us.

"How did you know about that December raid?" Milburn asked me.

"There are these things called newspapers and magazines, that tell you what's going on the world," I explained carefully.

"Funny," he said.

I hoped the intelligence the President, Secretary of Defense, and Joint Chiefs used to make their decision was good, because all we had was a stack of satellite photos of the village, the location of the three houses the terrorists were supposedly sleeping in—based on God only knew what kind of intel, rumor, or hunch—and some passport photos and descriptions that could have fit three quarters of the 20-30 year-olds in the Middle East.

The S-2 section immediately built a 3-D terrain model of the village. It was something they did for nearly every operation, and they were really good at it.

The village was out of range of CH-46's. We'd have to use '53's. Fortunately, based on early Afghan lessons we'd deployed with six instead of the usual four. The escorting Cobras, also six vice four, wouldn't be able to make it with any realistic weapon load or time on station, so an isolated location would be found to set up a FARP, or Forward Area Refueling and re-arming Point. More complication was never good when planning a raid, but we practiced doing FARPs quite often. We'd also have a KC-130 tanker available to refuel the '53's in flight. The MEU commander burned up the airwaves demanding another backup KC-130. Planes broke. You never took only one of anything you needed.

As is usually the case, life threw a monkey wrench into the planning process. O'Brien received a Red Cross message telling him he had a son. Fantastic news, except there were complications. The father's presence was requested at home.

Jack and Captain Z talked privately. The Captain gave him the option, but O'Brien said he was going on the mission.

Rumor control went crazy when the ship shut down the E-mail and satellite phone systems. Americans had zero security consciousness. A sailor who went out on the flight deck catwalk to see if he could get a cell phone connection from a land station ended up in the brig, squawking that he just wanted to call his wife.

We only stopped for meals, and they were quick ones. Once the MEU commander signed off on the plan we issued the operation order to the troops, using the satellite photos and terrain model.

Their reaction? The usual 10% went—oh shit. Sixty percent were grimly satisfied to be doing what they'd signed up for. And about 30% couldn't wait to finally shoot someone. The squad leaders began conducting room clearing drills.

We were all so busy there wasn't time to dwell on any anxieties, not that they would have been discussed anyway. If you thought anyone was going to want to talk about their feelings before going into battle, then I haven't done a good job of describing the culture.

I was more worried than scared. About all the things we hadn't done. Not enough training time, not enough ammunition, not enough realistic live fire. And what hadn't *I* done? What hadn't I taught?

The hard core the platoon, the leaders and senior lance corporals, had trained together from day one. They were tight. The younger Marines had arrived in packets from the School of Infantry. Some at the four month mark in our training cycle, some at three, some at two. We'd given them as much extra work as we could. The MCCRES and Special Operations Exercises, being all-encompassing, had helped bring them up to speed. Some were there; some not quite. At least all Marines knew how to follow their leaders. Hopefully that would be enough.

But I had two brand new PFC's who'd arrived from the School of Infantry less than a month before we shipped out. They hadn't done a day's training with us. They were crushed when I told them they were staying on the ship, but I remembered PFC Francois's first time on the grenade range. It would have been criminal negligence to bring them along on the raid.

Everyone's gear had to be inspected. Nothing could be left behind, either forgotten or because the troops thought *they* knew best, like the Rangers in Somalia leaving the back plates out of their body armor. No personal effects but a military ID card. Fresh batteries in all the electronics. Inoperative night vision goggles hurriedly temp loaned from units that weren't going. More paperwork.

It was a madhouse. All the staff officers wanted to put their chop on our plan, so they could say later, "I was intimately involved in the planning process." Intimate was right: they were really fucking with us. As Captain Z said, "Now I know why, even though we train to do it right, everything always falls to shit when we go to war for real. All the staff pukes start running around like rats on acid. Okay, y'all do the pre-mission prep by the book, and I'll try to keep all the little helpers away."

We were just carrying ammo and water. We'd go in with our standard ammo load, with just a few modifications to fit the circumstances. Since we didn't intend to kill any noncombatants unless they absolutely insisted on it, we'd clear rooms with stun grenades from our non-lethal weapons package. These were always called flash-bangs because they blew with a deafening bang and brilliant flash, but no lethal fragmentation. But we'd still bring regular frag grenades. Captain Z wanted more claymore mines in case we had to defend a landing zone while waiting for the helicopters. He also insisted that everyone carry an intravenous kit in their butt pack. You should have heard the peacetime whining from the medical section when they had to break all those supplies out.

The banter got a little thick, at least among the lieutenants. We were loading magazines and Jimmy Nichols, trying to make a little light of the situation, was saying, "I wouldn't mind a Navy Cross." Which was next in line after the Medal of Honor for heroism in combat.

My Irish mother would have had a few things to say about tempting fate.

"Just make sure you get the bronze one they pin on your chest," O'Brien told him, "and not the white stone one they hammer into the ground six feet over your head."

The pile of empty boxes, cans, bandoliers, and packaging was amazing. The troops went down to the fantail by squads to test-fire weapons and check the zeros on their sights. Everyone else was waiting in the marshaling area in their helo serials. Force Recon and the SEALs in their sand-colored fireproof flight suits and balaclavas, high-speed lightweight helmets, combat vests, and shooting glasses. Their rifles were M-4 carbines—short barrel, sliding stock M-16's—with Aimpoint red-dot sights. Their squad automatic weapons were the new compact, collapsible-stock paratrooper model.

Echo Company was in desert camouflage with pile sweaters underneath against the cold of the desert night, faces camouflaged, carrying our old worn-out weapons. And I do mean worn-out. Our squad automatic weapons, long overdue for replacement, were literally held together with wire and tape.

I didn't give the troops a motivational speech about living up to our heroes, like Dan Dailey on the Peking Wall, Herman Hanneken and William Button at Grande Rivière, or John Ripley at the Dong Ha Bridge. I also did not recite the St. Crispin's Day speech from Shakespeare's *Henry V.* Instead I used the time to move along the line with a satellite photo, having each Marine tell me every move they were going to make once they got off the helicopter. This caused everyone else to be furiously studying the operation order in the little green notebooks the Staff Sergeant and I made everyone carry.

Staff Sergeant Frederick was walking around tearing strips off a roll of tape to secure everyone's grenade pins. In Desert Storm he'd witnessed a PFC snag the ring of a frag on a truck ramp and blow himself to pieces. "Just a little bit around the outside of the head, there, crazy," he was saying. "No tape around the spoon, or it won't come off."

O'Brien caught my eye and beckoned me over. I turned the job of quiz master over to Sergeant Turner.

I'd left Jack alone since he'd gotten the message. He didn't need any lame questions wondering if he was okay. Of course he wasn't okay. I waited for him to speak first.

"I had to go," he said.

"I know," I replied.

"The woman I love more than anything else in this world needs me, but how can I go home while my platoon goes into combat?"

The answer was self-evident, but unexplainable to anyone who hadn't felt that awesome and total sense of personal responsibility. Jack's tragedy was that he was caught between two of those responsibilities.

And maybe the unspoken thought in the back of his mind, and maybe everyone else's, that by the time he got home the medical crisis was going to be over, one way or the other unfortunately, so going home might just be a reason not to go into combat. Foolishly macho? Maybe. But reputation and self image were a major part of the profession.

"There's a letter in my desk," he said. "But you tell her, too."

Now we were deep into movie cliché. But life runs on clichés, and if it wasn't for movies and books we probably wouldn't know how to act. We all had letters in our desks.

"I'll be glad to," I said. "And how long do you think I should wait, out of respect, before I ask her out?"

His eyes bulged with fury, then as I stood there gazing at him placidly his face cracked into a grin. "You fucker."

"By the way, what's the little guy's name?"

"John Francis O'Brien IV."

"You must have lost a lot of sleep over that."

I returned to quizzing the platoon. Lance Corporal Turpin said, "Sir, how long before we go?"

I checked my watch. "Twenty minutes or so."

He raised his voice. "Hey, Francois? You better hurry up. You don't have much time left to go crazy like Thomas."

Francois flipped him off with a quick little rap: "We go down that rope, you be cryin' and I be stylin'."

The platoon roared their approval, yelling at Turpin: "He punked you down! He punked you down!"

I was so proud of them. America's Hessians. Because that's what they were to the majority of the public who'd never countenance *their* children joining the military. And that included the civilian officials responsible for sending us into harm's way. Little did they realize how safe they slept in the arms of the poor boys.

Captain Z gave his own little speech, and it wasn't quite George Washington's address to the troops. He finished up by saying, "We're going to go through these motherfuckers like a hot oil enema." The Marines loved it.

The serials were called. "Are we good to go?" I asked the platoon. I didn't bark it out like a football coach trying to jack up everyone's emotions with some empty motivation. I just asked the question with all the seriousness it deserved.

And the "Ooh-rah!" I heard wasn't like any other, either. No empty spirit but hard and low, equal parts pride and determination.

We began the walk up to the flight deck. Waiting outside the hatch for the final call to board the helos, the 1MC made the traditional announcement that every generation of Marines had heard. *"Land the landing force."*

It made the hairs on the back of my neck stand straight up.

CHAPTER SIXTEEN

The flight deck was all blacked out, nothing but infrared lighting visible only through night vision equipment. Before I buckled myself into the CH-53 I unsnapped my gas mask belt, got out of my flak jacket so I was only leaning back against it, and put on my life jacket. Making myself ready in case we happened to crash into the water.

The pilot got his takeoff signal and pulled back on the collective. We went straight up, hovered for a moment, then slowly drifted to the left to clear the flight deck and avoid the island. I hated that part, looking down and seeing first deck then water.

When we crossed the beach and went feet dry I snapped up the gas mask belt and put my flak jacket back on.

The only thing worse than skimming way too low over North Carolina pines in a blacked-out helicopter flying on night vision goggles was skimming way too low over rocky desert, then foothills, and finally up jagged mountains in a blacked-out helicopter flying on night vision goggles. My PVS-14 monocular made it possible to choose my view. If I didn't want to see how the flying was going I just closed my right eye and there was nothing but darkness out the starboard gunner's window. Open revealed all kinds of alarming green images.

It was like looking through a toilet paper tube at a flat image with very little depth perception. The other CH-53's in the formation looked dangerously close. The escorting Cobras were dancing around us farther out.

I was going over each step of the mission in my mind. We'd be fast roping right onto the roofs of the buildings we were hitting. The only thing that had changed in this part of the world throughout human history were the weapons. Someone was always fighting over something.

Because of this villages were built for defense. On the high ground, surrounded either by purpose-built walls or the flat stone sides of the buildings, the few windows high up out of reach. Only a few easily-defended gated entrances, usually accessible only along narrow winding paths. No way were we going to land outside and either infiltrate or assault our way in. A handful of defenders could hold us off all night.

Inside the village the houses were tower style, like individual forts. Stone, brick, mud. Always at least two floors, the biggest five or six. The ground floors almost always used for shops, storage, or stabling animals, so anyone breaking in had to fight their way up stairs.

We'd fast rope right onto the flat roof of our target house and fight our way down. Of course those big fat hovering helos would be totally exposed while we were sliding down, but there was no other way. At least it was better to start high and fight down than start at the ground floor and fight your way up.

I'd memorized the layout of the village, and not just from our planned direction of approach. The company was hitting three houses simultaneously. The three biggest and best in town, owned by the most influential men, who would accommodate the most important guests. But not mansions, not in a village that small. What Americans would consider regular sized houses.

Force Recon and the SEALs were the close quarters battle experts. They'd better be. A 22-man Force Recon platoon and a 16-man SEAL platoon each received more annual training ammunition than our entire battalion. Force Recon backed by O'Brien and 1st platoon had the most likely target. The SEALs and Milburn's 3rd platoon the next. Second platoon and I were batting third, hitting what intelligence considered to be the least likely house all by ourselves.

Each group also had a couple of explosive ordnance disposal experts, and an intelligence collection team to take photographs and fingerprints, and root around for documents.

There was no place for the helos to land inside the village and pick us up, and only one good landing zone outside. This would be secured by the 60mm mortar section and Lee Harvey Oberdorff's platoon from Fox Company. Paul Federico was securing the FARP site, a secluded and hopefully uninhabited spot miles away, where the Cobras would refuel and rearm.

It was going to be a complicated operation—everyone needed to have their shit together. I hoped I did. At least it had started well. We had a bump plan to redistribute personnel if a '53 went down with mechanical problems, but they'd all gotten off the deck all right.

I didn't have a communications headset. Of course the MEU, battalion, and squadron commanders were coming along on the operation. They were in the '53's with us, because the command and control Huey didn't have the range. And because they all had to listen in, I couldn't communicate with the pilot if he accidentally flew to the wrong building. I had to take my signals from the crew chief. From behind his .50 caliber machine-gun he signaled "five minutes."

I took out a loaded magazine, always 28 rounds instead of 30 so the flimsy magazine spring wouldn't jam, slid it into the well of my M-16, and tapped upward to make sure it was seated. I pressed the bolt catch and felt the metallic snap as the bolt flew forward, stripping off and chambering the first round. You could tell by the feel that a round had gone in, but I hit the forward assist to make sure the bolt was locked, just to complete the ritual. It was familiar and instinctive, and in a strange way comforting. The platoon followed suit.

I glanced at my watch: 0208. During planning Captain Z had gotten excited because the senior officers, in regimented fashion, wanted to hit the objective on the hour. Which would only make it easier on the enemy if they were waiting for us. He'd won. It was that golden time for raiding when the human brain, programmed for sleep, was at its worst.

I was going off the ramp first. Putting the platoon commander in position to get killed first was not the schoolbook solution. But I had two reasons. The first was that, except for Staff Sergeant Frederick, this was everyone's first time in combat. It was a hairy and exposed fast rope, with no assurance of surprise, and we couldn't afford to get hung up or stalled. And in training the platoon never had to do anything I hadn't done first, so now it was real we weren't going to change from "follow me" to "after you, boys."

My second reason was that I couldn't get the grenade range accident out of my head. If my legs froze again I wanted the whole platoon behind me pushing me out.

I might be going out first, but Staff Sergeant Frederick, Lance Corporal Vincent, and our precious platoon radio were coming out last.

It was a unique feeling to have before you were about to do your job, that if you screwed up someone was going to die. But from the time I issued the order it was like being under a spotlight. I had to be cool because the Marines kept looking at me to see if I was cool. They were still looking at me through their night vision goggles. It didn't make me nervous, it gave me strength. Even though my stomach felt as if it had shrunk down to the size of a walnut. And yes, I had to pee.

We came in fast. First the village like a jewel box image in the distance, then I was able to pick up individual buildings. That we were hitting the biggest and most prominent ones in town made the identification easier.

The helo nose pitched up, and we shuddered to a stop over the right house. Gripping the fast rope, I leaned out over the ramp into screaming rotors and a shroud of hot burned kerosene exhaust. We couldn't move so quickly we came down in the street instead of onto the roof.

Then I was out. I hit the roof, pushing the rope away with my right hand and bringing up my rifle with my left. There was a little peaked projection on a corner of the roof, covering a stairway down into the house. A man was silhouetted in the opening, with the light behind him. He was clutching an AK-47 across his chest. The silhouette was unmistakable. It was pitch dark, and his attention was fixed on that huge beating helicopter overhead.

I flicked on the PAC-4 laser aiming sight and thumbed off the safety as the M-16 came up. The laser dot settled on his chest. My magazine was full of tracers to mark targets; it was as if the stabs of light were absorbed into his body. I kept squeezing the trigger until he went down.

I was blinking hard to fight the tunnel vision from the quart of adrenaline pumping through me. It slowed everything down except my heart pounding through my chest the way it had the day of the grenade range accident.

I felt Marines all around me but stayed focused and advanced on the doorway, left foot forward and dragging the right so I wouldn't trip, rifle stock against my cheek. A short stairway down and a sharp right corner into the house. The lights were on so I was looking through my left eye, the one without the night vision.

Corporal Asuego's fire team passed by me, and I stepped back and changed magazines. A diesel generator was grinding away in one corner of the roof. I wanted the lights out, but was afraid my tracers would set it on fire. Then I remembered that I'd followed the rest of the officers and staff in signing out a Beretta just for this mission.

I drew the pistol and fired, hoping a ricochet wouldn't come bouncing back at me. That generator died hard. It took ten rounds before it screamed. Electricity snapped and popped, and the house lights went out. Contrary to Marine stereotype, I *had* looked for the on/off switch first.

I put in a fresh magazine, and as I holstered the pistol someone opened up on full auto from the window of a nearby building. Supersonic bullets passing nearby made a sound like a bullwhip cracking. It made you want to drop and curl up into a tight little ball.

We hadn't gone in under any preparatory fires from the Cobras. Under the rules of engagement the townsfolk had the first shot. Now they were going to have to live with their choice.

The helo doorgunner cut loose with his machine-gun. The window and surrounding wall were sawn apart by the stream of half inch diameter slugs. Hopefully that would make everyone else in the neighborhood think twice.

A flash-bang went off as Corporal Asuego's lead fire team started down the stairs into the house. I could see their flashlights click on. Fighting in enclosed areas like rooms peripheral vision was vital, and you had none with night vision goggles. So our SOP was to flip them up off our eyes and go in with the white lens flashlights attached to our M-16's. The lights were a special purchase by the MEU, as were our knee and elbow pads.

When Sergeant Harlin was done clearing this floor Sergeant Turner's squad would take the next one down. Sergeant Eberhardt's squad and the machine-guns were arrayed all around the roof, ready to shoot anyone who fired on us, and anyone who tried to run out of the house.

This had touched off a heated exchange between Captain Z and the MEU JAG when the lawyer was briefing the rules of engagement. We weren't supposed to shoot anyone who wasn't armed—no surprise there—but Captain Z made the point that all anyone had to do in that case was throw down their weapon and run away. So why even make the raid? This went around the table way too long, and was never satisfactorily resolved. Mainly because no one wanted to go on record with a decision. So Captain Z just told us later to shoot any adult male answering the terrorists' descriptions—which was basically all adult males—who ran out.

I hoped that the U.S. intelligence community was operating above their usual level of competence on this one, because otherwise I'd just killed some poor bastard defending his home. And probably more to come.

Now emptied out, the '53 increased pitch and pulled away. At least I could stop worrying about a flaming helo dropping into our laps.

More firing now from the other houses. And massive return fire from the Marine-held roofs, along with arcs of 20mm cannon tracer from the Cobras.

I saw the brighter beam of a laser pointer held by the Forward Air Controller flick out toward the heaviest source of fire. A few seconds later a brilliant flash and explosion as a Hellfire anti-tank missile from a Cobra went right through the window and took out the whole floor of the house. Like magic the volume of firing tapered off all around the village.

Then a roar of rifle fire from inside my house. I could feel it under my feet. But my job was to stay on the radio, call for fire, and direct traffic, not be a squad leader. There was so much shooting that I could barely hear the company radio. I didn't worry about the intra-squad radio. Our training in the cinder-block Combat Town at Camp Lejeune had proved that it was worthless inside buildings. You couldn't get reception even between adjacent rooms. So messages were shouted back along the line, just like in the old days.

And a shout did come up the stairs: "Sergeant Harlin's down!"

I tossed the SINCGARS handset to Lance Corporal Vincent, shouting, "Stay here with the Staff Sergeant." Who would need the radio if he had to call in the Cobras.

There was a traffic jam at the bottom of the stairway. Around the corner was a very short hall where everyone was jammed up, then another sharp corner that seemed to open into a longer hall. In the dancing beams of weapon flashlights, I saw Sergeant Harlin being dragged along the floor, his face covered with blood. Marines were hunched over, protected by the sharp corner as automatic fire whipped down the long hallway and slammed into the wall at the end, showering them with sprays of masonry.

"Get him up to the roof!" I shouted to the Marines dragging Sergeant Harlin. From the smear of blood he'd gotten nailed as he went around the corner into the hallway. The stupid son of a bitch! But you never stop for casualties when you're in the assault. Sergeant Harlin was Doc Bob's job now.

Someone yelled, "Don't go around that corner, sir!" Always listen to the troops. I dug a frag grenade out of my pouch, shouting over the deafening roar of the firing, "Flashlights off!" I flipped down my night vision goggle, edged closer to the corner, and pulled the pin. I flicked off the spoon and skipped the frag down the hall along the floor to make it hard to pick up and throw back.

It blew and the firing shut off. I stuck one eye and the goggle around the corner. The smoke made it hard to see, but it looked like the hallway ran the length of the whole floor, and at the end was another stairway leading down to the next one. A rifle barrel poked around the far corner, and I pulled my head back as the firing started up again.

We weren't just stalled, we were screwed. No way were we getting down that hall. If we raced right down to the end someone could jump out of a room and cut us down from behind. And if we stopped to clear the rooms all they had to do was stick an AK around that far corner.

Think. Fucking think. Easy lying in my rack back on the ship, but not here. There was a room on the other side of the wall I was leaning against. We had shotguns to breach doors—that wouldn't do the job. C-4 plastic explosive, like modeling clay, that we'd fabricated into breaching charges to take down any steel or iron doors. Time fuse to set that off, like Clint Eastwood using his cigar to light the cord sticking out from a stick of dynamite. Not the best choice when you needed to set off an explosion with precise timing. And we'd have to re-form the C-4 to make up the right sized charge. More time wasted.

Then my eyes fell on the cloth bag hanging from the back of the Marine next to me. A pound and a half of plastic explosive behind a matrix of ball bearings, already pre-shaped for directional blast. A masonry wall, a foot thick or less. It might work.

I grabbed Lance Corporal Francois, the nearest SAW gunner, and showed him how to hold his light machine-gun with his left hand grasping both bipod legs and his right thumb on the trigger so he could fire it around the corner without exposing his body. "Short bursts," I shouted. "Just keep 'em out of the hall."

Francois was so tentative I had to grab his upper arms and shove him forward to the corner, but after the first couple of bursts he got his confidence back and started yelling abuse down the hall as he fired.

I sent everyone back up to the roof except Francois and Corporal Asuego, who was now the 1st squad leader. I had them send Sergeant Turner and Sergeant Eberhardt down so they could see what I had in mind.

I dug the quarter roll of duct tape out of my butt pack. A grunt platoon commander would sooner go to the field without his weapon than some duct tape.

Corporal Asuego held the hardcover book-sized claymore anti-personnel mine to the wall at belt height, and I taped it in place. Then I screwed the blasting cap into the fuse well. It was too loud for a lot of conversation, but with hand and arm signals everyone got clear on the plan.

Sergeant Turner grabbed Francois. We all dashed up the stairs, with me last unreeling the blasting wire.

I looked back to make sure everyone was out of line of the stairwell, plugged the wire into the hand-sized electrical generator we called a clacker, yelled, "Fire in the hole," and squeezed the lever.

The house rocked. Even in the open air and wearing earplugs, the blast overpressure was like getting hit with a brick.

I ran back down the stairwell through the choking acrid high explosive smoke. There was a jagged hole in the wall big enough to get through. Good thing it was a solid stone house or we might have ridden the roof right down to the street.

Corporal Crockett's clearing team went by me and ducked in. Francois went back to firing down the hallway.

I'd just wiped my ass with the rules of engagement. I didn't know how many unarmed civilians or babies in cribs had been inside the room I just blasted my way into. And frankly I didn't give a shit as long as no more of my Marines got hurt.

Crockett's fire team worked their way down through the rooms, staying out of the hall. If there were doors connecting each successive room, they used them. Otherwise a claymore blew a hole in the wall. Once the first room was clear a second fire team used it to sprint across the hall under the cover of another frag grenade and began clearing the rooms on the other side. The third team covered the hallway in case anyone tried to escape a room or come up the stairs, ready to reinforce the other two teams if necessary.

I wasn't anxious to send anyone down the angled stairway to the next floor. So once 1st squad had cleared through I placed a claymore on the floor of the first room we'd entered, piling on furniture to tamp the blast downward. Sergeant Turner quickly rehearsed his squad.

We moved up the stairway again and blew the mine. Rushing back in through the smoke, two Marines, each holding the carrying strap on the back of the flak jacket of a third, lowered him down through the hole in the floor while Sergeant Turner kept chucking in flash-bangs. Then another Marine right after him, followed by the rest of the squad. By being lowered rather than jumping the first pair landed ready to use their weapons.

There was firing down below me, and then firing up on the roof. The word passed down to me slowly from Staff Sergeant Frederick. "Three males ran out. Three down." Passing messages was another little thing we'd practiced over and over again. Otherwise even a simple message, reinterpreted through ten different mouths, bore no resemblance to the original.

Sergeant Turner was going to be fine. I moved forward through the rooms to join back up with Corporal Asuego. Doing so I bumped into the intelligence team, moving through the cleared rooms in 1ˢᵗ squad's wake.

One was rummaging around, while the other was on his hands and knees puking on the floor. Inside the room were pieces of one body and another that only existed from the chest up—and the AK-47 he'd been carrying was embedded in that. I knew there were two of them only after counting the arms and legs. The one corpse's face was glaring at us, full of fury. I haven't been able to get that out of my head yet.

The sight was hardly worse than the smell. It was a slaughterhouse stench of blood, shit, bile, and urine, cut by burned gunpowder and high explosives. And now vomit. Even though the Claymore had blown out all the windows, I wasn't that far from puking myself.

The intel specialist checking the carpet was a corporal. "Find anything?" I asked the other, a Gunny.

"A briefcase full of papers," he said. "Bunch of passports. Two laptops. Claymore didn't do them any good, like that guy over there, but we might be able to recreate the hard drives."

Good news. It was looking as though we had hit something more than a local Kiwanis Club meeting.

Lance Corporal Vincent entered the room through the hole, and the Gunny and I nearly shot him.

"Goddammit Vincent," I shouted. "Sound off before you come into a room."

"Sorry, sir," he said, puffing a bit under the radio and handing me the handset. "The Six wants to talk to you."

Captain Z was notorious for always wanting to talk directly to his platoon commanders. He figured that if he was on the radio you ought to be too. "Put on the actual," was his usual gruff reply to the radio operators.

We had to stick the antenna out a window to get decent comm. The stone was swallowing up radio waves. "Six, this is Two Actual, over," I said into the handset.

"We're ready to Diane," Captain Z said. "What's your status, over?"

All the code words for the operation were the senior officer's wives first names. I couldn't believe everyone else was done clearing their buildings and ready to leave. "Only halfway, over."

"What's the problem, over?"

I also couldn't believe Staff Sergeant Frederick hadn't told him. Maybe the Skipper couldn't believe it. "Six, we're in the middle of a major firefight here. Sitrep line Juliet: six confirmed so far, over." I'd just told him that we'd killed six enemy.

"Roger, you still have only one line Hotel, over?"

One friendly wounded. "That's affirmative, over." If Sergeant Harlin was still alive.

"You need help, over?"

I thought about it, but they'd have to fight their way down an open street to get to us, and then break into the ground floor. "Negative, Six. Just time. My Five will keep you informed, over." Five was the Staff Sergeant.

"Roger. You're on the spot—you make it happen. Call me if you need anything. Six out."

I gave Vincent the handset. "Go back up to the roof. Tell the Staff Sergeant to keep the Captain informed. And give a heads up before you go jumping out at them."

"Yes, sir."

That ever-reliable indicator of my level of anxiety, my bladder, was about to pop. I would have gone right there—nothing was going to make that room any worse—but I had a disturbing vision of getting shot with my dick out.

Another figure appeared in the hole. I thought it was Vincent again. I was just opening my mouth to chew his ass when I realized there was no lit flashlight on his rifle, and that the rifle wasn't an M-16.

My hand had never left the pistol grip of mine, but I was still slow. The full auto muzzle flash in front of me looked like a flame-thrower. I thought I was dead.

I dropped to my knees, centered the flashlight beam, and squeezed the trigger so fast it felt like automatic even though I was firing semi. At the same time bullets passed so close I could feel the wind. Then he was on the deck and I wasn't—though I had no idea why. "Cease fire!" I yelled. I didn't know if the Gunny and Corporal were firing or not, but I didn't want to get shot as I moved.

I walked up to the figure on the ground and squeezed my trigger again. Just a click; the magazine was empty. But two rounds from the Beretta made sure he wasn't getting up.

I picked up his rifle, just to give my hands something to do until they stopped shaking. Then I ran my flashlight over the wall I'd been standing in front of. The rifle and the bullet holes told the story. The rifle was a German G-3, that fired the big 7.62 NATO round we used in our machine-guns. That powerful a round in a light rifle on full automatic was a bitch to control. The first couple of rounds had gone right between the Gunny and I, and the rest over my head as the recoil pushed the muzzle up. If he'd been carrying an AK-47 we'd have all been dead. Oh, and I didn't have to go anymore. He'd taken care of that by scaring the piss out of me. At least it was dark. I disabled the G-3 by bending the barrel, and inserted a new magazine into my rifle.

In urban combat a bad guy popping out at you could happen even if you'd been thorough in clearing rooms—there were plenty of places to hide in a house. The Corporal was still on the deck. The Gunny was as shaken as I, and he reacted like a Gunny. "Get the fuck off the floor and provide some goddamned security!" he bellowed at the Corporal.

"Let's get this done as fast as you can," I said to them. "As soon as we clear the ground floor we're out of here."

We were moving much slower and more deliberately than we'd planned. But that probably always happened when the bullets were real. At least we were compensating by making unexpected moves.

Corporal Asuego had finished clearing the floor. Corporal Crockett inched his fire team down the stairwell until they had a clear shot at anyone trying to escape from Sergeant Turner on the next floor. A good ambush position, flashlights off and night vision goggles on. Two bodies were already sprawled on the stairs.

The house rocked each time Sergeant Turner touched off a claymore.

Farther down the stairs someone started screaming, "Surrender! Surrender!" in English. A figure appeared in the stairway. A young guy in his twenties, wearing only trousers. He had his hands behind his head, and was feeling his way up one step at a time in the darkness. Laser aiming dots that he couldn't see settled on his chest.

Corporal Crockett shouted the phonetic Arabic phrases we'd all memorized. *"'aqif!"* Then "Stop!" in English.

Before he could say "hands up," the man kept moving. I could sense the hesitation, as if the Marines weren't quite sure what to do. "Shoot him!" I yelled.

Crockett and the SAW gunner both fired.

Hit by about ten rounds simultaneously, he was dead before he finished falling back. And the grenade he'd been holding behind his head came free and bounced down the stairs. There was a shrill scream right after it exploded.

I yanked a frag grenade out of my pouch, rushing to get the pin out. The spoon off, I darted out into the open and threw the frag down the stairwell.

"Eat that, motherfuckers!" one of the Marines shouted.

It blew amid more screams. Probably the wounded and whoever was trying to drag them away.

"Floor clear," came the word from Sergeant Turner.

I sent Corporal Asuego's squad up to the roof a fire team at a time. Sergeant Eberhardt's came down.

More shooting below us. Whenever that happened the one thing I didn't do was start issuing a lot of demands to know what was going on. There's a special place in hell for officers who pull that shit, as if a leader in the middle of a firefight had a spare moment to answer questions.

A couple of minutes later Sergeant Turner reported that rounds were coming up through the floor at him. One of his Marines was hit, and he'd moved the rest out of the way.

The bad guys were getting wise to our pattern—it was time to change it. I sent down a couple of Sergeant Eberhardt's claymores.

And how Sergeant Turner used them was pure genius. He placed one on the floor of a room at the opposite end of the house from the stairwell we were on.

He blew the claymore, and from out in the hall tossed a flash-bang through the hole in the floor. This was answered by a torrent of fire from below, probably aimed from the room next door.

It would have caught them, except all Sergeant Turner's Marines were still out in the hall. And as soon as the bad guys started shooting Corporal Reilly blew the other claymore right over their heads and tossed a couple of frag grenades into the hole.

What this did to the shooters caused the rest of the enemy on the floor to bolt for the stairway. They ran right into Sergeant Eberhardt's squad coming down.

The firefight took place at a range of ten feet. The first two Marines had just led around the corner with their weapons. Up the stairs I heard another roar of gunfire.

A fragment or a ricochet split a Marine's cheek, but three more bad guys were down.

It was a roll of the dice that Sergeant Eberhardt's squad ended up clearing the rooms on that floor in the traditional manner, breaching doors and tossing in flash-bangs. Because one room was full of women and children, huddled in the corners and screaming in terror.

You disapprove of shooting women and children? Join the club. But try charging into a pitch dark room filled with them, not knowing if a guy with an AK-47 was hiding behind them, and *not* shooting everyone. That Sergeant Eberhardt and his Marines didn't amazed me. I'm still not sure whether it was a gutsy and heroic call or a moment of hesitation and indecision that could have been fatal, but it turned out to be the right thing. When I got there all the noncombatants were lying on the floor, searched and cuffed. Scared but alive.

So were two more terrorists. They'd caught some grenade frags and used it as an excuse to give up. We searched them, stripping them naked; handcuffed and gagged with duct tape, bandaged, and strapped into stretchers.

One look at the ground floor told me how incredibly lucky we'd been when everyone decided to make their last stand on the floor above. It was a warren of spaces that would have been a nightmare to clear. A combination garage/workshop, filled with Rover and Land Cruiser vehicles, drums of gasoline, about 50,000 rounds of ammunition, cases of AK-47's, and about twenty pounds of mixed civilian gelignite and Czech Semtex plastic explosives. A few stray rounds or a grenade and the whole house and all of us in it would have gone up in smoke. The intel team went nuts snapping pictures and taking down serial numbers. Besides the two laptops we ended up with four packs full of documents.

There were twenty-two adult male bodies with weapons in the house and on the street outside. Close to the number of Marines in my platoon. If we hadn't had those claymores—almost by accident—we would have been in very serious trouble.

I called Captain Z, gave him the rough inventory, and asked him what he wanted me to do. "I've got to go higher for permission," he said. "But get ready to blow it, over."

"Roger that," I said. "Be advised that there's not going to be much standing around here after it goes off, over."

"Understood. Wait, out."

There was a gap while he talked to the MEU commander. I pictured them stopping to get a ruling from the lawyer. Don't laugh, that's how it was really done in these ass-covering days. I had the Explosive Ordnance Disposal team begin rigging the ammo and explosives for demolition with all our remaining explosives. They were as good at disposing of ordnance by blowing it up as they were at defusing it.

Captain Z came back on the net. "You're clear to blow it, but make sure you give yourself enough delay, over."

"Roger, out."

The charges were rigged and we were finally ready to get out of there, but Captain Z had us wait. He wanted all the helos refueled and the Cobras rearmed before we made our move. They weren't all back on station yet.

This gave me a chance to get together with the squad leaders and platoon sergeant and make sure we were straight on the plan. It also gave the Marines a chance to reload magazines from their extra bandoleers.

We'd leave the house by bounds. First Sergeant Eberhardt and Staff Sergeant Frederick, covered by Corporal Asuego on the roof. Then Sergeant Turner with our wounded and the prisoners. Sergeant Harlin had been shot clean through the face but was still alive thanks to Doc Bob doing a tracheotomy by flashlight. Lance Corporal Bamburger had taken a round through the leg when the bad guys started firing into the ceilings. Corporal Asuego and I would bring up the rear.

I was up on the roof with Corporal Asuego. Through our night goggles we saw the Cobras coming back and knew we'd be getting the call soon.

The Captain Z gave the code word over the radio. The platoon commanders acknowledged in succession.

"Go, go!" I yelled down. Sergeant Turner released the women and children down the street, pausing to strip the ID and weapons off the bodies lying out there. At the same time Sergeant Eberhardt's squad broke out in the opposite direction. By twos, on each side of the street, well spread out.

They started taking scattered rifle fire from nearby buildings, but it was obvious the Yemenis didn't have night vision equipment.

We did, and opened up on every muzzle flash with everything we had.

When Sergeant Turner with the casualties and the intel team to help carry them moved out, we came down off the roof. The two EOD Marines were waiting beside their handiwork. When only one fire team was left in the house, I told the EOD Staff Sergeant, "Pull fuse."

They pulled the rings on the two friction fuse igniters screwed onto the ends of two coils of time fuse. "Smoke," they both reported, meaning the fuses were burning properly. You always lit at least two fuses per charge. Doing only one and having it go out would be very embarrassing. I would have lit more, but we only had enough fuse cord for two 15-minute delays. We'd only anticipated using small charges on short time delays. I set my watch timer to keep track of the delay.

While we'd been waiting to move out, the EOD guys had rigged up a couple of anti-handling booby traps in case someone got in after we left and managed to cut the fuses. As soon as anyone started rummaging around the whole thing would go up. Since their job normally entailed defusing someone else's booby traps, they were ecstatic about the shoe being on the other foot.

Once the fuses were burning I sent them along. Then Lance Corporal Vincent and I left with the last fire team.

Fortunately we weren't taking fire other than a few random rounds here and there. The Yemenis seemed cowed by the Cobras beating overhead, and confused about where we were and what we were doing. We were within two blocks of linking up with Milburn's platoon.

I didn't even hear it. I just saw the whole street ahead lit up in blooming flashes, and Sergeant Eberhardt's squad go down under fire.

CHAPTER SEVENTEEN

I grabbed the radio handset from Vincent. "Break, break, break, Two in contact, over." That cut through all the chatter. The Cobra pair shadowing my move through their thermal sights came up to request that we mark our front.

I had to break through the chaos of the intra-squad net to tell Staff Sergeant Frederick to throw some infrared chemlights out in front of him.

He did, and the two Cobras popped up high to get a clear shot between the buildings. We needed them badly. We were in two files going up either side of a street. There was practically no way to employ more than a few weapons to our front, and no cover other than doorways and front steps.

We were taking only automatic rifle fire. They hadn't dug their machine-guns or RPG's out of their hope chests yet.

The 3-barrel 20mm gatling guns in the Cobras' noses sounded like metal zippers being drawn up. The armor piercing rounds in their ammo mix threw up showers of sparks as they hit the masonry.

I ran up the street under the cover of the cannon fire, pulling Vincent behind me with the handset cord like a leash. On my way I grabbed the two machine-gun teams and the two SMAW rocket launcher teams.

I kept hollering over the radio to the Cobras, "Keep it up! Keep it up!"

Staff Sergeant Frederick was right up front directing fire. Third squad had been ambushed crossing the intersection of two streets. My stomach clenched up again when I saw two Marines lying motionless out in the road. Wounded were being dragged into doorways.

Some Marines were huddled under cover. Enough weren't. Lance Corporals Conahey and Westgate were putting out fire with their Squad Automatic Weapons, standing tall even though they were dangerously exposed. Lance Corporal Hiller was pumping out M-203 grenades one after the other, putting them right through the windows of the houses across the street. Until his grenade launcher broke like the plastic piece of shit it was, and he went back to his rifle. The noise was incredible.

"Smoke?" Staff Sergeant Frederick shouted to me, meaning to use it to screen the street and recover the bodies.

"They'll fire through it!" I shouted back. They probably had their weapons zeroed on the two Marines, just waiting for us to come and get them. Smoke would only signal our move.

Then I remembered reading about the battle of Hue City in Vietnam. Smoke hadn't worked then, but something else had.

I told him my plan. He rushed off to get ahold of everyone in 3rd squad carrying an AT-4. I positioned the SMAW's and machine-guns, all the while on the radio imploring the Cobras to keep firing. They were running low on ammo, and everyone and everything was moving so agonizingly slowly.

It was then I noticed Lance Corporal Vincent shaking like a leaf in a hurricane. "You okay?" I yelled.

"Do you know how much fire we're taking, sir!" he shouted back at me.

I won't pretend I wasn't scared. But at that moment I happened to be more scared of losing control of the situation and presiding over disaster than getting killed. Just a small difference in focus between Vincent and I. There were rounds cracking all around, but none close enough to pin us down. What stuck in my mind was that even in that situation he was still using proper military courtesy.

The noise was so overpowering the intra-squad radio was next to useless. The difference between a platoon shooting blanks and a firefight with live ammunition was the difference between listening to an acoustic guitar in a coffeehouse and standing directly in front of the speakers at a rock concert. I signaled the nearest AT-4 gunner to fire.

The two SMAW and three AT-4 gunners fired their rockets into the buildings across the road. The world rocked under the impacts, and the road filled with dust and smoke. Four Marines rushed out into the road and dragged the two bodies back to us. They all made it. Everyone firing at us who hadn't been knocked off their pins by the impacts of the rockets had certainly ducked for cover.

Now we had to break contact and get out of there. All I could think of was Somalia. If we sat still too long they'd start boxing us in on all sides and we'd be trapped. I sent Staff Sergeant Frederick back to Corporal Asuego. We'd turn the whole show around, the rear becoming the new point. They would cut over three streets and then head back up. We had to hurry. It would take us back in the direction of a house full of explosives that would be detonating in just a few minutes.

They began moving out. The SMAW teams reloaded. The 83mm rocket was pre-packed in a sealed fiberglass tube that screwed right onto the rear of the launcher, the whole thing looking very much like the old bazooka.

The SMAW's would fire; everyone in Sergeant Eberhardt's squad who still had one would throw a frag grenade, and we'd all turn tail and run back down the street. Everyone signaled that they were ready, and I gave the signal to fire again.

The SMAW team across the street from me had fired late the last time, and now I knew why. The SMAW had a 9mm spotting rifle attached to the tube, just a naked barrel and a simple action. A magazine of six 9mm tracers came with each rocket. The spotting rifle showed the gunner exactly where the rocket would be going, allowing him to adjust his aim in the telescopic sight. In training the gunners were told to fire all six spotting rounds so they wouldn't have to turn in any live cartridges.

And now my gunner was squeezing off tracers slowly and carefully, as if he was back on the range at Lejeune. Wrong training becoming habit, and habit taking over in combat.

"Fire the SMAW!" I shouted into the radio. Because of the rocket backblast the gunner had to stand relatively exposed. And while tracers told you where a round was going, they also told everyone else where the round had come from. It was like watching an auto accident you knew was going to happen but couldn't do anything about.

Bullet strikes blossomed in the stone wall all around the SMAW team, and they both crumpled to the ground.

"Everyone freeze!" I yelled into the radio, into the air at the top of my lungs, and using a hand signal. Then into the other handset, talking to the Cobras, "I need Hellfires, one at a time, at my command, over."

"What's the target?" the Cobra leader replied.

"I'm using all tracers. Fire on my impacts. My radioman will give the command. This is going to be closer than danger close, but don't argue with me."

Then some moron came up on the net with a routine message, and the Cobras and I had to shout him off. Finally the Cobra leader came back with, "Standing by, Two."

I could see the Cobras climbing higher so the laser beam that would guide the Hellfire missiles into the target would be unobstructed.

I know, I was going to do the same thing that had gotten the SMAW team nailed, but I couldn't think of anything else.

I told Vincent and Sergeant Eberhardt to move back the hell away from me. "Raise your hand to tell me if they've got the target," I said to Vincent. "When I drop mine, that's fire one." To Sergeant Eberhardt, "When the Hellfire hits we go grab the SMAW team. Then I'll call for another one. When that hits we get the hell out of here."

They both gave me thumbs up. When they'd moved away I raised my rifle and scooted as far back into the doorway I was hiding behind as I could. I started squeezing off tracers into the most troublesome building across the street. The best thing would have been to ignore the fact that everyone in the world was shooting at me. Easier said than done, especially with a sound all around my head like a big pot of popcorn popping at high speed. All the incoming rounds that hadn't hit me. Yet. I looked back. Vincent's hand was up. I raised and dropped mine.

A few seconds later came loud clicking and a violent *whoosh*. The Hellfire hit the building and knocked me clean off my feet. I got up fast and ran across the street to the SMAW team, joined by most of 3rd squad.

Everyone grabbed an arm or leg, and I dropped my arm again. The air was full of suspended dust.

We crouched over the wounded until the next Hellfire hit. Something hot jabbed me in the back of the arm, but I wasn't about to stop and look. We were up and moving. I picked up the SMAW launcher. As soon as we were out of effective small arms range of that damned intersection we halted for first aid.

In the dark, even with night vision goggles, you had to feel all over a casualty's body for holes. If you missed even something small they could bleed to death in a very short time. The assistant gunner had taken rounds in the shoulder and both legs. His vest had stopped one in the chest area. He was screaming from the pain, but as soon as we controlled the bleeding and hit him with a morphine syrette he'd be all right.

The gunner had caught a round in the side as he was poised to fire, and it seemed to have gone into his chest. He was out of it, limp and unresponsive, his eyes rolling around. It didn't look good, but all we could do was get a battle dressing on the entrance wound.

Linked back up with Vincent, I talked with the Cobras. "Great shooting. You saved our asses. Can you get eyes out in front of my lead squad, over?"

"Affirmative."

I stepped out into the street, checked behind me, yelled, "Fire in the hole!" and fired the SMAW back at the intersection. It wasn't bravado. The SMAW was another flimsy piece of shit weapon. It had a habit of not firing when you pulled the trigger, and it wasn't unknown for it to go off when the trigger wasn't pulled. An Israeli design rammed up our ass by their whores in Congress and never adopted by the Israeli Army, who preferred captured Russian RPG-7's that worked. I didn't want a rocket firing by accident while I was carrying it, and definitely didn't want to lug the full thirty pounds of loaded launcher if I didn't have to.

Then someone fired an RPG back at me. The rocket hit in the middle of the street with a blinding flash magnified by my night goggle. A Marine went down yelling, "Corpsman!"

Doc Bob and I ran up at the same time. PFC Cerullo was peppered with fragments, and my little Doc, who had turned into quite the tiger, kicked him hard in the ass, shouting, "Get up and walk, goddammit! You ain't hurt bad enough to carry." Cerullo sheepishly got to his feet and limped down the street.

"Move out," I radioed Staff Sergeant Frederick.

No more RPG's, though I didn't know the reason why until later. The weapon gave off a huge backblast when it was fired. You couldn't shoot an RPG from inside a room or the blast would bounce back off the walls and take out the operator. They had to be fired from a roof, a balcony, or a street. And as soon as anyone did that the Cobras pounced.

Sergeant Eberhardt got his people ready to go, but the column in front of us wasn't moving. I couldn't get a straight answer on the radio, so I ran up ahead to see what was happening, poor Vincent loping along behind me.

"What's going on!" I shouted as I reached Sergeant Turner's squad.

"That little fucking coward Peterson flipped out, sir," a Marine called from a darkened doorway.

There was a knot of Marines a little farther up the street. Lance Corporal Peterson had his arms and legs wrapped around an iron fence grate, screaming and crying hysterically. Three Marines were trying to pry him off.

"We can't get him loose, sir," Sergeant Turner shouted to me.

The three Marines were beating and kicking at Peterson, to no avail. You have no idea how amazingly strong someone in the grip of hysteria can be.

"You've got to," I shouted back. "We can't lose contact with 1st squad, and the house is going to blow in…," I looked at my watch, "four minutes. You've got to get moving now."

I ran up ahead to make sure we were still connected to 1st squad, yelping over the radio to the Staff Sergeant at the same time. We still had contact. On my way back I ran into Sergeant Turner with Peterson draped over his shoulders in a fireman's carry.

"Move out," I radioed the Staff Sergeant again.

Once we got going I went down the column counting heads, making sure no one hadn't got the word or been left behind in a doorway.

During the *Mayaguez* rescue operation of 1975, a 3-man machine-gun team had been left behind as Marines pulled back onto helicopters at night and under heavy fire after assaulting Koh Tang Island. The team presumably disappeared into the killing fields of Cambodia.

The thought of this happening to anyone under my command made me a fanatic on the subject. So whatever we did, the team leaders physically counted every head. They reported to the squad leaders, who reported to me. "Have we got everyone?" was my never-ending refrain. "I think so," was banned from everyone's vocabulary.

We were moving, but the adrenaline drain combined with the over 6,000 foot altitude was wiping us out. We seemed to be crawling.

I kept one eye on my watch. Less than a minute left on the fuses.

We cut back on our original direction. I stayed on the radio, making sure we didn't end up in a firefight with Milburn's platoon. Trying to link up like that, in contact and under fire, was incredibly dangerous. If we started shooting at each other we could do a lot more damage than the Yemenis had been able to.

Corporal Asuego's point fire team snapped infrared chemlights in their helmet bands. We took it very slow. Milburn's Marines saw it and let him know on their intra-squad radio. Milburn told me over the company net, and I passed it down on my intra-squad radio.

Sergeant Eberhardt's squad was being pursued by a few die-hards. Third squad had to have one fire team set up and shooting while the others moved, rotating positions as they made their way down the street.

As the last man came in one of Milburn's machine-gun teams, positioned and ready, opened up and sprayed down the street. Even the die-hards weren't up for that. I made another head count—we had everyone.

Just as we linked up the house blew. A white flash that washed out our night vision gear again, then a shock wave that felt like an earthquake and knocked us off our feet again. Everyone took what cover they could as big pieces of debris began to rain down.

The village must have thought they'd been nuked, because that was it—they'd had enough. All the firing just shut off.

As soon as pieces of the house stopped falling Milburn's Marines lent a hand with our wounded, and we moved a lot faster.

We passed through a hole in the stone village wall O'Brien had blown with two 20-pound satchel charges of plastic explosive. It said something about my night that I'd never even heard them go off.

As I brought up the rear into the landing zone perimeter, there was Staff Sergeant Frederick counting us all in.

"Have we got everyone?" I asked him.

"Yes, sir. Including the prisoners."

I clapped him on the shoulder and ran up to Sergeant Turner to help him get Peterson off his back. Peterson's neck was all wet where I grabbed him. There was blood on my hand. I felt a wound on the back of Peterson's neck just below the helmet, and either an entry or an exit wound in his face. Another pair of dead eyes stared back at me. Sergeant Turner and I just looked at each other. I didn't know what to say. All I could think to do was walk off to the command post to report in.

I have no idea what I looked like, because the first thing Captain Z said to me was, "You all right?"

"Yes, sir."

"Change of plan. You're going out on the first bird with all the wounded."

We discussed the technical details, and soon the '53's could be heard coming over the mountains.

The LZ was tight—one helo at a time. The '53 landed amid a hurricane of dust.

As I walked by the prisoners one of them was trying to shout something through his tape gag. And Lance Corporal Francois was telling him, "Shut up, motherfucker. Your juice is water right now."

I counted everyone aboard. The stretchers went on the deck down the center of the fuselage. Only one corpsman stayed behind at the LZ. Doctor Patel and all the rest were aboard.

The '53 lifted off, shuddered, and then dropped like a rock, wheels bouncing on the ground. We all held our breath as it took the pilot two more tries before he could get enough of that thin high altitude air under his rotors to get airborne. We seemed to go up a foot at a time until we cleared the peaks.

Then the village was gone. Even sealed off from it inside the familiar throbbing fuselage of a departing helicopter, it's wreckage lay at our feet.

When we went feet wet over the ocean I passed the word to unload, clear, and lock all weapons.

The SMAW gunner with the bad chest wound was Corporal Cushing, whose wife's flowers Captain Carbonelli had stolen a million years ago. Over the ocean they began giving him CPR.

Our helicopter was flaring to land when the doorgunner yelled over the intercom that we were still over the water. Then he threw himself spread-eagle face down onto the floor. I was the only one in the back with a headset, but everyone else knew that it was not a good sign when the crew assumed the crash position.

I found out later that the copilot—a first lieutenant whose uncertain hand we felt every time he took the controls—had gotten confused and almost landed us on the water instead of the flight deck thirty feet away. These things happened sometimes while wearing night vision goggles.

The pilot immediately grabbed the stick and put us on the deck. Major pucker factor, as the aviators liked to say.

As soon as we landed and the ramp went down we were inundated with corpsmen in white reflective vests and flight deck helmets. We all sat still as they hurried the wounded out.

I sent two Marines with them to guard our prisoners, afraid some well-meaning doc would cut off their handcuffs and hand them a scalpel or something.

Then I stood up and 2nd platoon followed me off the helo. When we were all in the passageway on the 02 level, the hatch dogged shut behind us, I went down the line and shook every Marine's hand, looked him in the eye, and thanked him for the job he'd done.

"Does this mean we get the Combat Action Ribbon, sir?" Corporal Crockett asked me with a smile.

"You earned it tonight," I told him. My tough guys had really taken it to them. And no one who hadn't been there with us would ever know what we were feeling then.

"Don't forget that five dollars a day hazardous duty pay, Crazy," Staff Sergeant Frederick said, smiling.

"Yeah, we're fucking rolling in it now," Corporal Reilly said sardonically.

The Staff Sergeant took charge of the platoon then, and I went to sickbay.

After calling down for a couple of the ship's Masters at Arms to take over guarding the prisoners, there was nothing for me to do but wait for word. Sitting in a hard plastic chair amid all the rushing activity, I could hardly even sense my own body. It felt as if I'd spent the whole night getting electric shocks and would never be able to rest again. I begged a handful of aspirins for my headache.

Then the 1MC blared out: *"All Echo Company Marines report to the troop marshaling area ASAP. All Echo Company Marines report to the troop marshaling area ASAP."*

CHAPTER EIGHTEEN

All the other lieutenants had gone from the flight deck right down to the marshaling area, so I was the last to show up.

Something was going on, because Marines and Sailors were dragging fresh cases of ammunition off the hoists from the magazines.

I broke into the huddle. "Sorry, sir, I was at sickbay."

"The FARP is in trouble," said Captain Zimmerman. "As they were pulling out they came under fire. One helo's down in the zone. We're going back in."

"Casualties, sir?" said Nichols.

"Forget about all that," Captain Z snapped. "The situation's changing by the minute, and whatever reports we've already gotten are out of date by now. I'm not going to base my planning on them. We'll fly in, I'll talk direct to Paul Federico and take a look at the ground, then let you know what I want to do."

I saw in everyone's eyes exactly what I was feeling. We'd gotten out, we were safe, we'd allowed ourselves to give in to the exhaustion, and now we had to go back in. It was a major psychological hurdle.

I'd leap it by taking my Marines over it. When I told them there were wide eyes and disbelief. Everyone seemed to sag. I could always tell from the undertone of muttering how they were feeling about something. Bitching meant everything was good to go. But they were sullen and silent, and that was contagious. Time to be a lieutenant.

"Listen up!" I said sharply. "We've got Marines in trouble. *Marines in trouble.* I'm not taking anyone with me who doesn't have the balls to get them out. Anyone who isn't up for it," I said, pointing, "pick up your trash and stand over by that bulkhead. We don't fucking need you."

Everyone looked at each other. Even the couple who'd been looking at the bulkhead didn't move. I said to the Staff Sergeant, "Tell Mitchell and Hauser to gear up. They're coming along." The two PFC's I'd left behind. It was going to be a daylight fight, and we were going to need everyone.

This was why the Marines and I didn't play cards together. A platoon commander had to have some distance, because some of the Marines I'd just manipulated into coming with me were going to lose their lives because of it.

Now I was spitting out orders to the squad leaders. "It's going to be hot. Everyone get their pile off and fill their canteens and Camelbak's up full. Take NVG's but put them in the butt packs. Full basic load, plus double bandoliers and double frag grenades. Any flash-bangs left, leave 'em here. We're short one SMAW team, so everyone who doesn't have a SAW or 203 carries an AT-4. SAWs and 203's carry a claymore."

And then, because the 90% always have to pay for the 10% who just can't seem to do what they're told, for whatever reason, I took out a 1-quart canteen and led the platoon in downing it. Forced hydration, crucial in any hot weather environment—vital in the desert.

The water must have given me a brainstorm. "Corporal Asuego, take your squad down to the mess deck and get some doughnuts or bread or anything we can eat fast with our hands. Enough for the whole company. Okay, move."

Remember what I said about giving Marines orders? I don't want to paint with a broad brush, because there were Sailors who dropped everything and broke their asses to get us back into the fight. But when the mess officer told Corporal Asuego there was no way he could have one tray let alone trays of doughnuts and danish, not to mention ten cases of cold soda, he found himself looking down the barrel of a loaded M-16.

And, of course, being Marines they didn't return with their booty in a spirit of quiet satisfaction. They came back whooping, "We jacked the motherfucker!"

Another officer got the M-16 treatment when he protested our pulling metal-frame Stokes stretchers off the bulkheads to handle extra casualties. "That's Navy property," he said.

"Fuck off, sir," was the reply given at gunpoint. Typical of Marines, it was still quasi-respectful despite the circumstances.

We loaded up the stretchers with ammo cans in case we needed resupply.

Our refueling and rearming took longer than the helicopters, the time being divided between loading magazines and ramming pastry into our faces. It was amazing the morale effect from one tiny detail. Sugar, caffeine, and a fresh load of adrenaline pumped everyone right back up.

As we stood by in our helo serials I was going down the lines inspecting everyone's gear. Captain Z walked over and said, "Good work on the chow, 2nd platoon." He slapped an embarrassed Corporal Asuego on the back of the helmet. "The Marines were hungry enough to eat the ass out of a rag doll."

Everyone in the vicinity cracked up. "Better not thank us too fast, sir," I said. "You may have to deal with some fallout."

"Oh?"

"Well, for starters, there may be some squids filing claims for post-traumatic stress disorder."

His reply was one voiced often in the Corps, but almost never by company commanders. He winked at Corporal Asuego and said, "Fuck 'em if they can't take a joke."

CHAPTER NINETEEN

The FARP site was a relatively flat valley sandwiched between two long jagged ridges that were sealed at one end by a shorter cross-compartment ridge that left the ground in the shape of a U. Every piece of land in that part of Yemen flat enough to land helicopters on was surrounded by high ground.

I was sure Federico had put outposts on those ridges. They'd either been driven off by a larger force, or someone had waited until the platoon pulled back to get on their helicopter.

All we had going in with us was a pair of Cobras. To keep two continuously over the target area meant that one pair had to be on deck refueling and another enroute.

Dawn meant no more advantage from night vision equipment. They could see us just as well as we could them. We circled out of small arms range, the rising sun to our backs. Too high to make out Marines on the ground, but a '53 was burning in the middle of the LZ.

This was the maddening part. I had a pretty good idea what ought to be done, but had to sit and wait for someone else to make the call. And even if theirs was fucked up, I'd have to do it anyway.

Since none of the battalion staff was on my helo I could actually listen in to the discussion over a headset. I know the responsibility was crushing, but it took them forever to pull the trigger.

At least they came to the right decision. Combat in mountains was a lot like urban combat. You never wanted to fight your way uphill if you could start at the highest point and attack down.

I acknowledged my orders over the headset and waved Staff Sergeant Frederick and the squad leaders up to the starboard gunner's window. I pointed and shouted what was known as a fragmentary, or frag order.

"We're going to take, clear, and hold that ridgeline. We'll fast rope onto the high open end and sweep down. First platoon will be doing the same on the other side of the valley. Third platoon is in reserve."

With proper dispersion between the Marines, there was only room for two squads on line going down the long axis of the ridge, so I said, "First squad on the left. Third squad on the right. Third is the base squad." Then to Sergeant Turner, "I want you behind us, far enough back to be out of our AT-4 backblast area. Cover our rear and take care of any fire we get from the flanks. Remember we've got 1st platoon on our right, but keep a close eye on that short ridge to our right front." He nodded. Then to the machine-gun squad leader, "One gun on the far left flank, one on the right." I crossed my arms to show him how I wanted his fire to be able to cover our front. He nodded. And to the Staff Sergeant, "You stay with Sergeant Turner. I'll be with Corporal Asuego." Then to them all, "Everyone understand the plan?" They did. "Questions?" There were none. "Okay, go tell the troops. Give me a thumbs up when you're ready."

They went down the lines of seats and briefed their team leaders. When the thumbs went up I reported over the headset that we were ready.

A few minutes later the helos broke from the racetrack pattern and went down. I had an immediate uneasy feeling because we were heading straight in with no maneuvering or jinking. That shit was okay at night, but it wasn't a good time for Marine helicopter pilots to be acting like peacetime bus drivers.

As we bore in tracers began rising up at us. An optical illusion made them seem deceptively slow, almost floating. I signaled the platoon to get ready.

The port side doorgunner opened up with his .50 cal.. I kept hearing pinging sounds and thought: what a great time for some engine trouble.

Then I saw the little dots of sunlight appearing in the fuselage and realized that the pinging was bullets punching through the skin.

Lance Corporal Carter, who'd obviously seen *Apocalypse Now,* took off his helmet and sat on it. Until Sergeant Turner shouted, "You can live without your balls! You can't live without your brain, dipshit!" Carter thought that over and put his helmet back on.

"I don't want to live without *my* balls," Lance Corporal Vincent muttered beside me.

We came in with our nose facing down the ridgeline. Which meant that after we fast roped out the back we'd have to pass underneath the helicopter to get into position. I tried to persuade the pilots to turn the bird a bit sideways to take care of that and allow at least one of the door guns to fire down the ridge, but if there was one certainty in life it was that pilots never listened to anyone, especially not infantry lieutenants.

Just as the '53 slowed and flared to a hover, PFC Mitchell seemed to launch out of his seat. The safety belt caught him and threw him back. His upper body fell forward onto his knees.

I'd let the poor kid come along and he hadn't even made it out of the helicopter. And now I had to do worse. "Leave him!" I shouted, signaling the fast rope out.

The ridge was typical desert terrain: sand and knee high scrub bushes broken by rocks and rock outcroppings. I stationed myself at the bottom of the rope, directing Marines to go around the helicopter left and right, staying as far away from it as possible. If the helo had hovered a little lower they wouldn't be as much of a target, but I'd given up trying to reason with pilots.

Fire was coming in heavy. The only way to suppress it was to send heavier fire back, but I had less than a squad on the ground. Only the fact that nearly everyone was shooting high at the helo kept us from being pinned down while we were all strung out. It was a fucking mess.

I looked up to see the '53 lurch and drop. I grabbed the Marine coming off the rope and threw him down the slope out of the way. The helo slammed into the rocks, and I fell back as the tail rotor came down like a screaming circular saw, so close I could almost taste the metal.

I landed hard on the AT-4 rocket strapped across my back, and it tangled up in my legs because I was rolling as if I was on fire, something

I expected to happen as soon as the helicopter blew up.

But when I stopped and looked up through the rotor wash sandstorm I could see the helo tilted on one side on the rocks, rotors still intact and beating though barely missing the ground. I also saw the rest of the platoon charging out the back ramp, making the hard right to avoid the tail rotor, asshole to elbow like cattle going though a chute, the Staff Sergeant driving them hard from behind.

To say that chaos reigned would be an understatement. That it reigned for such a brief period of time was really due to the fear that the '53 was going to continue tipping over and send a million shattered fragments of rotor blade among us. This made everyone sprint down the slope on each side to get around and away from the helo. And at least on the side of the ridge we were masked from most of the incoming fire.

Loud whooshing sounds overhead. As I scrambled back up the slope I saw that one of the Cobras had fired half a pod of unguided 2.75 inch rockets down the ridge. Some were white phosphorus, and the spreading blooms of white smoke gave us some screening.

The rounds snapping overhead had us crawling until we reached the protection of a rock outcropping. And made us very thankful for those urban warfare knee and elbow pads.

The cover gave the squad and team leaders a chance to shake their troops out and give me a head count. I thought we were in deep shit, but except for Mitchell, who was still on the helo, I had everyone present and, though banged up, none incapacitated. I actually had one extra. One of the helo crew decided that staying in the bird wasn't the best course of action. He was on the ground in flight suit, gloves, and helmet, the smoked visor still pulled over his eyes, his Beretta in his hand.

"Welcome to the grunts," I shouted, then pointed to Staff Sergeant Frederick. "Stick to him like glue."

He watched forlornly as the '53 increased pitch and shuddered into the air, the crew visibly fighting to keep it from pitching over. I had to give them credit for not trying it until we were out of the way. The bird actually stayed up, one engine blowing black smoke. An empty '53 was overpowered even with only two out of three engines working.

The undercarriage was all smashed up, one wheel dangling like a broken leg. Good luck landing back on the ship. That was their problem, but one less '53 was ours.

And now I had to go into the attack. It was like going into the attack after just finishing a marathon.

CHAPTER TWENTY

All the clever maneuvering, night fighting, raiding, and infiltration we did in training was wonderful, but now I knew why the experience of combat always led military units to load up on firepower. Because no matter what you'd prefer, you were eventually going to find yourself in a stand-up daytime fight with no room to maneuver.

The noise rose as the two squads spread across the ridgeline and set out to gain fire superiority. My binoculars turned out to be invaluable. The sun was behind me so I didn't have to worry about reflections glinting off the lenses. You rarely see a clear target to shoot at on a battlefield. Too much exposure is a death sentence, so everyone stays well under cover.

I picked out the likely spots based on the terrain where I'd be taking cover, movement I could see, or muzzle blast dust signature. I fired a tracers into those areas, the squad leader whose sector of fire it was followed with a few more tracers of his own, then the team leaders fired a 40mm grenade whose prominent explosion brought their Marines on target. Soon there were 3 squad automatic weapons, 10 M-16's, and 3 M-203 grenade launchers concentrated together.

Which caused the amount of return fire to really taper off. I wouldn't be sticking my head up either with all that lead flying in. And no one had to shout orders that no one would have heard anyway. It worked perfectly, but never would have if Captain Z hadn't made us practice it on the range.

While the Marines were shooting I was on the radio with my Cobra. O'Brien and I each had one in direct support. We were out of range of naval gunfire. The company 60mm mortar section couldn't carry a lot of ammo, and Captain Z wanted to conserve it until we really needed them.

I'd rather have my own Cobra anyway. The two-man crew had high-powered optics and the best seat in the house.

"Grinch, are you on our tracers?" I asked into the radio.

"Affirmative."

"Okay, give me a short cannon burst to confirm." Our conversation was taking place on the company net, at the same time Jack O'Brien was talking to his Cobra. While hitting the village we'd realized that using the squadron callsign and tail numbers had too much potential for lethal confusion, so we started using the pilots' personal callsigns. Living with them aboard ship made such things so much easier. The Grinch was a 1st lieutenant whose old man's face did vaguely resemble the Dr. Seuss character.

The 20mm cannon rattled from high up off to our right, and through my binos I could see the shells explode among the rocks. "Beautiful," I reported. "Now some rockets, HE and Willie Pete."

That familiar whooshing sound again, and my eye followed the black airborne arrows right into the target. White smoke spread from the sailing flecks of burning phosphorus, and I shouted into the intra-squad radio, "Go! Go!"

The squads began to fire and move, and it was beautiful. When I'd first taken over the platoon the squad leaders stationed themselves behind their Marines, screaming, "Prepare to rush! Rush!" And everything soon degenerated into chaos.

Now the squad leaders were out in front firing and moving, with their fire teams alongside them. When the leaders stopped or started or shifted left or right, so did the Marines.

Each fire team bounded forward in pairs, one Marine shooting while the other moved. Vincent and I covered each other. I was in the line near Corporal Asuego, but otherwise left it to him and Sergeant Eberhardt.

The previous night had proved to me that combat was just barely controlled chaos. Anything else was Monday morning spin from commanders who, when the dust settled, were usually amazed to discover all the strange ways everything had turned out. The idea of winning or losing resting on one or two almost random moves didn't sit well with them, or the writers and historians trying to make sense of it later. So they ended up imposing an order that didn't really exist.

The sheer noise, not to mention the dispersion necessary in the face of modern weapons, meant you could scarcely influence events farther away than you could see—about thirty feet or so, depending on the terrain. Especially since a sky full of lead made it inadvisable to raise your head more than a foot above the ground.

So you couldn't direct the troops like chess pieces once real bullets started flying. Call the main moves, yes, but otherwise you had to let the small unit leaders execute. And mine had shown me they could. The leader of a 4-man fire team was the most important man on the battlefield, even though he got the least training.

My job was complicated by the need to stay on the radio, even as Vincent and I fired and moved along with everyone else.

There was no cover except for the occasional dip in the terrain, just sand and scrub. Our fire was going to have to get us forward.

The Grinch sent two Hellfire missiles into the rocks, then peppered them with his cannon as we got closer. "I've got people bugging out in front of you," he reported.

"Don't ask me, just take 'em out," I gasped into the handset as I threw myself down yet again.

The cannon rattled, but I couldn't see what he was shooting at.

Our two machine-guns, shot from the bipods while firing and moving along with us, were literally chewing the rocks into pieces. The smaller arms weren't nearly as impressive. No matter how used I was getting to the woodpecker tapping of incoming AK-47 rounds, every vicious whine of a ricochet skipping by made every muscle in my body spasm involuntarily. Almost as bad was the visual evidence of tracers hitting ground and rock and sailing off in every direction.

Asuego's squad was closing in on the rocks. We were still taking fire. At first it scared the living shit out of you, until you realized how little of it was really effective. That is, until a machine-gun burst kicked up sand right between Vincent and I.

Pretty sure I could see where it was coming from, I shrugged the AT-4 off my shoulder and opened up the sights and handgrip. After a quick peek to check that the backblast area behind me was clear, I cocked the rocket and aimed at the space between the rocks. Letting half my breath out, I pressed the firing button.

No sensation that the rocket had fired other than seeing it leap out in front of me. It hit the rocks with a massive bang. I left the empty fiberglass tube behind in the sand.

The Grinch kept up with his cannon until we were less than 30 yards from the rocks, then he ceased fire. In peacetime an attack helicopter pilot would have shit himself at the thought of firing his cannon within 200 yards of advancing troops. But you had to risk casualties and lean into your own supporting arms, not giving the enemy any chance to get in some unhindered shooting.

We were still firing, though, approaching through the dispersing haze of white phosphorus smoke. Corporal Asuego's eyes were a foot wide, and his mouth was open. As I'm sure mine was. I pulled a grenade from my pouch and showed it to him. He took one out and showed it to his team leaders, who were all watching him.

We didn't have a firing range back at Lejeune where we could maneuver and use small arms, AT-4's, and grenades all together, so it wasn't the Marines' habit to use them. And only habit worked under stress.

I pointed to Asuego that it was his move. I rolled onto my back as I thumbed off the safety clip, then pulled the pin.

When Asuego's left his hand I pitched mine over the rocks. As they blew we went over, me pumping my hand toward the ground and yelling over the intra-squad radio, "Stay low! Stay low!" I didn't want the Marines to skyline themselves as they came over the high ground.

I scrambled between two rocks and almost stepped on a body. But the guy wasn't dead. He'd been aiming his AK between the rocks, and he tried to roll over and bring it to bear on me. My rifle hung up in the enclosed space. I had to knock the stock up over my shoulder as I fell backward to get some room. I fired about six rounds down into him, almost putting one into one of my own feet. Once I stopped hyperventilating, this prompted another order into the intra-squad radio, "Make sure these bodies are really down and not faking!"

I took the radio headset back from Vincent, telling him, "Search this guy for documents."

I smelled burned meat. Had these fuckers been barbecuing in their defensive positions? Then as I looked around I realized that what I was smelling was human flesh, cooked by white phosphorus.

The squad leaders came up on the intra-squad with ammunition and casualty reports. We didn't have any wounded. Most of the credit for that was the Cobra's, and an unfair fight was fine by me. We'd used quite a bit of ammo. Taking the extra bandoleers had been a good call.

The combination of raw fear and acrid high explosive smoke had sucked every last bit of moisture from my mouth, and I pulled hard at the drinking tube of my Camelbak.

The Grinch came up on the net to tell me he had to go refuel and rearm. "Come back with more Willie Pete," I told him. "They don't like that." The phosphorus seemed to get in between the rocks the way high explosive didn't.

Before they left they fired the rest of the rockets in their pods down the ridge. His replacement came on station and I was talking to The Reverend. Which was what he was going to be when he got out of the Corps. The quietest, most mild-mannered guy on the ground, and a wild man in the air.

If it had been training I would have continued tearing down the ridge after the enemy. But the Marines had to catch their breath and reload magazines, and I wanted to get all my ducks in a row before starting again.

Scanning though my binoculars, it seemed we were taking fire from about four positions farther down the ridge. Mostly single shot and short bursts. They might be running low on ammo, and either lost their machine-guns or were keeping them under cover. I'd seen at least one Russian 7.62mm PKM and two Yemenis with ammo belts wrapped across their chests Pancho Villa fashion lying among the rocks.

The Reverend called me and said, "I need to make sure exactly where you are. Can you mark your pos?"

I didn't want to pop a smoke grenade and let everyone else know, not if I didn't have to. I dug the little survival mirror that I always used for shaving out of my accessory pouch. I held it under my eye, reflected the sun onto my outstretched finger, and flashed it at the Cobra.

"He's got your mirror, sir," Vincent said, the radio handset screwed into his ear. A headset for him and a separate handset for me would have saved us both a lot of trouble, but that's the kind of little thing grunts never get because it doesn't meet the cost-benefit test.

I took the handset back from him and began coordinating our next assault with The Reverend.

Then Captain Z broke it. "Stand fast, 2nd. We've got Harriers coming in."

We were finally close enough to the ship for the jets to put in an appearance. The aviation generals loved the Harrier because it could take off and land vertically, but that very characteristic gave it piss-poor range and load-carrying ability.

O'Brien came on the net and asked the question that was on the tip of my tongue. "Six, one. What's the ordnance?"

"Two ships inbound," Captain Z replied, "with 6 GBU-12's."

Six 500 pound laser-guided bombs. And that was all the two planes were really carrying. Just to reach us they both had to have two big auxiliary fuel tanks under their wings. And all the payload capacity left over was two bombs and a Litening laser targeting and designation pod on one aircraft, and four bombs on the other. Pretty pathetic. I would have sent them home and stuck with the Cobras, but of course someone must have insisted they get into the show.

I heard them coming in, but otherwise had nothing to do with the process. Enlisted Special Forces guys were calling in Air Force and Navy air in Afghanistan, but the Marine pilot's union had decreed that only pilots could call in close air support. Either forward air controllers (FACs) on the ground or Cobras in the air. I knew how to do it but it was a work rules issue, even more ironic because the Corps was the only one of the services that took close air support seriously.

No one even asked me about targets. I guess our FAC, who was located with Captain Z, had the same know-it-all attitude.

O'Brien's Cobra fired a white phosphorus rocket down the other ridge as a target mark. I didn't see the Harrier weapon release, but a cloud of black smoke appeared on the ridge, soundless like a silent movie. Then the noise of the blast and the pressure wave reached us a few seconds later.

When The Reverend fired a smoke rocket about 800 yards down the ridge, I told the platoon over the intra-squad radio, "Get your heads down." Of course in typical lieutenant fashion I kept looking through my binoculars.

No whistling noise or anything like that. I kept looking, expecting to see an explosion, when it went off right behind us. I went from lying on the ground to being lifted up a foot above it, then gravity slammed me back down into the sand.

Feeling physically sick, as if someone had just kicked my balls up into my body, I spoke into the intra-squad radio, "You still there, 2nd?"

The silence confirmed that my 2nd squad had just been wiped out. Then Sergeant Turner's voice, "Here, sir."

My relief was indescribable. "Any casualties?"

"Negative, but I'm looking at a frag the size of a dinner plate that almost parted my hair."

I was about to suggest he save it so we could both jam it up the pilot's ass when Captain's Z's voice in the handset said, "Come in, 2nd?"

"Still here, Six. No casualties, but it was close. We could live without any more airstrikes."

"Don't worry, I sent them home."

All that laser-guided bomb footage from Desert Storm? You only saw the ones that hit the target. And the targets were all high contrast like buildings and tanks. Low contrast ground didn't work as well.

"Six, this is two," I said into the handset. "I'm continuing my assault."

"Go ahead, it's your call."

We increased our rate of fire, and The Reverend worked over our front with rockets.

This one was like opening night compared to the dress rehearsal. The squads moved even faster; any weapon bigger than a rifle got an AT-4 fired at it; and the grenades went into the air as soon as we got close enough.

One poor fool shot an RPG-7 at us. He misjudged our rate of movement and the rocket boomed over our heads to land behind us. The Reverend saw the blue-gray smoke backblast signature and put a Hellfire right on top of him. A 100 pound, 65 inch long missile designed to take out a 50 ton main battle tank. When we reached the spot there was nothing left but scorched stones and some splatter.

Sergeant Eberhardt had one wounded, not too bad. They left him for Sergeant Turner to pick up.

We paused again to reload magazines. I cursed the cheap-ass Marine Corps for only issuing us six each. The sun was almost all the way up. The sand felt blistering hot, like a persistent fan blowing heat up at you.

The white phosphorus left a smog-like haze over the ridge. There were bodies scattered throughout the position, but not many. The staring twisted corpses with bullet holes were a relief compared to the ones torn into pieces by the rockets, or with basketball-sized wounds from 20mm cannon shells. More were splayed out farther in front of us, cut down by The Reverend as they tried to pull back.

Fire began to snap at us from the short ridge to our right front. I guess they'd been waiting until we were in range. Return fire from Sergeant Turner's squad behind us. We could have used the Harriers to deal with that, but I wasn't asking them back.

I took the handset from Vincent to give Captain Z a report. And just as I pushed the button to transmit something blew up right beside me.

I came to being dragged by the carrying strap on the back collar of my flak jacket. At first unable to figure out what the hell was going on, then aware of the bushes going by my face.

This triggered another explosion, inside me this time, and I had to roll over and throw up immediately. I hoped I wasn't in danger of dying, because for about a half a minute I wasn't capable of anything except projectile vomiting on a creosote bush. I sensed Marines rolling away from me.

Another explosion, though not as close this time, and again I was grabbed by the back of the flak jacket with the admonition, "Sorry, sir." And my ass was on a sleigh ride across the sand and rocks again.

I think my eyeballs were bouncing around more than I was—they were having trouble focusing. I'd had my bell rung before, but not like this. When my forward progress finally stopped I felt like I was still moving.

Staff Sergeant Frederick appeared in my field of view. "Sorry, sir." Everyone was apologizing.

My left ear was working fine, but the right was a little off. My Camelback was gone. I reached back for one of my canteens. I got it out, so the hand to eye was still working. I took a drink and didn't throw up again. "I think I'm ready to hear what happened."

"They dropped some mortars on us, sir. We had to get out of there fast."

"We got everyone?" I demanded. The platoon commander's never-ending refrain.

"Yes, sir. All accounted for."

"We lose anyone?"

"No sir. Three wounded. No emergencies."

"Am I one of them?" I noticed that my right sleeve was ripped to pieces and bloodstained, and a battle dressing was on my arm.

"Better make it four then, sir."

"Do we need to move again before they adjust onto us?"

"I don't think so, sir. As soon as they started dropping both Cobras went after the tube."

They weren't fools. Once again they'd figured out my pattern. Waited for us to pause on the position we'd taken, and then hit us with their mortar. I'd broken a rule: always assault through and beyond an objective, just in case the enemy had mortars or artillery targeted on their own position.

I hadn't forgotten, but their positions were the only spots on the ridge with any cover. Assaulting through would have meant stopping out in the open. Well, they'd made me pay anyway. No right answers—you just had to pick one and live with it.

"Did the Cobras get the mortar?" I asked, looking around for Vincent.

"That's the bad news, sir," the Staff Sergeant informed me matter-of-factly. "We lost the radio."

"Vincent?" I said sharply, rising up on my elbows.

"He's okay, sir, but the round that landed near you tore the radio to shit. Maybe saved Vincent's ass."

And there was Vincent popping into view, showing off his perforated set. I looked it over. It was a write-off.

"You better dump that, Crazy," Staff Sergeant Frederick advised him. "No sense carrying around the dead weight."

"But I'm signed for it!" Vincent protested shrilly.

Even with rounds still passing overhead, everyone within earshot cracked up.

When he regained his composure, the Staff Sergeant said, "It's a combat loss, Crazy. No one's going to make you pay for it."

Vincent turned to me as the honest broker. "No shit, sir?"

"No shit," I said. "Lose the radio." His packbag was shredded too, barely holding together. "The pack, too." I didn't think the Yemenis would get any intelligence benefit out of it. Even if they managed to repair it, they probably had better FM radios than we did.

"I been dreaming of this," Vincent said as he took off his pack.

No radio communications meant no Cobra. I doubted that the intra-squad radio had the range to reach Jack O'Brien across the valley, but I consulted the list of frequencies I'd written on my left forearm and changed to 1st platoon's. No go. Then the Cobras' UHF push. Nothing but static.

"Anyone got any ideas?" I yelled. "Anyone?"

The helo crewman crawled over, still wearing his crash helmet. Just as I'd told him, he'd stuck to the Staff Sergeant like glue. He unsnapped a pocket in his survival vest, rooted around, and handed me something green. About the same size and shape as a paperback book. Yes. His survival radio.

I leaned over and slapped him on top of the helmet. "Fucking A!"

He gave me a thumbs up.

Ironically, Captain Z had wanted each platoon commander to carry one of these on the raid, but the squadron never coughed them up in time.

I opened the tape antenna and turned it to the guard channel that every pilot monitored as a matter of course. "Warrior zero-three, this is 2nd platoon. You up there, over?"

The Reverend came back immediately. "Good to hear you, 2nd. Lose your radio?"

"That's affirmative," I replied. "Let the Six know we're okay. Had some trouble with the mortars—three routines. You find the tube?"

"Negative." It was hard to pick out something like that on the ground, especially since it could be anywhere within about a five mile radius. "I'll relay your traffic."

He also had me switch off the emergency frequency to keep it open. Captain Z had been pissing up his toenails since watching the mortars drop and hearing us go off the air. Now I was clear to continue.

Corporal Asuego's squad had taken all the casualties, so I brought Sergeant Turner's 2nd squad into the line and had 1st fall back to carry the wounded. Our stretchers could be dragged even easier than carried. We took the ammo off the casualties and sent it over to Sergeant Eberhardt.

While all this was happening I got out my cleaning rod and punched the packed sand from the barrel of my M-16. Vincent looked like he didn't know what to do without a radio droning in his ear.

"Were you awake for the mortars?" I asked him.

"Jesus Christ, sir, you should have seen it. The first one went off right next to us, and then they started dropping all over the place. We couldn't do anything except suck sand. I about shit a cold purple Twinkie."

That was my second combat laugh. A cold purple Twinkie? Never heard that one before.

Vincent was still rolling. "It was fucked up, sir. But it was like the rounds were going into the sand before they blew. We would have been in the hurt locker otherwise. As soon as they stopped we got the fuck out of there, but then they started up again, dropping 'em between us and 2nd squad. You should have seen the Staff Sergeant and Sergeant Turner, sir. As soon as the mortars slacked off again they all got up and ran, fucking ran, right up to us. We put out rounds for cover, but they didn't give a shit about anyone shooting at them; they didn't want to get trapped by those mortars."

Well, I was filled in on everything I missed, my rifle was working again, and the platoon was ready to go. With that mortar still operational

I wasn't about to stay in one place any longer than I had to. The only good news was that a Western 81mm or Russian 82mm mortar round weighed about ten pounds each, so there couldn't be an infinite supply of them waiting to be shot at us.

The Reverend was replaced by Thor, who was black instead of blonde and Viking. He came up on my survival radio frequency, and I briefed him on what had worked with the previous teams. Mainly keeping an eye on our distance to the objective and not bugging me for permission every time he wanted to engage a target.

We were almost down to the end of the ridge. There seemed to be only one more obvious spot where the Yemenis could get any cover from our fire and that of the Cobras.

Thor saturated the area with rockets and we went into the assault. My new handheld radio was great. Although hours of practice had made Vincent and I a ballroom dancing team to rival Fred and Ginger, life was much easier not being connected by that handset umbilical.

Unlike the previous two times the return fire didn't slacken as we got closer. If anything it increased.

I had an idea why. The Yemeni tribesmen were snipers and bush-whackers. They shot up their enemies, and when they no longer had the advantage faded away to fight another day. Close combat wasn't their thing. But every time they'd previously tried to bug out the Cobra had gunned them down. Now they were trapped on the end of a ridge with a steep downward slope of open ground behind them and nowhere to run. Stand or die time for them.

Our method had been to soften them up and blind them with high explosive and white phosphorus 2.75" rockets, use the Hellfires sparingly against particularly stubborn resistance, then keep their heads down with 20mm cannon as we closed in.

Now I got on the radio and told Thor, "Keep putting in Hellfires until we get danger close. Use them all if you have to, or I tell you to cease."

"Roger," he replied.

They came booming in on a steady rhythm like very expensive 155mm artillery shells. Even though we realized the benefit outweighed the danger, advancing toward those explosions was a contrary act you had to force your body to perform. Their noise was so intense that even with earplugs it felt like two hard thumbs pressing into the little mastoid pockets behind my ears.

It was only when I could feel the missile parts zinging by that I shouted into the radio, "Thor, cease fire on the Hellfires, keep it up with the cannon." I looked over and Vincent had blood running down his face. He'd taken a piece under the eye. Maybe I'd waited too long.

Something had happened. Our assault seemed to hesitate and stop. I sprang forward to get the line moving, but it didn't. I almost stood up right then. An officer gets more money, and salutes, and the bill comes due when an attack stalls and you have to set the example by making yourself a target to get things going again.

But then I realized we hadn't stalled. The Marines, sensing the opposition, were pausing to fix bayonets.

Jesus. The line lurched forward again. An RPG blew up right in front of Sergeant Turner and I. While I was shaking the sand from my eyes he readied and cocked his AT-4 in two bounds and fired a rocket right back at them.

He'd fired from the prone, and when I looked over his trousers were smoking. The backblast had set his cammies on fire. I rolled toward him and shoveled sand onto his legs. Totally unaware of the reason for it, he looked back at me as if I'd gone nuts.

I'd stopped hearing cannon fire from the Cobra. "Thor," I shouted into the radio, "keep that cannon going."

"We're jammed," was the response.

Fuck. We were on our own. "I'll be off the air for a while," I said, turning the radio off and stuffing it into my accessory pouch.

Just like the MCCRES, it was time to put our heads down and assault. My head was thick and my stomach wobbly, but the cure seemed to be an overdose of adrenaline.

Every time the Yemenis increased their rate of fire we matched it and surpassed it. Well-aimed single shots were the way to go 95% of the time, but at that moment we all should have been firing full auto to suppress them. Unfortunately our M-16A2's were capable of only semi-automatic and 3-round bursts. The ordnance experts and rifle range geeks were afraid that too much ammunition would be wasted otherwise. They were the lineal descendants of those who had taken repeating rifles away from the 7th Cavalry just before Little Big Horn.

It felt like I was only receiving slices of sensory input, not knowing whether what I was hearing had just started up or I simply hadn't noticed it before. Like the screaming. Angry screaming, and it was coming from the Marines around me. The same sound had probably been heard crossing the wheat field at Belleau Wood or the airstrip at Peleliu. The sound of the decision to hurl yourself forward rather than run away.

Our grenades went out. It was almost choreographed by now. Another little hitch in the line as we waited for them to go off.

They blew and we were up. Then back down quick as dark balls came sailing back at us. Explosives blow up and out, and all we could do was suck dirt. Blasts like bone-jarring shocks, ringing my bell again.

I didn't know if I'd caught any frags. The adrenaline was roaring so hard I may not have known if I was missing a limb. I shook my head to try and clear it, but felt like I was wearing a fifty pound helmet.

I sprang forward to get the line moving again. I know that sand is brown and explosive smoke gray-black, but I seemed to be in the middle of a cloud of yellow.

I didn't even think about not being able to see anyone, didn't worry about Marines not being with me. I think I was screaming too.

We had to climb a low rise of jagged black basalt to get at them. Having learned the lesson from the last time I'd jumped over some rocks, I fished my next to last frag grenade out of a cloth bandoleer pocket.

C'mon, c'mon. My swollen fingers felt as stiff as wood. I yanked the pin and the whole grenade popped right out of my hand. Still dangling from the pin, fortunately. Christ. I shifted it over to my left hand and finally worked the pin out. I yelled at myself to hurry before Sergeant Turner's squad got out in front of me. Pin out, spoon off, a long count of three for a short throw, and then shouting, "Frag out!" with a spectacularly dorky left-handed toss over the rocks like a basketball free throw.

Another jarring blast, then scrambling over. A figure dashed across my front. I snapped off two quick shots, doubting I hit him, and didn't follow up for fear of hitting unseen Marines.

I crept forward, then dropped into a crouch as some of our own 5.56mm rounds passed overhead with sharper, higher-velocity cracks. "Watch your sectors of fire," I hissed into the intra-squad radio. Not that it would do much good besides make me feel better. It was just a part of combat you had to accept.

Movement off to my right that seemed to key off my voice. My rifle was pointed the other way. A long burst from a SAW while I was still turning. First in my peripheral vision, then straight on: a Yemeni fallen onto his back. Vincent darting forward, screaming like a banshee. And not stopping, not shooting, but driving his bayonet into the man's chest. A boot on the neck, a twist of the rifle, and he yanked the blade out, his eyes wild.

Holy shit. Why didn't he just shoot the guy? And I guess the answer is that in combat we get unrestricted access to the dark part of our hearts that wonders what it would be like to stick a bayonet into someone.

It had been Conahey with the SAW. Everyone seemed to be yelling their heads off, but I remember him coming over those rocks dead silent as usual, flicking an opaque gaze first to Vincent and the Yemeni, then to me, then continuing on.

We all did now, cautiously, not knowing where the rest of the platoon was with the rocks obscuring side-to-side vision. The roar of gunfire had pretty much stopped, but random shots still rang out all around.

The rocks tapered down into sand and scrub again. We stopped before we reached it. The sun was almost at its apex, and the heat was blinding. Mirage shimmered up from the sand. It had to be over a hundred degrees. Yeah, it was a dry heat—but so was an oven.

I knew I ought to move down the line and see what was happening, but my legs felt like jelly and I just couldn't make myself move.

I also knew if I sat down it might take more will than I had at that moment to get me back up. I leaned against the rocks and waited for the ammo and casualty reports to come in, trying to marshal my strength. The water in my canteen tasted even more like plastic when it was hot, and it was very hot.

CHAPTER TWENTY-ONE

Nothing like nagging guilt over your personal responsibilities to help you get your second wind.

I turned the survival radio back on as I made my way down the line. The Grinch was back overhead.

Sergeant Eberhardt, as always, was looking crushed under the weight of his burdens. I'd learned not to read anything into that, because he always looked that way. He had one more wounded. Hauser, one of the new PFC's. Who, the Sergeant told me, had probably run into the blast of his own grenade.

Sergeant Turner had two wounded, one of them bad. Lance Corporal Donato had taken a burst right across the chest. One round went through his vest and nicked him in the side, two were stopped by the ceramic ballistic plate, which then shattered and let the third into his lung.

Doc Bob hadn't arrived yet, but the rest of Donato's fire team had gotten a battle dressing on him. I checked their work, and it was good. They'd slapped the plastic dressing packaging over the "sucking" chest wound, which, with the chest cavity pierced, breathed whenever he did. The plastic resealed the chest, allowing the lung to reinflate. Then the battle dressing tied on tight over the plastic.

Doc Bob, who'd been everywhere all day, jogged up and started an IV. "We've got to get him out of here as soon as we can, sir," he told me privately as soon as he'd finished.

The Grinch relayed my message to Captain Z, and came back with an order to move all the wounded down into the valley.

I didn't care much for dragging badly wounded Marines down a hill, but had learned how to choose my words to keep from getting into arguments I'd inevitably lose. "I've got seven wounded, only two of them walking," I said to the Grinch. I didn't include myself of course. "I've got enough men to carry them down the hill, or hold this ridge. But I don't have enough to do both. We've got to take them off from up here."

A time lag while that was passed and considered. Then an order to prepare a landing zone on the ridge. Staff Sergeant Frederick got moving on that.

There were no prisoners, not even any wounded ones. I wasn't particularly shocked by that. If you were in the assault and someone popped up in front of you, and you waited to see whether their hands were up, then you were slow enough to die. And every body on the ground got two rounds as you went by, or you were asking to get shot in the back. Marines in the assault were not necessarily in their right minds. The idea that the savage violence of close combat can be controlled by rules probably sounds reasonable to anyone who hasn't experienced it.

I had a word with each of the Marines as I went down the line, to get an idea how they were doing. Just like me: both tired and wired, if that was possible.

"Do you know how much ass we kicked, sir?" Lance Corporal Francois shouted to me.

"All *they* had, Francois," I said, patting him on the back. "All they had."

Corporal Reilly had been shot through both legs. The Marines in his team told me he'd paused to tie on two tourniquets, then resumed firing until the squad was too far ahead.

He was conscious, but full of morphine. "What, did you slip on the deck?" I asked him.

"No, sir. I got shot in both legs."

Note to self: no joking banter with Marines zonked out on painkillers.

Huddling with the squad leaders, I told Sergeant Eberhardt to push down and across the small connecting ridge until he made contact with Jack O'Brien and 1st platoon. Sergeant Turner would head back to secure the far end of the ridge. And after we got the wounded out Corporal Asuego would hold the center.

"Whatever you do," I said, "stay the hell away from all these rocky outcroppings we had to take away from them. They'll be targets if that mortar opens up again. Keep good eyes on the downhill slope and surrounding terrain, but just observation posts. Keep most of your people in defilade on the valley side. Okay, anybody have any better ideas?"

A shaking of heads.

"You've done a great job so far," I said. "Let's not get cocky and careless—or fall asleep."

I turned to the helo crewman who'd been dogging the Staff Sergeant's footsteps all day. "You can go out with the wounded. Thanks for the radio. I'll get it back to you aboard ship."

He actually shook my hand, saying, "I'm never bitching about my job again, sir."

I grinned at that. Too bad the Marine Corps didn't give out a combat infantryman badge like the Army. I would have gotten it for him.

Retracing our steps was even more grisly than the original trip. Starved of everything in that harsh environment, clouds of flies had appeared to frantically attack the moisture of the spilled blood. Sergeant Turner detailed a fire team to collect all the weapons and documents. The barrels and RPG launchers would be bent between a couple of boulders, and the bolts scattered in the sand.

As I was giving the incoming '53 a zone brief, we experienced some conflict over the LZ marking. I wanted to keep using my mirror, feeling that a smoke grenade was just a way of announcing to everyone in the vicinity that a helicopter was about to land. Not to mention a really handy aiming point. But the pilot, worried about landing atop a ridge, insisted that he needed something to gauge the wind. So a smoke it was.

The sky was pure azure, not a cloud in sight. We could see the two incoming helos a long way off.

A faint pop seemed to come from some hills about a half mile away.

Thinking it was the mortar, I shouted, "Take cover!"

But a thin plume of smoke rose from the ground, corkscrewing upward. I thumbed the survival radio to the guard frequency. "SAM in the air! SAM in the air! SAM in the air!"

I knew I'd gotten through when I saw the '53's bank so hard they almost looped, simultaneously popping twin streams of white magnesium flares, countermeasures to decoy the heat-seeking missile. The helos dove toward the ground as the missile came up. The SAM didn't follow them, instead chasing after the flares. Probably an old Russian SA-7, since the newer ones had more sensitive seeker heads that could tell the difference between flares and hot engines.

I tossed my smoke grenade, wondering if they were going to keep coming in or pull back and regroup.

They kept coming in. One right into the valley, the other toward me, blurting out, "I see your green smoke," as a mere formality. Roaring down the ridge at full power, hugging the ground, aimed right at me standing with my arms outstretched. Then nothing but gray helo belly as it reared up and slapped down in front of me.

They kept the rotors on full power instead of feathering them. I could sympathize with wanting to get into the air immediately if anything else happened, but the rotor wash was like hurricane velocity wind. The stretcher bearers were leaning into it, bent forward almost horizontal, literally moving forward one step at a time against its force.

I had the radio to my ear, and the pilot was yelling at me to get going. That was about as effective as my signaling him to cut his power down. They were going to have to wait, because we couldn't let our stretchers fly away. Or just dump the casualties out of them.

Corporal Asuego and squad finally emerged from the '53's belly, carrying one of the Stokes Stretchers filled with ammo.

The crew chief must have told the pilot, because they were in the air before I could raise my hands to signal take-off. Not very high, though, before sliding down the ridge and following the slope down into the valley to join the other helo.

"Get your squad spread out," I told Corporal Asuego. "Leave a team here to move your ammo." I radioed down the ridge for Sergeants Turner and Eberhardt to do the same.

Vincent and I helped Staff Sergeant Frederick break down the ammo. A wooden case of frag grenades. The 40mm high explosive dual-purpose grenades for the M-203, that look like bullets the size of juice cans. Belted 7.62mm and 5.56mm for the machine-guns and squad automatic weapons. And 5.56mm in 10-round stripper clips pocketed in 140-round cloth bandoleers. All these in green metal ammo cans we left littering the ridge.

A few minutes after the teams staggered away under their burdens, there were three crisp, spread-out booms down on the valley floor.

The Staff Sergeant and I ran to the edge of the ridge. The mortar was in action again. With no observer to adjust the fire, they were traversing along the valley, hoping to get lucky.

They almost did. One round exploded about 50 yards away from one of the '53's. I held my breath—I think everyone else did too, waiting to see how the mortar crew would twirl the dials. The next round dropped about 100 yards farther away.

The tube kept firing even though the Cobras were furiously hunting it.

It definitely speeded things up on the ground. Paul Federico boarded his platoon and his wounded. The helos took off one after the other, and the valley was empty except for the smoking skeleton of the '53 whose destruction had brought us back from the ship.

The two helos had taken off in the opposite direction from the mortar's path, toward the open end of the valley.

Sand sprayed up along the ridge, followed closely by a rapid string of deep hard pops. I was back down on my face, along with the rest of the platoon. Heavy machine-gun. Probably a Russian 12.7mm, the equivalent of our .50 caliber Browning.

We weren't pinned down, but we were under cover. "Hold fire, hold fire," I said into the intra-squad radio. Just in case they were trying to get me to open up and reveal the location of my machine-guns. Our snipers would have been ideal in this situation. Too bad we hadn't brought them along.

I'd leave it to the Cobras, who were already lunging toward the source of the fire.

In combat everything happens so fast you almost never see the action, only the results. I heard at least two more 12.7's open up, followed by a thump, and only then saw one of the '53 fighting for altitude, belching smoke and trailed by two strings of tracers.

I had to give them credit, they'd played it perfectly. Flushed the '53's with the mortar, distracted us and the Cobras with the one 12.7, then ambushed the '53's with two more while they were still low and slow.

But the '53 was still flying. And the Cobras were firing rockets down into the origin of the tracers.

There was no more heavy machine-gun fire, though that didn't mean anything. If any of the guns had survived, they wouldn't give away their location unless they had another good target. Like more '53's coming to fly us out.

CHAPTER TWENTY-TWO

With that in mind, Captain Zimmerman called me over for a face-to-face meeting on the short connecting ridge. I took Vincent along. We walked along the interior slope, since we were still taking sporadic, though poorly aimed, long-range sniper fire from the adjacent hills.

"How are your Marines, Mike?" was Captain Z's first question.

"Running on adrenaline, sir. But still good to go."

"What's your estimate of the situation?"

"Well, sir, now that Federico's out I don't see any reason to hang around here. But if we give up the high ground and go down into the valley to extract we're going to end up like Paul. Seems to me we've got to land a '53 on each ridge. Get all the Harriers back and time the extracts with airstrikes on the surrounding hills."

"That's what Jack and I think," the Captain said. "But there's no place to land a '53 on Jack's ridge."

"My ridge is higher anyway, sir. Even if they get back up on the other, they're still firing up at us. We can hit them with air as we pull out."

"The longer we wait," said O'Brien, "the more neighborhood minutemen are going to be showing up."

"The timing'll be crucial," said Captain Z. "I want to hold both ridges until I know exactly when this is going to happen. We'll have to do it right the first time—we're running out of '53's.'"

"Did the one that got hit make it back to the ship, sir?" I asked.

The Captain nodded. "But I don't know about any additional wounded. Sorry, Mike."

I really didn't want to know anyway. Not when I couldn't do anything about it.

Captain Z sent the mortar section back with me. Sergeant Lenoir picked a spot on the edge of my prospective landing zone. With him barking at them, his section broke out their entrenching tools and started digging three mortar pits like rabid badgers.

I took advantage of the interval to get together with the squad leaders and platoon sergeant and let them know what was in store. We worked out what we wanted to do, knowing of course that all of it could be instantly overruled by what Captain Z *decided* to do.

When they got the order to move, 1st platoon very slowly crawled back onto the reverse slope of their ridge so as not to be observed. Then they trudged around to us on the interior slope, again to keep out of sight. My platoon was in a semicircle half-perimeter on one side of the open landing zone area, and O'Brien's was arrayed the same way on the other side.

To have the maximum number of Cobras overhead at the extraction, Captain Z decided to send our overhead pair back to the ship to refuel. A few minutes after they left, the Yemenis started moving around openly on the surrounding hills.

This was when the Marines came into their own, because the one thing the Corps did better than anything else was teach you how to shoot a rifle. The machine-guns and squad automatic weapons stayed quiet, and the rifles went to work.

Over the sound of the shots I could hear the Marines calling back and forth, telling each other what range they were using on their sights, and how many clicks of windage.

It's incredibly difficult to hit a moving man-sized target with a rifle at any range, but particularly so at the 500-700 yards we were shooting at. And with "iron" instead of telescopic sights. The average man could move five yards in the time lag between the trigger squeeze and the bullet reaching 500 yards. But we were hitting close enough to make that movement much more hesitant. An occasional figure dropped. Then more as the Marines got the idea for a fire team to all concentrate on one target, and word of the technique passed around the perimeter.

Captain Z and his command group of Jimmy Nichols, Gunny Harris, Captain Donohoe the forward air controller, and their radio operators stationed themselves close to me. It eliminated the disadvantage of not having a radio, though I'd grown fond of not being supervised. And I didn't much care for the antenna farm of radio operators following the command group around. They seemed bound to draw fire.

Nichols had Sergeant Lenoir training his binoculars on the ridge 1st platoon had just evacuated. The mortars would open up on the first signs of life over there.

Word came over the radio that the air was on the way.

Jack O'Brien and I had bucked up. He'd lost, so he was going out first. We had our extraction order arranged, boarding the helo a squad at a time, the platoon sergeants counting each man in.

However, the only constant in the history of warfare was that no operation ever went down the way it was planned.

We saw the helos coming in. Being much faster, the Harriers had taken off from the ship at the last possible moment. Everything happening at the right time was going to be critical.

It didn't start off well. One desert hill looked like another from the air. I guess the lead '53 got confused and didn't make the approach Captain Donohoe had told them to.

Captain Donohoe was yelling into his radio. It was that helpless 'watching the car crash' sensation. Amazing how far a helo could fly in the time it took to make a radio transmission.

Those big 12.7mm tracers sprouted up again, one stream right under the descending '53. It shuddered and veered, two more streams reaching out for it. The Cobras dove, firing rockets. One stream of tracer shut off, but another continued.

The wrong approach screwed up the Harriers, who were coming in on their own heading and on a time hack. Fearing a collision, Captain Donohoe had to abort the run, which packed on yet another layer of complication. Things began to snowball.

Our mortars began their hollow metallic banging. Sergeant Lenoir must have seen some movement on the opposite ridge.

My eyes went back to the sky, and the '53 was veering away. Smaller green AK tracers were going up now. They were a hell of a lot closer to us than we wanted them to be. The Yemenis must have found a concealed avenue of approach to our ridge.

Over the noise I heard Captain Donohoe say to Captain Z, "They're losing hydraulics. They've got to head back while they still have them."

How quickly could things fall apart? That quickly. All we had left were two '53's. And one of them was filled with our reserve, Frank Milburn's 3rd platoon with Dick Herkimer and the First Sergeant.

So we would have to put two platoons, the mortar section, and the command group on one '53. I did the math, and for the first and only time was happy about the number of casualties we'd already evacuated.

I heard Captain Z say to Captain Donohoe, very calmly, "We've got only one more chance to do this right. So get on the radio, make sure everyone is on board, with their shit together, and then let's fucking do it."

A sentiment I echoed.

Captain Donohoe said, "Squadron commander and battalion commander were on the lead '53."

"Maybe that'll cut down on the general confusion," Captain Z said. Then, louder, "You didn't hear that, Mike."

"Hear what, sir?" I called back. Wish I had a buck for every deaf ear and blind eye I've turned in the Corps.

The next '53 came in, on the right approach this time. The first pair of Harriers streaked across our front, firing 5 inch white phosphorus rockets into the hills. Someone had made a good call on the weapons load. A bomb could hit or miss, but you couldn't see through white smoke.

The incoming '53 began popping flares. The flares acted like pointers, making the helo easier to see in the sky, but I guess they were more worried about another SAM.

The next pair of Harriers came in with unguided 500lb bombs. The shockwaves rattled my teeth. I hoped the 12.7 gunners were eating some dirt.

The Cobras flitted around firing their own rockets. Some at the end of the ridge. It made me even more uneasy, since they had to be firing at something.

The '53 rotors blew up another sandstorm. Despite the danger the pilot landed gingerly, as if walking through an unfamiliar pitch dark room.

He was cool. He cut back on the power, and the sandstorm dissipated. The rear ramp dropped, as did the starboard side hatch near the nose.

I signaled 1st squad to board. This was a dicey moment. Nothing in this world is more disciplined than a Marine, but there was still human psychology to contend with. One unit pulls back, and a guy in an adjacent unit thinks that maybe someone forgot to give him the word, so he pulls out too. Soon there's a stampede for the helo, and no protective perimeter left.

I needed a clear signal. The intra-squad radio might not cut through all the noise. My solution was a good old fashioned police whistle, whose use was still encouraged in officer training in defiance of technology. Its sound rose above everything. One whistle blast and Corporal Asuego and 1st squad handed over their claymore clackers, rose up, and fell back to the helo.

Our mortar section fired their last rounds, grabbed the hot tubes with asbestos gloves, levered the baseplates out of the sand, and followed Corporal Asuego into the helicopter.

O'Brien's lead squad was boarding the front side hatch on the other end of the '53.

A mortar round detonated on the slope leading down into the valley. A stroke of luck that meant the Yemenis couldn't observe its fall and adjust the next rounds onto the '53.

By now we were doing the combat spaz. Every loud noise had us all flinching and ducking in unison. Every close loud noise had us instinctively throwing ourselves onto the ground.

Bullets were passing overhead and kicking up the sand. We were taking plunging fire from farther up the ridge.

Another mortar landed, this time on the forward slope. Not good. A couple more adjustments and they'd be right on us.

Two whistle blasts and Sergeant Eberhardt's squad passed their clackers to Sergeant Turner and pulled back to the helo.

A surge of fire from Sergeant Turner's squad. Holy shit, had the Yemenis gotten that close?

I rushed up to them but the sonic cracks soon had me crawling. This was why lieutenants were always getting killed out of proportion to their numbers: always rushing back and forth making themselves inviting targets.

The Yemenis weren't assaulting us, they were pressing us. I had to give it to them again, almost anyone else would have bugged out of the neighborhood long before. Cannon shells from a Cobra were sparking among the rocks.

I threw myself down next to Sergeant Turner and screamed into his ear, "We can't bolt for the helo. We have to pull back bit by bit."

He nodded, and as he turned to signal his fire team leaders a figure rose up in front of us. A Yemeni had one of our claymores in his hand; I could see the firing wire draping down. He reared back to throw it at us.

I brought up my M-16 at the same time Sergeant Turner mashed the clacker and the Yemeni disappeared in a thunderclap of rolling black cloud.

"Blow the claymores!" I yelled, pantomiming the motion. Seconds later they all went off in ragged succession.

Taking advantage of the shock value of the explosions, we pulled back. It was like firing and moving in reverse, bounding back ten yards at a time.

On one bound I threw my last frag grenade. I was getting rid of everything. A yellow smoke went next.

A massive blast behind us. We all threw ourselves onto the ground. The mortar had gotten the range. Through the smoke I could see the '53 still intact, rotors turning.

We had to be gone before the mortar fired for effect.

The smoke cleared enough to see the havoc the round had wreaked with the command group. They were sprawled over the rocks, but there was no time to see who was wounded and who was only stunned.

Sergeant Turner and I laid down fire while his squad dragged the command group to the helo. A machine-gunner fired his last belt but pulled out his pistol and kept firing until I grabbed his shoulder and spun him toward the helo.

More rifle shots barked at my other side, which I thought was open. Jack O'Brien had tucked his platoon away on the helo and rushed back out to stay in the fight.

We gave ground a step at a time, keeping ourselves between the Yemenis and 2nd squad dragging the casualties.

A Yemeni popped up from the rocks and in the same motion fired his RPG. Perfectly silhouetted against the billowing blue-gray backblast smoke, we shot him down. Only after he'd fallen did I look back. He'd rushed his aim. The rocket had sailed right over the '53 and landed in front of the nose.

Almost at the ramp, and rounds flying everywhere. Jack and I were firing and changing magazines so fast we let our empties drop to the ground.

Sergeant Turner snatched at his hip and went down. O'Brien and I grabbed him under the armpits and dragged him up the ramp, ducking under the howling tail rotor.

Staff Sergeant Frederick was there, signaling me that we had everyone. "Fucking go!" I screamed at the crew chief.

He was screaming into his microphone and slapping at the switch to raise the ramp. The '53 lurched up, spilling us onto the deck atop the command group.

Rounds zipping through the fuselage. Explosions on the ground as the Cobras covered our takeoff.

The '53 fought for speed and altitude. Something nicked me on the helmet as it went by. Everyone who was ambulatory began untangling themselves from the pile of bodies on the deck.

Still climbing, and still taking fire. Both doorguns blasting forward. Only ground visible through the opening between the top of the ramp and the top of the cabin. The crew chief was braced against the frame, one foot on the ramp.

Then he was gone. A round through the wiring must have caused the ramp to drop. All I could see was the green nylon strap of the gunner's safety belt, taut as a bowstring against the ramp.

And Jack O'Brien throwing himself onto the ramp. Christ, we were climbing and he didn't have a safety belt. I sprang onto his legs, getting both hands on his belt. Now we were both sliding down the slick oily metal.

I decided in less than an instant that I'd rather take the ride down with Jack than let him go and have to live with the fact that I'd let him go.

Someone thudded onto my legs, and we stopped sliding. This only solved our most immediate problem. I wasn't what you'd call fresh, and my arms were getting tired.

Jack's chest was over the ramp. Then he hiked himself back, and a sand-colored flight-suited leg swung up and over.

"Back, back!" O'Brien was yelling.

I took up that call, trying to shimmy back, but it was easier said than done.

We were gradually pulled back, inch by inch, for what seemed like an hour. Somewhere in this process the helo leveled out, making our job easier.

Then were all off the ramp, O'Brien clutching an ash-white crew chief. I finally looked back to see that it was Captain Z on my legs. Probably a case of: I can't lose these lieutenants—I'm signed for them. Gunny Harris was on the Captain's legs, part of a daisy chain that stretched back into the fuselage.

"You crazy fuck!" I shouted at O'Brien.

He rolled around and looked at me. "What was I supposed to do?" he shouted back over the noise of the engines. "Let him dangle out there the whole ride back?"

"He gets flight pay," I shouted.

We both started laughing. Harder than the remark deserved, but it was more about how good it felt to be alive.

"Jesus Christ," Jack exclaimed, looking around for the first time. "This is one seriously shot-up helo."

He was right. The fuselage looked like the sides of a cheese grater.

We got busy attending to the command group wounded. Surprisingly few; most just had their bells rung. Vincent was right, the sand absorbed most of their mortar blasts. If the Yemenis had been using VT airburst fuses we would have been in trouble. I probably would have been dead.

Fighting to get IV's going in a shaking and wobbling helicopter, the corpsmen had to jab some Marines three or four times.

As we gained altitude the blast furnace air turned beautifully cool. The word came down from the front that we were going to have to refuel in mid-air. Probably due to the greater than anticipated weight of a greater than anticipated number of passengers. Not to mention the ramp hanging down in the slipstream like an air brake.

The two KC-130 Hercules transports were the unsung heroes of the operation. They'd been on station since before midnight the previous evening, refueling '53's and relaying communications when the inevitable radio failures occurred, leaving the scene only to refuel themselves in Saudi Arabia. An unromantic aircraft, usually sneered at by the silk scarf types, but little happened without them. I hoped they at least got an Air Medal out of it.

It was possible to look through the open tunnel from the fuselage to the cabin and get a glimpse of the view through the windshield.

From one of its outer wing tanks, the KC-130 unreeled a long hose with a basket drogue on the end. Our '53 extended the refueling probe from the starboard side of the nose like a metal straw.

Our pilot approached the drogue carefully, because it would be very unpleasant if the rotors cut the hose. It took three tries, then a little thump when he completed the coupling by inserting the probe into the basket.

We all breathed a sigh of relief. Until a sound like the popping of a champagne cork, and a spray of fuel erupting from the ceiling. The wind from both doorgun windows turned that into an aerosol stream down the length of the cabin.

There was nowhere to go. All we could do was sit glumly under the hard kerosene rain. The looks of dismay on the Marines' faces can only be imagined.

Eventually the crew shut off lines and wound tape around the break, but we were still soaked in fuel. It was one thing to have hydraulic fluid dripping on us in mid-flight, but this was really a bit much.

Jet Propulsion fuel isn't anywhere near as volatile as gasoline, but it was still fuel. The crew wasn't about to go screwing around with electrical wiring in the present situation, so the ramp stayed down. And no one was looking forward to the metal on metal sparks as we tried to land on the steel flight deck with it down.

Once I wiped kerosene off my glasses and could see again, I unzipped my notebook, popped the cap off an alcohol marker pen, and wrote in big letters on one of the laminated pages: NO SMOKING. I held it up, and the Marines gave me that smirky look: real fucking funny, sir.

The Red Sea came into view. One of the helo's plastic water cans was being passed hand to hand, and the troops were guzzling it like cold beer. The officers only drank after everyone else had, the Captain last. It was the same when eating chow in the field. Inviolate Marine Corps ritual.

For the first time since morning I looked at my watch. It was 15:48. Amazing. I had no idea it was that late in the day. Pretty soon we'd see whether our streak of surviving everything that could possibly go wrong would hold up.

The Harriers had all landed. Then the Cobras, as we circled the ship to burn off fuel. Normally we'd all be buckling ourselves in and arranging gear. But there were more Marines than seats, and by now everyone was too tired and too jaded.

As always, we approached from the stern, even with our landing spot over the water, then slipped in sideways until we were over the flight deck. The pilot literally brought it down inch by inch. I could see the regular crash crew out on deck, as always, along with a lot more sailors with fire hoses at the ready. No foam on the deck—they probably didn't want us slipping off.

Both doorgunners were halfway out their windows, calling directions to the pilot and copilot. The crew chief at the back, watching that ramp.

A metal clank and swaying as the bottom of the ramp made contact with the flight deck, then creaking as the helo settled down.

As soon as all the slack had left the wheels the pilot shut everything down. The Navy could tow this bird to wherever they wanted it.

Once again the medical teams rushed aboard. Then the white shirts of Combat Cargo led us off. O'Brien and I, the Gunny, and the Captain were the last ones off. My adrenal gland had stopped pumping now. I'd been tired at dawn. Now I could barely put one foot in front of the other.

Sitting on the flight deck with engines off and rotors drooping flaccidly, that '53, which had been both savior and nemesis, looked almost benign.

Down in the marshaling area it was back to mundane routine. The first thing we did was collect all the remaining ammo. It wouldn't do to have live rounds floating around the ship. A forgotten or souvenir bullet might end up being used to settle a score in the heat of a moment. And a Marine wouldn't be dumb enough to take a live grenade home and put it on a shelf, would he? Believe me, any action that could possibly be conceived of had happened in the past.

A detail took all the ammo and pyrotechnics down to the fantail and threw it into the sea. Shipboard fire regulations required that only fully packaged ammo with unbroken seals could be stored in the magazines.

All the papers and documents collected from the Yemeni dead were turned over to the intelligence officer.

There was no *Top Gun* high-fiving—everyone was too pooped. The Marines were swaggering, and rightly so, but with more calm and quiet pride than I'd thought them capable of. I guess everyone had grown up overnight.

The next ritual would have been to start cleaning weapons. But with everyone reeking of fuel Captain Zimmerman sent the company to shower and change. And just to keep our streak intact, the ship's water was off. The engineering department had turned it off so they could work on something.

Which well and truly summed up the Navy amphibious fleet for me. There was nothing dishonorable about being in support—three quarters of the U.S. military supported the one quarter in the combat arms. But when the support thought it was the be all and end all you had something like a ship's engineering department totally oblivious to the fact that a company of Marines had spent the better part of the last 16 hours fighting for their lives, most of it in hundred degree heat, and just might appreciate a shower.

Instead Captain Z had his company lock up their weapons, uncleaned. Then he led them down to the mess deck, as if the meal line and everyone in it didn't exist, and stood with crossed arms while his Marines were served.

The mess officer Corporal Asuego had drawn down on that morning was nowhere to be seen. When one of the messmen timidly told the Captain that they had to go by the meal pass system, he said, "Son, you've got two choices. Dish it out, or call the bridge and get me the Captain on the phone."

I didn't know whether to admire the messman's dedication or pity his ignorance. The company was grimy; sweat and dirt-streaked. The torsos of our cammie blouses, that had been underneath the flak jackets, were soaking wet from sweat. The rest had been baked dry in the desert heat. Most of us were wearing dried blood. Unfocused "thousand yard stares" from fatigue, but also something grim and potentially vicious. If I hadn't been out there with them, I would have been really careful how I ordered the Marines to do anything.

After some loud whispering back in the kitchen they dished it out, as much as the troops wanted. And after not eating practically anything for 16 hours, they wanted a lot. What the hell, the Navy was going to hate us anyway.

I really felt awful. I thought it was the stink of the fuel, a smell that's never agreed with me.

Frank Milburn was livid about missing the fight, not to mention spending all day with his platoon flying around, and throwing up, in the back of a '53.

We were watching the troops being served, and he said, "You don't look so good."

"I don't feel so good," I said. "I...." I stopped, as the mess deck spun around. Then everything clicked off.

CHAPTER TWENTY-THREE

I woke up in sick bay. One nice thing about shipboard sickbays, you'll never wake up in one and think you're in the afterlife.

"Okay, what's the damage?" I croaked to the first person I saw, a cheerful looking black corpsman.

"You've got a really bad concussion, Lieutenant," he informed me. "At first the doctors thought you had a fractured skull."

Too thick for that, I thought.

"They were amazed you walked around with it for so long," the Doc continued.

Nothing like the power of adrenaline. As soon as the word got around that I was awake I had to undergo a very long and annoying battery of neurological tests. The doctors were surprised and, it seemed to me, a little disappointed that my memory and reflexes seemed to be all right. I think they were looking forward to drilling a few holes in my skull.

Because I'd been unconscious, twice, I had to spend three days in sickbay under observation. My roommate was Paul Federico, who'd picked up a bad infection from the mortar fragments he'd also picked up.

Captain Z was my first visitor, in checking all his wounded. "What are you doing screwing off in here?" he demanded.

"Just felt like I needed a little vacation, sir."

"God-damn, Mike, you're already on a cruise. What more do you want?"

"Terrible how some people are never satisfied, isn't it, sir?"

"You caused quite a stir on the mess deck. Should have at least had chow before you passed out."

"I wish I did too, sir. You should see the pablum they're giving me."

"Serves you right."

"Care for one of these, sir?" said Federico, offering him a glass jar. Lee Harvey Oberdorff had already smuggled in some jalapenos.

Captain Z examined the jar carefully. "Thanks, Paul, but if I eat one of these I'll end up standing in the middle of a passageway and shitting into the rooms on both sides."

Laughing made my head hurt bad.

Staff Sergeant Frederick showed up next, telling me about attending the mission debrief in my place. Clearly it was going to take a while before he forgave me for that.

"It was a fucking nightmare, sir. They went on for about an hour about you violating the rules of engagement. You know, when you used the claymores to blow through the walls of that house? I was starting to sweat, big time, then that intel Gunny did the PowerPoint of all the pictures he snapped inside the house. That, and the Cobra gun camera film of us on the streets, shut them up."

"How did we look?" I asked.

"Studly, sir. Very studly."

"So they didn't give you any more heartburn?"

"The BLT staff was on our side, sir. The MEU staff was dishing out the heartburn. Like why you didn't ask permission to use the claymores. They kept asking me that, and I kept saying I didn't know. So you better stand by for some shit on that, sir."

"I didn't ask them because they would have said no. They were circling around up in a helo, not stuck at the end of that hallway, and besides it violated the rules of engagement. Most of the time, Staff Sergeant, it's better to beg forgiveness than ask permission."

"I'll leave that to you, sir. I don't ever want to go through one of them fucking debriefs again."

"Don't worry. The MEU staff is just positioning themselves. If Washington thinks we fucked up, I'm the scapegoat who panicked, exceeded his orders, and killed some poor civilians. If we're heroes, everyone's reservations will be forgotten."

"Fuck, sir."

"Ah, you thought lieutenants just played polo and drank gin fizzes at the Club? Didn't realize all the shit we have to take on a daily basis, did you?"

"Grass is always greener, sir. I'll stick to being a platoon sergeant."

I snuck out of bed and visited my Marines. Damn near half the platoon had some kind of wound. Most were minor and would recuperate on ship. The more serious cases would be flown off to Djibouti, then on to Germany.

Sergeant Harlin was going to make it; he was flying off.

Corporal Cushing, the SMAW gunner who'd taken a round in the chest in the village, had died on the operating table. He and Peterson were our only dead. The corpsmen had done brilliant, heroic work, but the Interceptor flak jackets with the ceramic ballistic inserts were worth their weight in gold. And the 16 pound weight, even in the desert. Without them we'd have been burying a lot more Marines.

There was some good news about the two Marines who'd fallen in the ambush at the intersection. Lance Corporal Nolan had been kissed by five or six rounds that shot his canteens and gas mask off but didn't even touch him. With the nearest cover a long way off he decided to play dead. It saved his life. PFC Getz took two rounds that were both stopped by the ceramic ballistic plates in his flak jacket. Another hit his helmet and did nothing but knock him out cold. He woke up with only a concussion of his own and some deep bruises. Everyone was talking about taking him to Atlantic City once we got back.

Sergeant Turner had a bullet in his hip, lodged near the femoral artery. He was going to Germany for surgery.

I had some business to take care of before he went. I honestly didn't know whether Peterson had been shot in the heat of the moment because Sergeant Turner thought there was no other way to get him off that fence, or Sergeant Turner had embraced a heaven-sent opportunity to pay off an asshole who had continually provoked and disrespected him.

That was one question I was never going to ask. I knew Peterson and I knew Sergeant Turner. And I knew who I was going to back. I pulled my chair very close to his bed so I could speak into his ear. For the first time in my life I was about to embark on a criminal conspiracy.

"Just listen to me," I told him. "I don't want you to say a word, because if anyone asks me I intend to say that you never spoke to me about this. You will say nothing of what happened that night in the village except to the Colonel, the Captain, or as part of the process of a formal investigation. Anyone else: the First Sergeant, the Gunny, or your five best friends, you either don't want to talk about it or I've told you not to pending an investigation.

"You were trying to pull Peterson off the fence. It was total chaos, pushing and shoving. You're not sure how he got hit. That's it. Now, if—and only if—someone tells you that Peterson had an American 5.56mm hole in his head, you will say that in the middle of the struggle to get him off the fence your weapon accidentally discharged. You don't know if you had your hand on it or the safety was off and the trigger snagged on your gear. You never thought that the bullet hit Peterson. But if it did it was a tragic accident; at night, under fire, and in a very confusing situation.

"I don't know if there's going to be an investigation. But if there is, what I just said is all you say. Period. Nothing more; no added details. You got that?"

He nodded.

"You want me to repeat it again so we're straight?"

He shook his head.

"As far as I'm concerned you did what you had to do, and it probably saved all our lives. I'm not going to leave you hanging. All right?"

He nodded again, and we shook hands.

When the doctors finally let me go they ordered me to get my ass back to sickbay if I experienced any paralysis or mental lapses. And especially headaches, depression, or abnormal irritability. "I'm a platoon commander," I said. "What's abnormal?"

My roommates, with typical sensitivity, had modified our quarters to accommodate my brain-rattled condition. There was a Welcome Home Mike sign, of course. And everything was neatly labeled with post-it notes, in case I'd experienced any memory loss. My rack was labeled: RACK—SLEEP HERE. My pillow was labeled: PILLOW. The sink: SINK. My boots: BOOTS, and, helpfully, LEFT and RIGHT.

"This is *so* thoughtful of you," I said, trying not to mist up. "And you even broke out the dictionary to spell everything right."

One of the strange things about combat is that you never knew what had really happened until it was over and everyone gathered to put all the individual pieces together.

The other two houses in the village had been dry holes. Force Recon shot two armed men in one, taking one wounded in the process. They turned out to be part of the family who lived there, the rest of whom quickly surrendered. Anyone expecting the war on terrorism to be clean and simple and evenly divided between combatants and noncombatants with the ability to harm one and not the other was due for a major wake-up call.

First and 3rd platoons also had fights on the streets, but they hadn't gotten ambushed. A group trying to close in on Milburn had probably found itself between us and taken advantage of it.

All the terrorists—or whoever the hell they were, we wouldn't know until the prisoners were interrogated and the intelligence evaluated—had been in my house. The least likely one. Friday the 13th luck again, I guess.

Captain Z could hardly believe how many bad guys we'd taken out. "An attacker's supposed to have a 3:1 advantage in numbers over the defenders, Mike. You barely had 1:1."

"I didn't have any idea how many were in that house until it was all over, sir. And if I'd called for help you would have had to come in either the front door or at ground level." I explained what the ground floor had been like.

"Claymores to breach walls," he said. "God damn, Mike, that was slicker'n snot on a doorknob."

We rocked with laughter, and he said, "I'll never understand what you Yankees find funny." Though of course he always knew what he was doing.

Paul Federico had been preparing to pull out of the Forward Refueling and Rearming Point right after we left the village. Apparently just after he vacated the high ground to board his '53, an arms smuggler's caravan bumped into him. While the firefight was going on more Yemenis showed up, occupied the high ground, and proceeded to shoot up the area and set the '53 afire. Then the word went out all over the area. A unique aspect of societies without modern communications was that somehow the word seemed to move just as fast, though more prone to disinformation.

It didn't make any difference who we were or what we were doing. The rule of the Yemeni outback was that strangers got shot at.

The Yemenis had a fine time shooting up the helo and Federico's platoon, but their unfamiliarity with vertical envelopment meant they were caught by surprise when we fast-roped onto the ridge. And then they were stuck. They couldn't run without getting slaughtered by the Cobras, so they had to stand and fight.

And the longer we stayed the more locals poured into the area looking for a fight. That they had mortars and shoulder-fired surface to air missiles meant nothing. In Yemen such items were as common as backyard grills in the American suburbs.

We killed a hell of a lot of them. After Vietnam no one talked about body counts—that was an American military taboo. And apparently the government of Yemen, who had agreed to a nice quiet raid on one isolated village, was none too pleased about us shooting up the whole county in daylight. But they were keeping it quiet, not anxious to have word of American Marines killing a shitload of Yemeni civilians get around.

As were we. The entire mission fell under the shroud of secrecy that covered the war on terror. We were told to keep our mouths shut, and my expectations of that were about the same as liberty incidents. Especially once the wounded got to Germany.

I had to write letters. To the relatives of my wounded. Even though Cushing was weapons platoon I thought I ought to write his wife and parents.

Then there was Peterson's mother. What was I going to say there? *Dear Mrs. Peterson, I am writing to you because your son was an asshole who chickened out and lost it in combat. His hysterical panic put us all in danger, and rather than allow that to happen his squad leader shot him dead.*

Needless to say, that's not what I wrote. I lied about Peterson, I lied about the circumstances of his death. I lied to keep from destroying Sergeant Turner's life and career. It might be true that no mother needed to know that kind of truth about her son, but it was still a rationalization.

I don't know how often something like that happens in war. It's not the kind of thing that gets into the history books. It's the kind of thing that festers in the human heart until the day we die.

And it was all my fault. I knew that Peterson was a disaster waiting to happen, but I'd never been able to get rid of him. I should have thought of something, done anything; I'd failed in my duty to both Peterson and the platoon.

The same with Sergeant Harlin. I should have figured out a way to get rid of him, for his own good, but I didn't. At least he didn't get anyone else hurt when he screwed up the way I'd always known he would.

Both of them on my head, and not easy to live with.

Along with his Purple Heart Sergeant Harlin would be receiving a career-ending adverse fitness report, along with a special notation in his record book. Probably not the classiest move I ever made, but he might not come back to the platoon and I had to make sure he never commanded Marines again.

Jack O'Brien cut back on his stress-related routine of PT'ing twice a day and goring everyone who bumped against him. Lynn and the baby were fine.

My prediction to Staff Sergeant Frederick came to pass. We didn't get fired; Washington was very pleased with what we'd done. Three of the bodies my platoon left behind in the house turned out to be on the wanted list from the bombing of the destroyer *Cole*. Six more were the top Al Qaeda in Yemen. Everyone else was either Al Qaeda or its cover groups—Yemen Islamic Jihad and the Aden-Abyan Islamic Army—or their bodyguards.

The two laptop computers and the documents were said to contain significant intelligence. That's all we were told. All intelligence goes up, then sideways, but rarely if ever comes back down. Knowledge is power, so the more the intelligence agencies kept it to themselves the more powerful they were. Even though we'd collected it, we were no longer cleared for it.

The platoon and I held our own debrief, talking about everything we'd done right, and wrong, and the lessons that needed to be learned. I used the notes as the basis for the medal citations I'd begun to write.

It turned out to be surprisingly therapeutic. Instead of going home and bottling it up inside themselves for the rest of their lives, the Marines talked about what they'd done and seen with the buddies who'd been through it with them. In a couple of instances Marines torn up about making wrong moves or not doing what they thought they should have done were told by their friends they were full of shit, and to forget it.

I took one action right away. Held a platoon formation and gave Westgate back his fire team for standing tall with his SAW when we were ambushed. Just as I'd said after the MCCRES, he'd worked his way back to being someone I could rely on.

I gave Conahey a fire team at the same formation. He and his SAW had popped up in every tight spot we'd been in. Whether these appointments would last beyond our next liberty ashore was anyone's guess.

Both were promoted to corporal at the same time. And it was depressing how much we had to plead with Colonel Sweatman before he gave out the combat meritorious promotions. The senior officers were so paralyzed by the zero-defects system they were afraid to do *anything* without getting permission first.

The bodies were flown out along with the wounded. I had yet to hear anything about Peterson's gunshot wound.

Echo Company knew it would be a long time before we saw another mission. Not with our strength so whittled down. The other companies wouldn't be getting anything either, not until some replacement CH-53's were flown in.

It drove a real gulf right down the middle of the battalion. Echo Company, Federico and Lee Harvey's platoon on one side, the rest on the other. The jealousy of who had been in combat, and who hadn't. Paul and Lee Harvey had it the worse, because they had to live with Captain America. Who, they reported, couldn't stop talking about how he would have done it better. Sometimes you'd think Marines had never gotten off the playground.

It was nearly two weeks after the operation before the first mail came on board. In it was a videotape from Corporal Cushing's wife, addressed to the Captain. No letter, just the tape.

The Skipper had a TV and VCR hauled into the company office. The officers, the First Sergeant, and the Gunny assembled to watch it. Though there was plenty of discussion, no one had any idea what it might contain.

The images that blinked onto my TV screen were of a military burial. I think we all groaned at the same time. In combat the dead are taken away and disappear, so you can try to forget them, if you can. But thanks to technology we were watching a funeral that had taken place on the other side of the world.

"Why did she do that?" O'Brien wondered out loud. Not in anger but genuine puzzlement. "Was it to say, now watch what you did, you bastards? Or did she think this was the same as us being at the graveside, honoring him."

"We killed him," said Milburn. "She's doing this to get back at us." And I was inclined to agree with him.

"I don't know, sir," said the First Sergeant.

"All of you hush up," said the Captain.

I think we all wanted to leave, but of course none of us did.

The service. The folding of the flag on the casket, the neat triangle presented to the widow with the thanks of a grateful nation. Flinching at the firing party salute. Taps. *Day is done. Gone the sun. From the lakes, from the hills, from the sky. Rest in peace, soldier brave. God is nigh.*

Just when I thought the service was done a very small boy slid off his chair, and before his mother could get ahold of him ran over, put two little hands on that cold casket, and shouted loud enough to be heard through it, "Bye Daddy."

I felt as though my heart had been torn out of my chest. Everyone in the office had his hands over his face, so the others couldn't see him crying.

Maybe it's the curse of too much reading, because all I could think of was Lord Byron, *Don Juan*. That while all comedies are ended by a marriage, all tragedies are finished by a death.

THE END